Withdrawn

Born
of
the
Sun

Born
of
the
Sun

Holiday House / New York

© Gillian Cross 1983
First American publication 1984 by Holiday House, Inc.
Printed in the United States of America

Library of Congress Cataloging in Publication Data

Cross, Gillian
Born of the sun.

Summary: Paula's journey with her father to find a lost
Incan city becomes shadowed with mystery and danger, and
in the end the truths learned on the journey, not at the
destination, are what is important.
    [1. Fathers and daughters—Fiction. 2. Mystery and
detective stories. 3. Peru—Fiction] I. Edwards,
Mark, ill. II. Title.
PZ7.C88253Bo 1984   [Fic]   84-3740
ISBN 0-8234-0528-1

To Martin

Born
of
the
Sun

Altiplano

Imagine a dusty plain
Miles above sea
Where stunted bushes rise
Out of a scrawl
Of yellow grass.

The wind rasps, with a dryness
That chaps the skin,
And lungs unused to height
Struggle for breath
In the thin air.

But the eyes stride like giants,
Mastering space
As they skim over a harsh land
Of huts crouched
On grudging soil

To where, in a far wall,
The mountains rise
Stern above clouds, making
The world beyond
A matter of faith.

Chapter 1

'THE meaning of life!' said Mrs Logan. '*Very* thoughtful of you to explain it to me.' Her red pen jabbed down again at Paula's essay. 'All I asked for was a simple analysis of 'The Tyger', but you knew better. You decided I wanted this — this half-baked philosophical rubbish.' She waved the pages about as though they disgusted her. 'What did you think you were doing?'

Paula wriggled in her chair. 'I thought —' She hunted for words to defend herself. 'Well, I don't see how you *can* write about Blake without trying to find out what he means.' She knew her face was bright scarlet and she kept her eyes lowered. The rest of the class would be looking sympathetic, but they would be relieved as well. If Logan had picked on her, it meant that everyone else was safe for a while.

'What he *means?*' Mrs Logan snorted. 'I'll *tell* you what he means when the time comes. Until then, you can just take this rubbish away and write me a proper, detailed appreciation of the poem's structure and imagery. Come on. Get it out of my sight.'

Paula got to her feet, stumbled over her bag, and began to walk to the front, bumping against the corners of the desks. She was almost there when, from the corner of her

3

eye, she saw the car parked outside in the courtyard. The white Ford with the distinctive patch of rust on the roof. She stopped suddenly, as though someone had slammed her in the stomach, half sick and half excited. *But they're supposed to be in Rome.*

'Well?' Mrs Logan tapped her fingers on the desk. 'Have we got to wait while you stare out of the window for half an hour?'

'I'm sorry. I —' The words stuttered out. 'My father's car's down there.'

She felt the others sit up, interested for the first time since the lesson had begun. Logan felt it too, and her mouth pinched irritably.

'I suppose we can't expect a *celebrity* to keep the rules,' she said. 'Parents' Days are good enough for everyone else. Your father seems to think he can turn up whenever he likes.'

A little hiss of breath went round the room. Unexpected visits were not always welcome. They could mean a bankruptcy or a death in the family. Logan knew it, and the realization that she had been unfair did not improve her temper. When the knock sounded on the door, she snapped 'Come in!' with vicious emphasis.

Fettis lumbered in. A heavy, dark-haired boy with his hands in the pockets of his prefect's blazer. He took in the scene with his usual silent stare before he spoke.

'Miss Macdonald wants to see Paula Staszic in her office.'

'All right, all right.' Mrs Logan flapped a hand at the door. 'Go on then, girl. Don't stand there like a statue.'

Grabbing up her despised essay, Paula hurried out. As the door closed behind her, she heard Logan say, 'Now perhaps the rest of us can do some proper work.'

Fettis looked over his shoulder and grinned. 'Been chewing you up, has she?'

'A bit.' Paula grinned back, feeling battered. 'I was glad you came.'

'Always happy to rescue a damsel in distress,' said Fettis. 'Especially one like you.'

He gave her a slow, appraising stare and Paula felt herself growing pink. 'I'm not really in distress,' she muttered quickly. 'Not yet, anyway.'

'But you're expecting a bit of distress when Miss Macdonald gets hold of you?'

'No, it's not like that. It's just — my parents have come, and I don't know why.'

'Ah.' Fettis nodded, understanding. As they reached the door of the headmistress's office, he flicked Paula's cheek lightly with one finger. 'Cheer up. It might not be as bad as you think. Might even be something nice.'

Oh please, she thought. *Not trouble.* She knocked.

As she walked in, the first thing she felt was disappointment. Karel was not there. Only Jean, sitting in the big armchair with her knees together and her handbag in her lap.

'Hallo,' Paula said.

'Hallo, Paula.' Jean nodded, but she did not seem to expect a kiss. Paula crossed to the upright chair facing Miss Macdonald and sat down.

The headmistress cleared her throat. She sounded faintly annoyed. 'So we're to lose you for the rest of the term?'

'What?' Paula's head jerked up. 'I mean — I beg your pardon, Miss Macdonald?'

'Ah. I hadn't realized you didn't know. Perhaps you'd better explain, Mrs Staszic.'

'Of course,' said Jean, as though everything were quite ordinary. 'We're starting a new expedition in three weeks, Paula. I've come to take you home today so that you can have your injections and get ready to come with us.'

'But —' Paula faltered and stopped. They never took her with them. She did not even think about it any more. It had been explained to her so often that she knew it by heart. Her education was the most important thing. It

5

must not be interrupted. That was why she was at boarding school. And now, of all times . . . .

Jean answered the question before it was asked, with a queer, ironic smile. 'We're going to South America.'

It was like an earthquake. For a moment Paula could not see anything in the room. Instead, in her mind, she was staring at the jagged, snow-capped peaks of the Andes scoured by a savage wind. And the dark jungle, thousands of feet below, tangled with damp decay. *South America.* The words glittered gold in her brain — the gold of intricate Inca statuettes, of the eyes of great savage cats, of the brightness of the sun on the snow. She could hardly catch her breath.

Gradually she became aware that Miss Macdonald was speaking. '. . . can't say that I approve of this interruption to your work. Not now you've started on your 'O' level courses. But I assume your parents have good reasons. And it's certainly an extraordinary opportunity.' She nodded briskly. 'You'd better go and pack what you need to take. I understand that your mother would like to start as soon as possible.'

Still half dazed, Paula got to her feet and listened to Jean's crisp, unemotional instructions. As she came out of the room, she closed the door and leaned back against it, shutting her eyes for a moment to gather her wits. When she opened them, she saw that Fettis was still there, loitering in the corridor. He looked curiously at her.

'You all right?'

'Oh yes.' The words burst out. 'I've got to go and pack. I'm going to South America.'

'Ah.' Fettis did not ask any questions. That was not his way. But he fell into step behind her as she climbed the stairs and when they reached the box-room he clambered over the piles of trunks to pull hers out of the far corner.

'It's nice of you to help,' she murmured, 'but aren't you supposed to be in a class or somewhere?'

'Private Study.' He hoisted the empty trunk on to his

shoulder. 'And that's what I'm doing. I'm studying you. I want to find out why you looked the way you did when you said *South America*.'

It was not quite a question, and although she was bubbling with it all she did not know how she could begin to explain. So she stayed silent until they reached the dormitory. Fettis put down the trunk in the doorway and leaned against the doorpost. Then he smiled his slow smile.

'Come on. Cough it up.'

Paula dragged the trunk to her bed, just inside the door, and knelt down in front of the chest of drawers. 'It's hard to know where to start. Because it's always been so important. Ever since I can remember.' She started to shovel untidy heaps of clothes out of the drawers and into the trunk. Fettis did not say anything. He just waited. And after a moment or two she sat back on her heels.

'When I was a very little girl, my father used to sit in front of the fire with me — whenever he was at home — and tell me stories. My favourite one of all was about Atahualpa, the Inca ruler of Peru when the Spanish came. He received them with all his soldiers round him and all his glorious gold ornaments and coloured feathers and — oh, everything. The Spanish must have looked pretty rough and desperate, because they'd just come over the mountains. And they had horses. The first horses the Incas had ever seen.'

She shut her eyes for a moment, seeing the scene as clearly as she had seen it in the firelight, hearing Karel's voice telling the story. 'One of the Spanish soldiers put on a display of riding. And he ended it by riding straight at Atahualpa, at full speed. Imagine it. A great, huge animal that you didn't know anything about, charging straight towards you.'

Fettis nodded. 'Bloody terrifying.'

'Awful.' Paula shuddered. 'Atahualpa must have been scared out of his wits. But he never flinched. Never moved a fraction. Just went on looking steadily at the

7

horse until, at the last moment, it turned aside. And he's always been a — well, a hero of mine — ever since I first heard the story.'

She shook herself. 'It doesn't sound anything when I tell it, does it? You'd have to hear Karel. He could conjure it all up. The fantastic richness and organization of the Inca empire, up there in the mountains. The strangeness of that first, huge horse. The whole feel of what it must have been like. If you could only understand how he does it.'

'He's not your private property, you know.' Fettis sounded amused. 'I've heard him too. I'll never forget that television programme he did about the aborigine place in Australia.'

Paula pulled the last of her clothes out of the drawers. 'Yes, it was good, wasn't it?'

'Good?' Fettis said in an odd voice. 'It really shook me up. Made me feel —' He bit off the words and looked down at her. 'And you're going with him this time? Lucky devil.'

'He always promised I should. If he went to South America. That's why I did Spanish as my first foreign language. To get ready. But I never thought it would be so *soon*. I didn't even know he was thinking about it.' She reached up for the photo of Karel that stood on the top of the chest of drawers and Fettis followed her hand with his eyes.

'Bit special, isn't he?'

'I know,' Paula said softly. She looked down at the picture. Karel was standing at the mouth of a cave, laughing in the sun as he gestured towards the black entrance. 'Everything he does is like magic.'

'I think I'd be scared witless if it was my father. Don't you ever worry that he might get killed?'

'I asked him once. When I was about eight and he was going to the Middle East. I said, "You won't *die*, will you?" And he laughed. Like a great bear. Then he said,

8

"It's what a man's *for*, Tabby. To take his life in both hands and throw it into the unknown." '

'And that stopped you worrying?'

She grinned. 'Of course not. Haven't you seen me twitching round the school whenever he's off on an expedition?'

'Not twitching. You just look as though you're not really here.' Fettis gave her a slow, grave stare. 'It must take the edge off everything else. Having a father you can feel like that about. Other people must all seem very unexciting to you.'

'Well —' She could not think of a polite answer. 'A bit colourless. As if they're not quite real.'

'Or as if you're not quite awake,' murmured Fettis, oddly. 'A touch of the Sleeping Beauties.' Then he laughed. 'Shouldn't you be taking your trunk down? Before they send out search parties?'

'Help!' Paula flicked the catches shut and scrambled to her feet. 'Can you give me a hand? My mother said I should be quick.'

They carried the trunk between them, down the stairs and out into the courtyard. Fettis did not say anything else until she opened the boot of the car. Then he muttered, 'I'd like to know what happens to you. You might tell me about it. When you get back.'

His eyes rested briefly on her face and there was something about the look that pleased and embarrassed her, both at once. She glanced away. 'Of course I will.'

'Promise?'

'I promise.'

He nodded abruptly, lifted the trunk into the boot and then turned away, slouching off with both hands in his trouser pockets. Paula slammed the boot shut and clambered into the car. Jean was tapping her fingers on the steering-wheel.

'You were a long time. Been saying goodbye to your boy-friend?'

Paula felt the familiar scratchiness seeping into her. 'He was just helping me with my trunk,' she said coldly.

'Well, put your seat-belt on and let's get going. It'll be dark soon and I want to be home by midnight.' Jean swung the wheel and the car moved off down the drive, under the shadows of the trees. Paula waited for her to say something, but there was no sound except the steady hum of the engine and at last, as they pulled on to the motorway, she broke the silence herself.

'I thought you were both in Rome.'

'We came back last week.'

'Oh.' Paula looked at her. 'Aren't you going to tell me *anything*? Where are we going *exactly*? And what's it for? And why haven't I heard — ?'

Jean shrugged. 'I expect Karel will want to tell you himself. In the morning.'

'But it's all so *quick*. I thought it always took a year or more to organize an expedition.'

'This came up suddenly.' Jean overtook a lorry, not shifting her eyes from the road. 'Karel hasn't stopped working for three weeks. First in Rome and then here. All day and all night.'

'But how can he possibly get it ready in time? There's all the people. He took twelve when he went to Australia. And he had to interview fifty. He'll never manage it.'

'This is a different sort of expedition,' Jean said. 'There won't be lots of people. Just us and — a photographer.'

Something in her voice made Paula look at her. 'What do you mean *a photographer*? It'll be Uncle Alfred, won't it?'

'Not this time.' Jean pursed her lips. 'He's decided not to come.'

'But it's *always* Uncle Alfred.' Paula was bewildered. That was part of it. The names on the spines of all the books. On the television screen. *Staszic and Moon*. Like eggs and bacon. Karel, tall and golden and excited, in front of the camera and Uncle Alfred, stocky and dark and calm,

10

behind it. 'How can we go without him?'

'Well, we are,' Jean said, in a voice that squashed argument. 'And I shouldn't go on about it, if I were you. Karel's not very pleased.'

She stared out at the dark road, the speedometer's needle hovering steadily on the seventy mark. Paula frowned.

'Well, it all feels peculiar. I thought you were still in Rome and suddenly you're not and you're going to South America and I'm coming and Karel's quarrelled with Uncle Alfred and — and you won't *explain*.'

'You'll find out soon enough. Now why don't you get some sleep? There'll be a lot to do tomorrow and you won't be any use if you're tired.'

Paula sat upright, rebelliously, but Jean did not say any more and at last the silence and the darkness and the steady speed began to blur together and she dozed, curling round in her seat. At first she stirred from time to time, glancing secretly across at her mother and trying to surprise an expression on her face. But no one could ever tell what Jean was thinking. She sat there, concentrating on the road, her face a calm blank, and in the end Paula fell asleep properly.

She did not wake until the car slowed, turning into the drive that led up to their house. Blinking, she saw the familiar gabled front, dramatically shadowed by the sweep of the headlamps. The windows in the long frontage were curtained and black, and the creeper waved eerily round the front door. Jean switched off the engine and the lights.

'Wake up, Paula.'

'I am awake.' She sat up and rubbed her eyes, shivering slightly.

'Quietly, then.' Jean opened the door, letting in a whisk of cold air. 'Let's see if we can slip upstairs without waking anyone. We can bring your trunk inside in the morning.'

They tiptoed across to the front door, guided by the light in the porch, and Jean slid her key into the lock. Then, before she turned it, she put a hand on Paula's arm.

'I'm glad you're home,' she said abruptly. 'You ought to be here. For *this* journey.'

It was such an unusual thing for her to say that Paula was startled. Before she could think of a reply, Jean had opened the door and pushed her in.

'Go on,' she whispered. 'Straight up to bed.'

She did not turn on the light and Paula fumbled her way across the wide hall, wondering why Karel had not waited up to see her. Then she felt the smooth rail of the banisters under her hand and realized suddenly how tired she was. She pulled herself up the stairs and, ten minutes later, she was sliding into bed, ready to fall asleep as soon as she closed her eyes.

Then she heard the footsteps. Slow, heavy strides that went along the landing, down the stairs and across the hall. There was a quick murmur of voices and then the steps began again, purposeless and distracting. Across the hall to the kitchen. Back again. Up the stairs and along to the bathroom. And immediately back and down the stairs. A steady, restless tramping, not loud but perfectly audible in the silence. Paula sat up, wondering whether she should go out. But there was something about the sound of the steps that made her lie down again and pull the pillow over her head.

She fell asleep quite quickly, but the noise of the footsteps disturbed her dreams.

Chapter 2

THE morning came in a great burst of sunshine. Paula woke to the sound of birds singing and, leaping straight out of bed, she tugged the curtains back and opened the window, gulping huge breaths of fresh, cold air.

South America. She was going to South America with Karel. The day opened gloriously in front of her and she washed and dressed with excited speed, splashing water up the wall and pulling the brush through her thick, tawny hair until it floated and crackled with electricity.

As she raced down the stairs, she could hear Karel's voice from the dining-room. Throwing the door open, she stood for a moment on the threshold, looking at him. He had been sitting at the far end of the table in front of a huge plateful of eggs and sausages, but when he saw her he jumped up and spread his arms wide, smiling a welcome. His face seemed thinner than she remembered, but his hair and beard gleamed like a halo of gold in the sunlight that came through the window behind him.

Paula launched herself towards him, caught her foot on the edge of the carpet and went tumbling into his arms in a wild rush.

'Tabby!' He laughed as he hugged her, and rubbed his beard in her ear. 'Just as elegant as usual.'

'Oh, isn't it wonderful?' Paula laughed back at him. 'It's really happening? We're really going?'

'We're really going.' He took her shoulders and turned her round to face back down the room.

Immediately she was shocked into embarrassment. Standing at the sideboard, with the coffee-pot in his hand, was a perfectly strange man. He grinned at her.

'You might have warned me, Karel. I didn't know you had a comet in the family.'

He was quite young — around twenty — and as lean as a dancer. Over his sharp, intelligent eyes the eyebrows arched mockingly under a tangle of dark curls.

'I'm sorry,' Paula stuttered. 'I — I didn't see you there.'

'Gross invasion.' He shook his head apologetically. 'Strangers at breakfast. Positively uncivilized.'

'I always fall over things,' said Paula. And stopped, because it sounded so stupid.

Karel rescued her. Putting an arm round her shoulders, he introduced them. 'This is my daughter, Paula. Tabby, this is Finn Benjamin, our photographer.'

Photographer? Paula stared, too surprised to speak, and Finn grinned with relish at her embarrassment.

'Go on. Say it. I'm too young.'

'Well —' It was exactly what she had been thinking. She blushed and looked at Karel, who shook his head with pretended sorrow.

'Awful, isn't it?' he said. 'We needed a photographer who could speak Spanish and Finn was the first to answer my advertisement. So we've got ourselves saddled with him.'

But you don't just take the first one, Paula thought, bewildered. *You always interview lots of people before you choose anyone for anything.*

Finn had pulled an extravagant, outraged face. 'Saddled with me? What do you mean? You're lucky to get me.' He turned to Paula. 'I've been a camera freak since I was seven. I could have done this job standing on my head when I was fifteen. And now I've been to college as well, and got bits of paper to *prove* how brilliant I am. There's no pleasing your father. He *knows* I'm a genius and he's still not satisfied.'

'It's your modesty I like best,' murmured Karel. 'Remind me to take along a horsewhip to keep you in order.'

'You won't need *that*.' Finn looked dramatically solemn. 'You know I hero-worship you, Karel. I've been reading your books since I was in diapers. Your slightest wish shall be my command.'

They grinned amicably at each other, but Paula felt uneasy. She knew how important the photographs were. And, for all his cheeky confidence, Finn was very different from Uncle Alfred with his meticulous expertise. Why was Karel taking a chance on someone so inexperienced? For *this* expedition? Couldn't he have waited until he had a few more answers to his advertisement? Uncomfortably, she changed the subject.

'But what are we going to *do*? Jean hasn't told me a thing. Why is it all so sudden and — ?'

'Not yet.' Karel smiled teasingly at her impatience. 'Breakfast first and then I'll tell you and Finn, both at the same time.'

'You see what a monster he is?' Finn pulled a tortured face. 'I've waited a week, and it's been *agony*. He wouldn't say a thing until you came home. Oh Paula, if you knew how I've *longed* to see you.'

'Breakfast first,' Karel said again.

As though it had been a signal, Jean appeared in the doorway with a plate. 'But don't choke yourself,' she said, as she put it down in Paula's place. 'It'll keep till you've eaten.'

She knew, of course, Paula thought with a flicker of irritation, as she began to chew her way through two sausages and an egg. It was easy for her to be calm. And what did she care about where they were going? Jean never got excited about anything. She just sat sipping her coffee and making a shopping list, as though it were an ordinary day.

Finally Paula mopped up the last dribble of egg with the last piece of sausage and pushed her plate away. 'There. I'm ready now.'

'Let's clear this stuff off the table first,' said Karel.

'Fiend in human form!' Finn gave a loud, dramatic groan. 'You're enjoying it. Watching us eaten alive by curiosity.'

'He just needs the space, that's all,' said Jean, with a tinge of disapproval, beginning to stack plates. 'We don't want to get crumbs on the papers.'

Then they were all ready, sitting with their elbows on the table. Finn and Paula leaned forward eagerly as Karel reached for his brief-case and pulled out a folder. He waved it under their noses.

'Aha!' he said mysteriously. 'The treasure map!' Then laughed at their expressions. 'No, it's not quite like that. No sign of Long John Silver on the horizon. The whole thing's quite complicated. It'll take a bit of time to explain.'

'If you don't start,' murmured Finn, 'I shall explode.' He fluttered his eyelids at Jean. 'Will you sweep me up off the floor?'

She was not softened. 'Why don't you listen? You'll never find out anything if you go on talking.'

Karel pulled a sheet of paper out of the brief-case, suddenly businesslike. 'Right, we start here.' He pushed it across the table to Paula, pointing at the first line of typing. 'Recognize it?'

She looked down and saw the familiar opening words. *El Ynga Atabalipa.* 'Eugh! It's that beastly Diego Martinez and his horrible letter.'

'Never been a favourite of yours, has he?' Karel smiled at her fierceness. 'Suppose you tell Finn about him.'

16

Finn was peering over Paula's shoulder at the paper, looking puzzled. 'Who on earth's *El Ynga Atabalipa*?'

'It's the Inca Atahualpa,' Paula said. 'You know. The one that Pizarro captured when he marched into Peru.'

'Ah. The one who had a roomful of gold collected for his ransom.' Finn nodded.

'That's right. And then the beasts killed him anyway and —'

'Tabby, Tabby.' Karel wagged a finger at her. 'Don't get started on Pizarro or we'll be here till Christmas. Anyway, Finn knows all about him. I've been force-feeding him with books on the Spanish Conquest ever since he came. Get back to Diego Martinez.'

'He was one of Pizarro's men.' Paula gathered her thoughts. 'This paper of Karel's is a copy of a letter to his wife. He'd left her behind in Spain, of course. He starts off by telling her how they've nearly collected all the ransom and how they are watching Atahualpa, to make sure he doesn't plot to get away. They wouldn't let him talk in private to anyone. Imagine it.' She swallowed hard, steadying her voice. Even though she'd known about the letter for years, it still made her feel peculiar to think of Atahualpa imprisoned like that. When he'd been like a god. The son of the Sun.

Then she saw Karel start to tap his finger on the table and she began again.

'This Diego Martinez happened to be keeping guard one day while Atahualpa talked to his doctor. That wasn't so easy to spy on, because the doctors and the Incas had a secret language that the ordinary interpreters didn't know. So when the doctor sent his servant out of the city the next day, Diego Martinez had the servant captured and tortured. I told you he was a *monster*.'

Finn was glancing down at the paper as she spoke. 'I can't see anything here about torture. It just says, "After we had questioned the Indian for an hour".'

17

'Oh, *sure*.' Paula pulled a face. '*Questioned*. Can't you imagine it? They squeezed it out of him. He was being sent to the doctor's tribe — the Kallawaya — to get them to prepare an ancient city. Make it ready for Atahualpa to hide in when the Spanish released him. Only he never was released, of course, because the *pigs* took his ransom and murdered him.'

'A city for a god,' murmured Karel. He had been listening idly to Paula, stroking the folder with one finger. Now he sat up and spoke to Finn. 'What Paula *ought* to have told you, if she hadn't been so busy hating Diego Martinez, is that while the servant was being questioned, the doctor escaped to take the message himself. So Diego had another go at the servant and squeezed the directions to the city out of him.'

'But they're not in the letter?' Finn picked it up and read it through, frowning slightly. 'No. What do you think he did? Kept it a secret so he could sneak off by himself?'

'Only he couldn't!' Paula said exultantly. 'Because he died about a week later. *Before* they shared out the loot from Atahualpa's ransom. And serve him right.'

'We know the date because he made a will when he was dying.' Karel took another piece of paper from the folder and passed it over. 'There. What do you make of that?'

It was much shorter than the letter. Finn scanned it quickly and grinned sideways at Paula. 'How can you be so hard-hearted? All those poor little girls — Inez, Catalina, Isabella, Maria and Juana. Left with no father and a lot of debts.'

'Better off without a father like that,' said Paula. 'Anyway, you've missed the point. Karel didn't give you the will so you could feel sorry for the Martinez family. He meant you to notice this bit. Look, where he tells his wife that she should *conffiar a la Santa Trinidad, y a aquella cosa que ya le he embyado, su fortuna por venir.*'

'Trust her future fortune to the Holy Trinity and to that thing which I have already sent her?' Finn chewed his bottom lip, considering. Then he looked up at Karel. 'You think it was the directions that he got out of the Indian? That he'd sent them to her? He doesn't say so.'

'No.' Karel nodded. 'For years I've *thought* that that was what he meant, but I've never been able to prove it. I even went to Soria, where the family lived, and sorted through all their business papers. But there wasn't a sign of it.'

'Couldn't it have been used?' said Finn. 'After all, it was all Sēnora Martinez had by the sound of it.'

'You think she leaped on to a boat and took her five daughters on a treasure hunt to South America?' Karel grinned. 'Not a chance. She might have sold it, I suppose, but in that case, there ought to have been some record of someone trying to find the city. No, my bet was that she'd hidden it away somewhere, not really believing in it. It's a fairly fantastic tale, after all.' He grinned, almost smugly. 'And I wasn't far wrong.'

'Oh, go *on*!' Paula banged her fists on the table. 'What's happened?'

Karel leaned back in his chair. 'Remember my friend Peter Laban, Tabby? He's working in the Vatican Library. All sorts of strange things have landed up there and he came across the *domestic* papers of the Martinez family. You know, household bills and account books and so on. He's writing a book about them. And a couple of months ago I got a card from him. It just said, "Come at once," but I knew. As soon as I read it.'

'He's found them?' Paula caught her breath. 'He's found the directions?'

Karel nodded. 'Glued between two pages of a ledger.'

'Well, come on.' Finn flicked his fingers. 'You can't stop now.'

Karel put a hand on the folder, pressing it shut. 'Before I get this out, I want a promise. This could be a really big discovery. One of the great discoveries of South American history.' His face was grave. 'I intend to be the man to find that city. I don't want anyone to beat me to it. You must promise not to breathe a word of what I'm going to show you.'

There was a moment's silence and then Finn said lightly, 'Cross my heart and hope to die.'

'I'm serious.' Karel gave him a long, steady look and Finn stared back, his blue eyes unwavering.

'So am I.'

'Paula?'

'Of course,' she whispered. 'I promise.'

'Well, here you are.' Karel slid another sheet of paper out of the folder and laid it on the table in front of them. 'Read it carefully and see what you think. I would say it's a direct translation of the words of the Kallawaya doctor's servant. Written down more or less on the spot, while they were torturing him.'

Paula and Finn leaned forward, their heads close together, and tried to take in the unfamiliar words:

Segund es de todos sabido, junto al lago que dizen del Señor Viracocha comiença el camyno que atraviesa las montañas hasta los ayllus dellos Hampis Camaiocs. Dexando el camyno do se desbia hazia la salida del Señor Inti y los valles de los Calahuaios, el camynante que quisiere alcançar la cibdad occulta deve prosseguir por la loma de la sierra, la qual en su estremo se conuierte en un valle que se abre hazia adelante.

En el paraje do el arroyo que passa por dicho valle se desagua en otro mas grande, el camynante hallara al otro lado del puente un sendero. Aqueste sendero es aspero y difficil de passar y baxa por el bosque. Llegados al termyno de dicho sendero los ygnorantes desesperan y buelven atras, mas los sabios deven buscar la señal del Señor Illapa, la qual es el rroydo della gran huaca.

Es menester camynar rrio abaxo durante muchos dias, soffriendo las cuytas de la jornada, conffiando en la Pacha-mamma y rrechaçando toda duda hasta llegar, por terçera vez, a la boca de un rrio caudaloso que entra por la derecha

20

mano. En la rribera de enffrente, cerca del lugar do se ajuntan dichos rrios, es la torre de piedra hecha por el pueblo de antaño, la qual señala el camyno occulto que cruza la sierra de mas alla.

Despues de atravessada la sierra, el camynante porfiado vera al fin aquello que vos jamas vereys porque en breve morreys, el lugar occulto del bosque ado no llegaran syno los fieles despues de soffrir muchas penas, la cibdad secreta del Oryente do tornara a nascer nuestro Señor para destruyr a los invasores y bolver a traer la gloria del pueblo de Tahuantinsuyo.

★   ★   ★

Despues de pronunciadas estas palabras, murio el ynfiel, siempre sin creer.

Karel was watching them. Quietly he said, 'Translate it, Tabby. Let's make sure you've got it right.'

She began, stumbling a little. '*At the lake of the Lord Viracocha* — he was a god, wasn't he?'

Karel nodded. 'It's Lake Titicaca, in the Andes, between Peru and Bolivia.'

'Well, from there, *begins, as all the world knows, the road over the mountains to the ayllus* — villages? — *of the Hampis Camaiocs.*'

'They're the doctor's tribe,' Karel said thoughtfully. 'The Kallawaya. And the villages are still there. There shouldn't be any trouble about finding them. But the Kallawaya could be trouble if — oh well, never mind that for now. Go on.'

Paula started again. '*Leaving the road where it turns towards the rising of the Lord Inti* — I know that. He's the Sun — *and the valleys of the Calahuaios* — oh, the Kallawaya — *the traveller to the hidden city should follow the mountain ridge which, at the end, gives place to a valley stretching ahead. When*

21

the stream of this valley flows into a larger stream, the traveller will find a path on the other side of the bridge.'

'Bridge?' interrupted Finn. 'Do you think that will still be there?'

Karel shrugged. 'Probably not. The Incas went in for rope bridges. Go on, Tabby.'

'It is a hard path and difficult to travel and it goes down through the forest. At the end of the path, the ignorant despair and turn back, but the wise should seek the guiding-sign of the Lord Illapa, which is the sound of the great — the great huaca. What on earth does all that mean?'

This time, she and Finn both looked up, and Karel laughed at their faces.

'What did you expect? A street map? I don't know what it means. Illapa was the god of thunderstorms, and a huaca was a holy place — some sort of natural feature. But I've got no more idea what it is than you have.'

Paula felt Finn stir beside her, as though he were about to argue, and she plunged on quickly:

'It is necessary to travel downstream for many days, bearing the sorrows of the journey, trusting to the Pachamamma — she's a sort of earth mother, isn't she? — and ignoring all doubts, until, for the third time, a great river flows in on the right hand side. On the bank opposite the place where these rivers join, is the stone tower built by the people of before, which marks the hidden road across the further mountains. Phew! Well, that's fairly clear, anyway.'

Finn's mouth twitched, but he did not say anything.

'When he has crossed the mountains, the steadfast traveller will see at last that which you will never see, because you will die soon — what does he mean?'

'That should please you,' murmured Karel. 'He was talking to your favourite man, remember. He must have spotted that old Diego wasn't too well.'

'Good!' Paula said fiercely. She fumbled for a moment, finding her place. '. . . because you will die soon, the hidden place of the forest, which only the loyal shall reach, after great

22

hardship, the secret city of the East from whence our Lord shall rise again to destroy the invaders and bring again the glory of the people of Tahuantinsuyo.'

'Tahuantinsuyo,' Karel said softly. 'The Land of the Four Quarters. The Inca name for their empire. This city wasn't just a hidey-hole, you see. It was a spring-board. A centre for the rebirth of something splendid.'

'There's a line and then a bit more,' said Paula. 'Oh. *Having spoken these words, the infidel died, still unbelieving.* Poor man. He must have felt terrible. To have given it all away.'

She put the paper down and Finn leaned back in his chair and looked at Karel. 'Gee,' he said. 'Oh gosh. Golly. Coo, sir.' His eyes narrowed. 'And you're really taking this *seriously?*'

Jean glanced sharply at him and Karel gave a small, tight smile. 'You don't like it?'

Finn grinned, baring white, perfect teeth. 'I love it. It's like a boys' adventure story. But to *go* there? On the basis of all that stuff? It's a mishmash of gods' names, roads that might go anywhere, bridges that have vanished and the sound-of-something- only- we- don't- know -what-it -is.'

'You sound like Alfred Moon,' Karel said. There was a bitter edge to his voice and Paula burst out, before she could stop herself.

'So that's what happened! You showed it to him and he wouldn't go and you quarrelled.'

On the table, Karel's hands clenched. 'Something like that.' He was still watching Finn. And Jean was watching him. Suddenly Finn laughed cheerfully.

'*I* was like a kid, I suppose. I thought it would be all clear and simple. That we could just whip out a map of the place, compare it with the instructions and draw a big "X Marks the Spot".'

'Then leap into a helicopter and fly off there?' Karel grinned, loosening the tension. 'There was never any chance of that. Haven't you ever seen a map of that part of the world? Look, I'll show you.' He took the last thing out of the folder and spread it on the table. It was a huge sheet of paper, about four feet by six, and it lay across everything else. It was almost completely white except for a web of straggling blue lines. 'This is the most accurate map of the area. And here's our bit. North-west Bolivia, up by the Peruvian border. Where the Andes swoop down to the edge of the Amazon basin.'

Paula stared at it. 'But where is everything? There aren't any contour lines. No roads. Nothing much except rivers.'

'And even those they're not quite sure of.' Karel was laughing at them. 'Did you think the whole world was as well mapped as the middle of Birmingham? What do you think I've been doing all my life? I'm an explorer. Remember?'

'So the only way we can find out if the directions work,' Finn said slowly, 'Is to start at the beginning and follow them. To the letter.'

Karel nodded. 'That's right.'

'And the servant might have been lying.'

'He might.'

'And the landmarks might have vanished.'

'Yes.'

'And the Kallawaya might never have obeyed Atahualpa's instructions anyway.'

'That's possible. But it's not really important. Because there was a city there to start with. Just finding that would be worth it.'

'Phew!' Finn looked at Karel with reluctant respect. 'You *are* serious.'

Jean said, 'Of course we are. How do you think we got the money for the expedition? We've raised a loan on the house.'

Paula felt a quick nudge of fear. 'You mean we lose it if we don't make enough money out of the trip?'

'That's right,' said Jean.

24

For a moment, Paula could not take it in. Everything hanging on that single piece of paper. And Jean, dull pernickety Jean, was as calm about it as if they were going to Margate. When even Uncle Alfred thought the whole thing was impossible.

Karel began to fold the papers together, speaking quietly. 'That's it. You can back out if you like. No one's forcing either of you to join in. But I'm going, and Jean's coming with me. For twenty years I've known that that city was there, somewhere in the jungle, and I've always meant to be the man to find it. Now I've got the chance to go, I'm not going to hold back because it seems difficult.' He shut the folder and looked up at them. 'Well?'

Finn tapped his fingers together, trying to look precise and thoughtful. But his hands were shaking. 'Isn't it possible to wait a bit? To try and find out some more before you risk everything?'

Jean was suddenly very still, almost as though she were holding her breath, and Paula glanced at her, puzzled. But Karel's reply was matter-of-fact.

'No. If we hang on, we'll get caught by the rains, and it'll be a year or more before we can try again. By then, Peter will be publishing his research — including the directions — and there'll be a mad scramble. Other expeditions. Publicity. Not to mention the Kallawaya.' His face darkened for a moment. 'I shouldn't like them to get wind of the trip. You never know —' His voice drifted away and he frowned. Then he looked tauntingly at Finn and Paula. 'Come on. I'm supposed to be the old fogey around here, and I'm leaving in three weeks. What about you young fogeys? Are you coming with me?'

He had raised his voice slightly and the words echoed in the panelled room. For a moment they hung in the air like a challenge and then Finn caught his breath and jumped to his feet.

'Blast you, Karel Staszic! I thought I was a rational man, but if you make it a *dare* — I'll shrivel up and die if you leave me out.' With a great bound, he leaped on to his chair and flung his arms up above his head. 'I'm for Bolivia and the Andes!'

It was impossible not to laugh at him as he tottered on the chair, grinning down at them like a goblin. But it was the right gesture, thought Paula. Because this was not an ordinary journey. It was the one that Karel had waited for all his life. The one he and she had dreamed of, in all those magic, firelit evenings. Across the sea, in the forested foothills of the Andes, a golden city was waiting for them.

She scrambled up, knocking her own chair over backwards. 'Of course I want to come. Don't you dare leave me behind.'

'Well there's no need to break up the furniture.' Jean's everyday briskness shattered the mood. 'Get down before you fall off, Finn. We've all got an appointment at the doctor's in half an hour, to have our injections.'

Finn slid off the chair, pretending to grovel apologetically, and Karel put his brief-case away. But as he turned back he winked at Paula and Finn's words sang themselves in her head:

I'm for Bolivia and the Andes!

Chapter 3

At the lake of the Lord Viracocha begins, as all the world knows, the road over the mountains to the ayllus of the Hampis Camaiocs.

T̶HE Land Rover bumped down yet another pot-hole in the bleak, dry plain. Jean reached an arm over the back of the seat and pulled some oranges out of a bag behind, handing one each to Paula and Finn. Dropping her own into her lap, she began to peel Karel's and feed him with the segments as he drove.

'I'm sick of this wretched altiplano already,' she said. 'I can't see why you all thought it was going to be so wonderful.'

Paula knew what she meant. Wedged uncomfortably in the front seat, between Karel and Jean on one side and Finn on the other, she kept trying to glimpse the distant mountains through the cloud of dust the Land Rover stirred up. Kept trying to make herself believe that they were actually two and a half miles above the sea, in the place where the Incas had ruled. All she could really feel was the jolting and the icy wind that whipped through the canvas roof, but she was not going to tell Jean that.

'I think it's lovely,' she said.

Finn stared out at the sparse clumps of spiky grass and the huddle of thatched mudbrick houses in the middle distance. The huddle that never seemed to get any nearer. The knitted Indian hat he had bought in La Paz was squashed down ridiculously on his curls and, between the hanging earflaps, his face was gloomy.

'I just hope this is all worth it,' he said. 'I still don't see why we couldn't have picked up a guide in La Paz.'

'I've told you.' Karel sounded irritable. 'If we'd gone round La Paz asking for a guide to the Kallawaya villages, there'd have been questions. Everyone would have known which way we were going. And we'd probably have landed up with a Kallawaya guide.'

'But I don't think — ' Finn began.

'That's right. You don't think.' Karel cut him off short. 'You're the photographer. Leave the thinking to me.'

Tired, thought Paula. They were all tired. Even Karel was squabbling like a four year old. She opened her mouth to try and tease him back into a good humour, but before she could say anything Jean dug her in the side with a sharp elbow. Oh well, perhaps it was best to be quiet. She concentrated on peeling her orange and staring at the mountains, trying to ignore the village.

It was another half hour before they drew up beside the nearest house. Karel switched off the engine and opened his door.

'I'll go and see if I can find this man Octavio Quispe, that Philip Bellamy told me about. Tabby, you stay and keep an eye on the Land Rover. The rest of you can come if you like.'

Disappointed at being left out, Paula curled her legs up on the seat and stared out of a side window. All around her spread the plain, unrelentingly flat for miles and miles until, in the far distance, the mountains rose, floating above a great bank of cloud. Their peaks were jagged, carved out against the sky. Close at hand, the houses turned their backs, enclosed by high walls. The overhanging edges of the thatch shivered in the wind and, above the top of the nearest wall, a couple of llamas looked haughtily at her, chewing slowly.

A sudden noise from behind made her turn and she jumped. Two large, brown eyes stared at her through the opposite side window. It was a boy of about her own age, his hair blowing untidily under a knitted hat, his red and orange striped poncho pulled tight around him. She smiled quickly and pushed the window open.

'Good day,' she said in Spanish.

He smiled back, inquisitive but a little cautious, and said something. She had not had time to get used to the guttural Bolivian accent and she did not understand.

'Please?'

He repeated it, very slowly. 'It is an American car?'

'No.' She shook her head. 'It is English. A Land Rover.'

'Land *Rover*.' He tried out the syllables awkwardly. 'And it is not new. How old?'

'I don't know.' She felt stupid and ignorant. He walked round the Land Rover, peering closely at details and nodding to himself from time to time. When he reached the driver's door, she pushed it open.

'Do you want to come in? To look inside?' She waved a hand at the controls and the dashboard and he nodded gravely, climbing up into the seat. For a while he did not say anything. Just touched the switches carefully and pressed a foot down on the clutch so that he could move the gear lever.

'There are many gears?' he said at last.

'Lots, I think. But —' She stuttered to a stop. She knew hardly anything about cars and she could not even understand his next question, but had to shrug and spread her hands. He stared at her for a moment and then ignored her, leaning forward to study the dials. To get his attention back, she asked, 'This is your village?'

He pointed, without looking up from the dashboard. 'It is my house there. And my father is with the foreigners.'

Karel had come through a gap in the wall with three Indian men and was talking rapidly to them. From time to time he paused and the men put their heads closer together as though discussing what he had said.

'That is my father. He — ' Paula fumbled for the word. 'He finds new places.'

The boy looked faintly amused. 'This is not a new place. It is a very old place.'

'Yes. Of course.' Paula blushed, feeling that she had been rude about the village. As an apology, she waved a hand towards the mountains. 'They are very beautiful.'

'They are very wise.'

Was that really what he had said? It did not seem to make sense.

She was still puzzling when Karel strode across with Finn and poked his head through the window.

'You are Agustin?' he asked the boy. 'The son of Octavio Quispe?'

The boy nodded. 'You have been speaking with my father?'

'I have spoken to him. We have agreed that you and he will come on our journey with us. To guide us and to help us talk with the people.'

For the first time Agustin looked excited. 'We shall travel in this Land *Rover*?'

'At the start.' Karel smiled at him. 'You like it?'

'I like all cars.' Agustin gave a grin of pleasure and slid out of the door, running towards the group of men. Karel glanced after him.

'Octavio's the man Philip told me about. The father who took his son to a Kallawaya village. It was a stroke of luck finding him here. He could easily have been working away from home. And he's fairly hard up. Only too anxious to earn a bit of money by guiding us to the Kallawaya villages.'

'But I didn't think we were —' began Paula.

Karel put a finger to his lips. 'Plenty of time to break that to them later on. When we're clear of the village and they can't gossip.'

30

Finn raised an eyebrow. 'Is that really —'

'Keep your opinions to yourself, you young whipper-snapper,' said Karel. It was almost a joke, but not quite. 'You just concentrate on taking photographs.'

'Yes sir. Very good, sir.' Finn pulled an imaginary forelock. But his eyes were serious as he pranced round to the back of the Land Rover.

It crossed Paula's mind that, if she had been in Karel's place, she would have wanted to know what Finn was thinking. His jokes were a brittle crust, like the ice on a pond. What was moving in the black water underneath?

But Karel did not give her time to think about it. He nodded briskly.

'Out you get. Octavio's invited us to eat with his family tonight and Jean's sorting out some food for us to contribute. Nip round and see if you can help her.'

Paula slid out of the door. The wind whipped her face cruelly as she walked round the Land Rover and, although she pulled up the hood of her jacket, her ears tingled with cold. Almost immediately, her fingers were numb, and when she reached into one of the boxes of food she knocked a bag of dried beans on to the ground. The bag broke and the beans spattered out on to the dusty soil.

Jean sighed impatiently as she bent to scoop them up. 'Oh Paula, can't you be *careful?*'

'She's a natural disaster.' Finn grinned, but he had spread a quick protective hand over the equipment he was sorting. Now he pulled his camera out of its travelling bag and slipped it into one of the big front pockets of the padded waistcoat he was wearing. 'Watch out, folks. Here comes Hurricane Paula.'

'I think I'll get on better without you,' said Jean. 'Take these eggs — if you can carry them without dropping them — and give them to Octavio. He's over there, by the corner of the house.'

Paula blew on her fingers to warm them and took the eggs, walking across to the short, stocky man Jean had

31

pointed out. As she held out the eggs, he smiled, a slow, rather melancholy smile.

'Here are some eggs,' Paula said in Spanish. 'Please take them for the meal.'

He took them but, as he did so, he shook his head and said something incomprehensible, pointing to his mouth with his free hand. What he meant was obvious, but for a moment Paula could not believe it.

'That's right,' murmured Finn, coming up behind her. 'That's Octavio — and he doesn't speak Spanish. But he's the one your father's decided to take with us. To be our guide.' He shrugged. 'Ours not to reason why.'

'I'm sure he knows what he's doing,' Paula said quickly.

'Did I say anything? *Did* I?' Finn spread his hands. 'I'm only the photographer. Remember? Keep me in my place.'

He was smiling ironically and Paula felt herself go pink. She had not meant to be rude. But Karel *must* be right. Mustn't he?

For a moment the question made her uneasy. Then, as she turned to follow Octavio into the house, her eye was caught by the massive shape of the mountains, tinged pink by the setting sun, and her doubts were swallowed up in a swoop of wonder and happiness. As the wind raked her face, she felt, for the first time, that she was really in a high, alien place, at the beginning of an adventure. Tomorrow they would set off for the mountains and she would be able to watch the distant peaks all day, as they grew closer and closer.

But in the morning, when Karel had supervised the loading of the Land Rover, he pointed at the back. 'You'd better go in there, Tabby, with Octavio and Agustin. I want some elbow-room if I'm driving all day.'

'But I shan't see a *thing!*'

'You're not sightseeing.' Karel sounded sharp, but Finn gave a delighted crow.

'You've been exposed, Paula. You're nothing but a tourist.'

Karel grinned. 'She'll be wanting to buy postcards next.'

'And sticks of rock.' Finn shook his head teasingly. 'And funny hats with *Up the Andes* written on them.'

'I think you're both rotten.' Paula pretended to sulk. 'I'll just have to see what I can when we stop for meals.'

Karel frowned. 'There won't be time for that. It's a long way. Octavio says there's a village just after we get into the mountains. We should be able to leave the Land Rover there and hire mules, but we'll need time to chat up the villagers. So we can't waste any on picnics.'

He moved off to discuss it with Octavio and Agustin, and Paula pulled an exaggerated, despairing face at Jean. 'Is he *always* like this? In a mad rush?'

It was meant as a joke, but Jean looked stony 'He's in a hurry this time. Now get in the back and stop fussing.'

Paula climbed in among the boxes and bundles, curling her legs over a couple of rucksacks. Agustin and Octavio settled themselves opposite, between packages of dried food. Octavio seemed resigned to a long, boring journey. He leaned back and closed his eyes, his broad face peaceful.

But Agustin was excited. Ever since he woke up, he had been asking eager questions and examining things. He had even persuaded Finn to let him use his precious camera to take a photograph of Paula. She thought she would never forget his face, as he looked up from pressing the switch, nor the wonder in his voice as he said, 'I have done it? I have made a picture?'

Now he craned his neck to look through a gap in the back, watching as his village began to dwindle in the distance.

'This is a very fast way to travel,' he said.

Suddenly Paula remembered what Karel had told her the day before. 'Was it you who came this way with your father? To the Kallawaya?'

33

He nodded.

'Tell me about it. Is it a hard journey?'

'I was small.' He tilted his head thoughtfully. 'A *wawa* with my hair just cut for the first time. I remember that my arm hurt me. It was hot and heavy. And I cried when we got near to the mountains.'

'Because of your arm? Or because you were afraid of the journey? It must have been hard to cross the mountains.'

'How could I know that?' He looked scornfully at her. 'When I had never travelled in mountains before? No, I was afraid because they were the mountains.'

'But what *made* you afraid?'

She could see from his face that her question meant nothing to him. 'I was afraid because they were the mountains,' he said again.

Paula gave up and tried a different question. 'And was the journey difficult? Do you remember?'

'I remember that the sharp stones made my feet sore. And my mother told me afterwards that my father carried me in his arms for eight days. Even though I struggled when the fever took me.'

Eight days. Paula looked across at Octavio, who was sleeping. He was no taller than she was, and she had gasped for breath in the thin air even from loading the Land Rover. But he had carried a child for eight days through the mountains.

'He was good,' Agustin said unemotionally. 'They could have had other children instead of me. And it cost him the price of five llamas to pay for my cure. That is why he is a poor man now and must work for a *patron* like your father.'

Octavio stirred slightly, turning his face towards Paula. It was smooth and unwrinkled, but the bones stood out strongly and the skin was toughened by the wind.

Paula looked back at Agustin. 'Tell me about the Kalla-waya. What did they do to cure you?'

Agustin suddenly looked obstinately blank. 'I remember nothing. Only that I came back across the mountains and my arm was light and cool like the other one.' He shifted in his seat, as though the subject made him uncomfortable, and said in a different voice, 'This is a good Land Rover. When I am a man, I shall go to La Paz and learn to fix engines like this one.'

But Paula was still curious. 'Is it true then? What they say about the Kallawaya? They really can make wonderful cures?'

Agustin's face was expressionless as he pulled his poncho round him. 'It is a long journey. I shall sleep now.' Closing his eyes, he turned his head away from her.

Paula wriggled inwardly. He made her feel that she had gone crashing into something private. *Why don't you think first?* she scolded herself. But there was no way to apologize. Agustin's eyes stayed firmly shut and, with nothing to stare at except the endless plain behind, she found herself dozing as well. After an hour or so, she fell asleep properly.

She woke to the sound of raised voices. The Land Rover had stopped and outside Karel was shouting impatiently in Spanish.

'Tell your father to say that I do not wish to *buy* their starved mules. Only to hire them. And that I have not got as many dollars as they ask for. But I will leave the Land Rover here. And if they do not trust me to come back, I will give them a paper to say that they may sell it if it is still here in six months.'

'Calm down,' murmured Jean, very low, in English.

Paula climbed stiffly out of the back of the Land Rover. Karel and the others were standing among a crowd of Indians, in the centre of a bunch of battered houses with corrugated iron roofs. All around lowered the mountains, rocky and forbidding, but the little group of people had suddenly broken into smiles. Karel's last offer seemed to have been accepted. He was grinning and shaking hands with one of the men.

Agustin waved to Paula. 'It is agreed. My father is going to choose the mules. Will you come?'

Paula glanced quickly at Karel. He had turned aside from the group. Jean was talking quietly to him and looking in her shoulder-bag.

'The *patron* is not well,' murmured Agustin. 'I think he is asking for medicine.'

Karel did look very tired and grey-faced. Paula took a step towards him.

'Go away,' said Jean, without turning round. 'Karel's got a headache, that's all. He doesn't want people fussing round him. You go off with Octavio and look at the mules.'

She sounded almost too brisk. Paula shrugged and followed Agustin across to the nearest compound, where half a dozen mules stood staring dully towards them. Octavio was examining them with care, running his hands down their legs and forcing their mouths open to peer at their teeth. The owner of the mules was standing beside him, frowning and talking quickly.

Paula glanced at Agustin. 'Is there something wrong?'

'That is the *cacique* — the head of the village. He is worried that his mules will not be safe. He says that the foreigner is rich enough to take the mules and leave the Land Rover. Then the *cacique* will have money, but not the mules he has reared. I think he wants to change his mind.'

Octavio had straightened now and was speaking earnestly. He placed one hand on his heart and gestured up at the mountains with the other. Then he reached into the woven bag that he carried over his shoulder and pulled out a bundle of leaves. Selecting some carefully, he held them out to the *cacique*.

With great seriousness, the *cacique* took a few, dropped one deliberately on to the ground and rolled the others in his hand, working them into a small ball which he put into his mouth. Octavio took some more leaves for himself and, chewing companionably, the two men returned to the study of the mules.

'It is settled,' Agustin said, with a tinge of pride. 'My father has given his word that he will take care of the mules and they have chewed coca together. We shall have our mules.'

'Not *that* one, I hope,' said Finn. He had lounged across to them and now he pointed. Octavio had laid a hand on the head of the biggest mule. Rolling its eyes, it backed away from him, its teeth bared. 'That one looks ready to eat us.'

Agustin laughed and cocked his head sideways to listen. 'The *cacique* is saying that that is the best mule of all. His name is Atoc — the Fox. Where he leads, the others will follow. I think my father will take him.'

Finn shuddered elaborately. 'It will give me bad dreams to know that he is with us.'

'There are worse things than that in the mountains, Señor Finn,' Agustin said. His voice was grave, but the light in his eyes was teasing. 'There is the condor, who carries off young llamas. And the puma who attacks in the dark.'

'Don't! Don't!' With pretended terror, Finn cowered away. 'I am not a brave man.'

'And the *karisiris*,' went on Agustin, with relish, 'who suck the fat from sleeping children.'

'Why did I ever come?' wailed Finn, grinning. 'This journey will scare me out of my wits. I am terrified.'

The track they took the next morning was enough to terrify anyone. It was narrow and steep, climbing rocky valleys and curling along ledges cut into the mountain slopes.

Underfoot, the path was cobbled and uneven. Paula was glad of her heavy new boots. The small stones, set side by side into the ground, were rough to walk on and in places they had been knocked out, so that the earth was eroded into dusty holes. But at least there was no doubt about where the track went. It stretched inexorably ahead round the sharp shoulders of hills and into the distance where the view was cut off by yet another slope.

Walking along it was incredibly hard work. The mules kept up a steady plod and Octavio and Agustin walked easily beside them, as though they were out for a Sunday stroll, but Paula found herself panting after less than a mile. Her legs ached and she felt curiously light-headed, as if she floated somewhere high in the sky, watching the little procession wind its way, unbearably slowly, up one narrow valley after another.

Karel's impatience made everything worse. He was obviously trying hard to be considerate, watching the others to make sure they were all right, but he never suggested that they should stop. When they were forced to rest, or when Finn insisted on taking some photographs, he paced about irritably.

'This is the *easy* part of the journey,' he said. 'It's all straightforward until the road turns towards the Kallawaya villages. We can't afford to waste time on this bit. I want to get it over in two days.' He changed to Spanish, turning to Agustin. 'Ask your father. We shall reach the turning of the road in two days?'

But Octavio shook his head when the question was translated and held up three fingers. Karel frowned.

'No. Tell him I want to get there in two days.'

Agustin muttered to his father and then replied, 'He says that it must be three days or even four. With foreigners and with the mules loaded so heavily. Otherwise we shall have to rest for a whole day.'

'Perish the thought!' muttered Finn under his breath. 'A whole day doing nothing? Karel would burst.'

Jean heard him and pursed her lips, moving closer to Karel. 'I think we should go on as fast as we can. We don't know how difficult the way will be later on. When we get down towards the jungle.'

The conversation echoed uncomfortably in Paula's head for the rest of that day and all the next. However steep the path grew, she kept remembering that there was worse to come.

By the third day, they were all scratchy and exhausted. As though to mock them, the track became even more arduous. A high ridge ran straight across in front of them and they could see the path zigzagging up the mountain face and over the top. Paula felt herself shrinking with weariness as she looked at it. *I can't*, she thought, *I can't*. But she was tougher than she knew. Even while she was gazing in horror at the ridge, her feet were carrying her mechanically towards it, step by step.

The cobbled path grew gradually more derelict as they went. As they toiled up towards the ridge, Paula saw Octavio and Agustin start to shuffle their feet among the loose stones, staring down thoughtfully. Then Octavio bent and picked up a small, round pebble, turning it over in his hands as he walked on.

A moment or two later, Agustin did the same, pausing slightly to choose between two apparently identical stones. Glancing over his shoulder, he saw Paula watching him. As though he were embarrassed, he shrugged and let his fingers fall slack, so that the stone bounced away, clattering on the path. But Paula noticed that he picked up another one when he thought she was not looking.

Karel was about a hundred yards ahead, nearly at the top. He clambered the last few feet, past a great untidy cairn on the crest, and turned, his tall figure outlined against the sky, his hair golden in the sun.

'Hey!' he shouted.

It was the first sign of excitement he had shown in all the three days and the others began to walk faster, their feet skidding on the uneven ground.

39

As he reached the large heap of stones, Octavio stopped, with Atoc, the lead mule, nosing gently in his ear. Bending down, he placed the stone he was carrying carefully on the side of the pile and stood back for a moment, gazing at it.

Agustin, coming up behind, was less deliberate. But, all the same, Paula saw the stone slither from between his fingers to take its place on the heap. *It's a ceremony*, she thought, suddenly understanding. She turned to ask Finn what he thought, but he had reacted quite differently to the sight. Leaping forward, he shouted, 'A cairn! I love cairns!'

Dramatically he heaved a huge rock from the side of the track and staggered up to the pile, dropping it on to the very top. Paula felt obscurely shocked, wondering if he had made fun of something important. Perhaps they should have ignored the stones. Agustin had flushed, like a child caught in a foolish act. Looking apologetically at Octavio, Paula was amazed to see him smiling gently and shaking his head, as though he understood her feelings, and wanted to reassure her. *He is a kind man*, she thought, with a queer surge of surprise. It had not occurred to her to wonder what he was like.

Smiling back, she stepped beyond them, across the ridge to where Karel was standing. He was quite still, the wind blowing his hair into a great cockade. Without turning, he reached a hand backwards and pulled her to stand beside him.

'How about that?' he said softly.

In front of them, the mountain dropped away steeply in a downward swoop of rock, sparsely covered with grass. But far below, a dark tangle crept up the valleys, muffling the angles between the spurs.

And below that, thousands of feet down, a great sweep of green stretched away into the distance. It spread in a smooth blanket, broken by minute eruptions of colour — purple, crimson and yellow. Across the centre, cutting a

40

curling, silver line, ran a river, shrunk to a mere thread from the height at which they stood.

'The roof of the jungle,' murmured Karel.

As her eyes grew used to the huge splendour of the view, Paula picked out tiny, darting specks of scarlet way below as a flock of birds flew over the tree-tops. Then she tugged at Karel's sleeve. 'Look!'

Further along the ridge, almost on a level with them, a great bird was riding the up-currents, poised almost motionless over the immense drop. Its huge wings spread wide, a curve of black patched with silver with the long feathers at the tips fanned out, moving delicately to correct its balance.

'Condor,' breathed Karel. All at once he squeezed Paula's hand, so hard that the knuckles ground together. 'We're on our way, Tabby. We're going to find it. We're *here!*'

Paula was taut with joy. All her life, this had been promised to her. That she should stand in these mountains with Karel, the boring details of homework and hockey and Logan left behind and the dream of a golden Inca city ahead of her. And now, at last, they were on their way. She forgot the harshness of the journey and Karel's impatience. She even forgot her own clumsiness, her inability to say the right things. Her mind swooped and hovered like the condor, and there seemed to be nothing in the world except the austere mountains, the richness of the jungle and the powerful, relaxed flight of the great bird.

'If you'd left me behind,' she whispered, 'I would have *died!*'

Chapter 4

Leaving the road where it turns towards the rising of the Lord Inti and the valleys of the Kallawaya, the traveller to the hidden city should follow the mountain ridge which, at the end, gives place to a valley stretching ahead.

'This must be it,' said Karel. 'I was beginning to think we'd never reach it.'

It was the morning of the fourth day and ever since they struck camp they had been climbing a long, narrow tongue of land. The road had been mercilessly straight, grinding diagonally upwards, and even Karel had been forced to rest every half hour or so.

Now they were on top, exposed to the full force of the wind. Ahead of them, to the north, stretched a sharp ridge, with valleys falling away steeply on either side. But the path curved away eastwards, zigzagging down the slope into the nearest valley.

'That is the way to the ayllus of the Kallawaya?' Karel said.

Octavio caught the last word and, without waiting for Agustin to translate, smiled and nodded. 'Kallawaya,' he repeated, turning Atoc's head towards the slope.

But Karel put a hand on the halter. 'No,' he said. 'Agustin, tell your father that we do not go that way. We follow the ridge.'

'But Sēnor Karel —' Agustin looked puzzled. 'You will never reach the Kallawaya that way. We must keep to the road.'

'I do not wish to reach the Kallawaya.' Karel shook his head firmly. 'I told you our journey would be long. This road was only the start of it and here we leave it.'

Seeing Agustin hesitate, he added, 'I am paying you to take me where I want to go. You are not to decide. Only to obey.'

'You wish me to say that?' Agustin's chin lifted. 'To my own father?'

'Say it how you wish. As long as it carries my meaning.'

'Don't you think we ought to explain?' murmured Finn in English. 'Tell them what we're up to.'

'Not yet,' said Karel. 'Not until we're clear of the Kallawaya.' He pointed to the ridge again, to make sure that Octavio understood.

Agustin was talking rapidly to his father, spreading his hands and glancing over his shoulder at Karel. Octavio did not answer at once. Instead, he turned to the mules and began to examine their feet and the ropes that held their loads. Paula watched him, blowing on her gloved fingers. The stiff, formalized pattern of llamas on his poncho danced and wriggled as the cloth billowed in the wind, but underneath, his stooped back was steady and solid.

At last he straightened, muttered a few words to his son and stood with his arms folded while Agustin translated.

'We shall do as you ask. But it will be harder for the mules without a path. It may be necessary to rest them.'

'We shall do whatever is needed.' Karel nodded. 'The mules still have a long way to travel and we must take care of them. Now, let us start.' He stepped off the path and began to stride out along the ridge, with Jean hurrying after him.

'*Not* very well handled,' murmured Finn. 'They don't like it. He should have told them where we're going.'

'Oh, you always know best, don't you?' Paula rounded on him. 'Why don't you stop sniping? *You're* not leading this expedition.'

43

He grinned. 'You want me to be a faithful follower, like you? Not a question in my head?' Reaching out a hand, he ruffled her fringe. 'You're beautiful. Like a lovely golden labrador. A one-man dog.'

She jerked her head away. 'At least I haven't got to be right all the time.'

'Because Karel will do that for you?' Finn looked shrewdly at her. 'That's not a let-out, you know. Even a labrador has to stand on its own paws. And you could do it, if you tried.' He laughed at her uncomprehending face and leaped off the path, shouting, 'Forget it! Here we go. Into the unknown!'

Karel looked over his shoulder and frowned.

'Not so much noise. Do you want everyone within a hundred miles to know we're here?' He pointed down towards the valley that fell away on the right. Its lower slopes were patched with small fields and over the surface of one of them minute black-clad figures were moving, stooping as they worked. 'There they are.'

Finn clapped a hand to his forehead. 'Not,' he said, in a loud stage whisper, 'not the Kallawaya?'

'Of course.' Karel did not look amused. 'It would be better if they didn't notice us.'

But it was a hopeless wish. The little procession of travellers was moving along the very crest of the ridge, outlined against the sky, and it was not long before one of the black figures straightened and looked upwards. Putting a hand to his mouth, he gave a long, yodelling shout that echoed between the funnelling walls of the valley.

'Damn,' said Karel.

'It was bound to happen.' Jean touched his arm. 'I don't suppose it matters very much.'

'Let's hope not,' Karel sounded grim. 'But there can't be much to gossip about in these mountain villages. I'll bet the news travels faster than we do.'

One by one, the people below had turned to look up at the ridge. They stood with their hands on their hips, like a

44

line of dark pillars stretching across the stony field. All the time the travellers were moving across the head of the valley they did not stir and even later, looking back, Paula could see that they had not started work again. They had come together in a huddle, like a crowd of ants. But it was not possible any longer to tell which way they were looking. Paula imagined she could feel their fixed gaze.

For the rest of that day and half the next they toiled along the ridge. The wind scoured the ground, leaving them battered and exhausted. But there were still people about, even though the mountain was too high and bare for pasture land and they had left the Kallawaya villages behind. Once they came down a dip in the ground and surprised three boys herding llamas in a high valley. Octavio shouted something cheerful to them, but they gazed with hostile, inquisitive eyes and did not reply. And on the second day they saw an old man toiling along a path below with a heavily loaded mule. It seemed that, even here, on top of the world, they were not entirely isolated.

They were just into the afternoon of the second day when the ridge finished. A small stream oozed out of the earth. Unlike the other streams they had passed, it ran neither to the right nor to the left, but plunged north, down a steep valley.

Karel looked down it, nodding with satisfaction. 'That poor devil of a servant hasn't let us down. It's exactly as he said. That's our valley, and this is the stream we must follow.'

Finn ran up, jerked to a stop and raised his eyebrows. 'What do we do? Put on our parachutes and jump?'

The valley dropped away sickeningly, walled in by precipices of bare rock, two or three hundred feet high.

Karel chewed at his lip. 'We'll have to go down the stream. In the water. That's rather what I expected from the directions. At least it's not deep.'

'I bet it's cold.' Paula pulled a face. 'Will the mules be able to do it?'

Karel turned to Agustin. 'Say that we go down the stream. We must walk in the water. Can your father manage the mules?'

'It is very steep.' Agustin gazed down the valley. 'I will ask him.'

Octavio did not say anything. He smiled his sweet, melancholy smile and began to unfasten the coil of rope that the second mule carried. Carefully, he fastened one end to the harness on Atoc's shoulders. Then he moved to the other mules, tying them together in a train with lengths of rope left slack between. Finally he tested the knots, leaning against them with all his weight. When he was satisfied that they were secure, he picked up Atoc's halter and signalled to Agustin.

'I will take the second mule,' Agustin said. 'Someone should hold the third also.'

'I'll do it,' Paula said quickly, eager to be helpful. She slipped her hand round the strap and the mule turned to look at her, its brown eyes liquid and patient. With her other hand, she stroked its nose. 'Come on, boy. We can do it if we take it steadily.'

She felt that she was feeding the mule with her own determination. As they began to pick their way down the rocky, uneven bed of the stream, she kept her eyes on its hooves, checking that each foothold was firm.

Gradually the water deepened, oozing over the tops of her boots and squelching icily round her toes. Her bones ached with the cold, and her knees and the fronts of her thighs knotted, bracing her against the downward slope. But she tried to ignore the pain. The mule. She had to take care of the mule.

After about half an hour, Karel began to grow restless. He had been leaping ahead, jumping from one large rock to another and then standing with his arms folded listening to the crunch and scrape of the mules' hooves while they caught up. At last he signalled to Octavio to stop.

46

'We are not going fast enough. It is the ropes. They slow the mules down. Agustin, tell your father that he must untie them.'

'It is for safety,' protested Agustin. 'If one should fall, the others will hold him — so.' He caught at the rope in front of him and dragged on it. Immediately, Atoc planted his feet wide apart and strained forward, taking the weight.

Karel frowned. 'It is not necessary. Do as I say.'

Octavio listened in silence while Agustin repeated the command and then shrugged and began to untie the rope. From time to time he glanced ahead, but he did not say anything and, when the rope had been coiled and loaded back in its place, he took up Atoc's halter again and began to move.

Inexplicably, Paula felt less safe. She had not needed the rope, but the sight of it had given her confidence. Now they were moving faster and her mule, without the gentle tugging from in front, jibbed more often when the way grew difficult. Once or twice she had to pull with all her strength to urge it over a particularly large boulder.

All the time they were going down, the stream had been growing larger and noisier. Paula had imagined that it was because they were now walled in. The rocks rose almost sheer on either side of them and, between them, the clatter of the water resounded deafeningly. But Octavio was looking worried and as they came round a curve in the stream he stopped and pointed. At last Paula understood what had been bothering him.

'There's a waterfall,' she said to Finn. 'What do we do now?'

Five yards ahead, the stream bed stopped suddenly, in a jagged lip of rock, and the water crashed fifty feet into a pool below. Beyond that, for another twenty yards, the stream frothed white over a series of ledges like steps.

'You're asking *me* for an opinion?' said Finn. 'Ttt ttt, you don't catch me that way. You know that's the Great

47

White Chief's job.' He laughed at the expression on her face. 'You're going to hate me by the time this journey's over, aren't you?'

'I don't hate anyone,' she said primly. 'And I'm sure Karel's got a plan to deal with the waterfall.'

He had. He had walked on a little way and was studying the bank. Almost level with his head, there was a fault in the rocky cliff. It made a narrow, grassy ledge that ran sloping downwards past the waterfall. He studied it for a moment or two and then turned to the others.

'It ought to be possible to get up there. If we pile up some of these boulders —' he waved at the edges of the stream '— we can make a sort of ramp for the mules. You three keep hold of them. The rest of us will move the stones.'

Jean and Finn began to heave at the boulders, dragging them splashily through the water. Within minutes, Jean was white-faced and pressing a hand to her side.

'Don't try too hard,' said Finn. 'You have a rest. Karel and I can do this.'

He put a hand on her shoulder, but she pushed him away crossly and then gave a tight smile. 'I'm O.K. You can treat me like a china doll when you hear me start to moan.'

'And that's never, I suppose.' Finn shook his head at her. 'You ought to leave it to Karel. He'd make five of you.'

'He's not lounging about either,' said Jean.

She was right. Karel seemed to be finding it very hard work. Paula looked at him in surprise. He was so strong that she had never seen him struggle to lift anything, but now he was labouring, his face bunched as though he were in pain. *It's the altitude*, she thought quickly. *The thin air.* But it still seemed odd. Although Finn was sweating, he moved far more easily than Karel.

She could not watch them for long. Her mule was jittery, shuddering nervously at the closeness of the waterfall, and

48

she had to concentrate on holding it steady. Atoc clearly did not like the noise either. Octavio was soothing him and whispering into his ear. Only Agustin's mule was unconcerned. Bending its head to the stream, it was drinking, taking no notice of the roaring beyond or the grinding and rattling as the stones were piled higher.

It took the best part of half an hour to build the ramp and test each stone to make sure it was steady. As Finn, perched on top, settled the last one in place, Octavio reached for the coil of rope.

'Not *now*,' Karel said. He knocked Octavio's hand aside to make his meaning clear. 'We haven't got time to start fussing with ropes.'

For a moment it looked as though Octavio would argue. He muttered a few words to Agustin, pointing up at the ledge and down at the waterfall. But it was difficult for him to have a complicated conversation with Karel, because he could not speak directly to him, and in the end he shrugged and picked up Atoc's halter.

The mule whinnied loudly and planted all four feet firmly on the stream bed, its eyes rolling. Octavio frowned and then smiled, tugging gently at the thick mane. Then he spoke to Agustin again.

'My father will take my mule first. Because it is not afraid. When Atoc sees that all is well, he will follow. He is not stupid.'

They exchanged halters and Octavio led the second mule forwards, clicking his tongue encouragingly and jumping on to the first stone to show that it was safe. The mule hesitated for a moment and then lumbered forwards obediently, stepping carefully up on to the rock. Inch by inch, Octavio coaxed it upwards until, with a final scrabble, it lurched up on to the ledge, pushing its soft nose into his face as he praised it.

Immediately Agustin led Atoc forwards, imitating the encouraging signs that Octavio had made. But Atoc was still uneasy. He sidled around, baring his teeth and whinnying in protest.

'Oh, for Heaven's sake!' With a splutter of annoyance, Karel stepped forward and slapped the mule's brown rump. With a scrape of hooves on stone, Atoc lashed out bad-temperedly with his back legs. Then, as if he had made enough of a complaint, he scrambled up on to the first layer of stones.

But Paula's mule was startled by the sudden movement, and one of Atoc's hooves had flicked its leg. With a toss of its head it jerked backwards, its eyes rolling. Before she could regain control, its back hooves skidded and slid over the edge of the waterfall.

Automatically, she heaved on the halter, trying to pull the mule back to safety. But, instead, she found herself dragged after it, its weight sending her sliding across the loose stones towards the waterfall.

Finn reacted instantly. Not bothering to speak, he hit her hands sharply upwards so that she cried out and drop-ped the halter. There was a long squeal and a rattle of stones. The mule scrambled desperately at the edge with its front hooves and then plunged over, hitting the water below with a great splash.

'You made me let go!' Paula screamed at Finn. 'I was trying to save it!'

'It would have pulled you after it,' Finn said. He was white and trembling. 'If you hadn't let go, you'd have been down there as well by now.'

Sick with shock, Paula looked over the edge. The mule was lying in the water, almost completely submerged and whinnying with pain. It raised its shoulders and planted its front feet down. But as it attempted to heave its body up its voice rose to an agonized shrillness and it fell back.

Octavio, his lips pressed tightly together, was taking the coil of rope from the mule on the ledge. Without looking at the rest of them, he looped one end round a projecting rock, testing the knot carefully. He tied the other end

50

round his waist and took a knife from his bag, gripping it between his teeth.

'What will he do, Agustin?' murmured Paula.

Agustin stared down at the water as, very slowly, Octavio began to lower himself down the bank, planting his feet against the sheer rock and keeping the rope taut to brace himself. 'He will kill the mule. It has broken its leg — perhaps its back also — and it suffers. It is in his care.'

Horrified but unable to turn away, Paula watched as Octavio reached the water. He waded out into the pool, the water coming almost to his waist, his body braced against the eddying current. When he was close to the mule, he began to stroke its head soothingly, his hand running over its eyes. With his other hand, he reached for the knife.

'Don't look, Tabby,' Karel said quietly.

'I can't help it. I —'

His hands gripped her hard and he turned her away from the waterfall, towards him. With a sob, she buried her face in his chest and pressed her fingers into her ears. But she still heard the shriek of the mule and she began to shake.

'It's all right,' murmured Karel. 'It's done. Octavio's just cutting the load off its back.' His arms were round her now and she leaned against him. But it seemed hours before she heard the noise of Octavio climbing up the bank again, dragging the heavy bundles after him.

'You can look now,' Karel said.

Keeping her face turned away from the pool, she lifted her head and saw Octavio heave himself up on to the bank. His face was expressionless. Karel moved across to the ramp of stones and jumped up them, reaching Octavio in time to help him to his feet.

'It was my fault,' he said. 'I bear the blame. Agustin, tell your father not to distress himself. At least it was not your own mule.'

51

Agustin stared at him scornfully. 'If we had lost our own mule, it would be bad. But this is worse. My father had pledged his word for the safety of that one. He chewed coca with its owner.'

Karel hesitated, as though he wanted to say something else, but Octavio turned his face away and began to untie the bundles he had brought up from the pool. They were wrapped securely in groundsheets and most of the things were still dry. Squatting back on his heels, he started to sort through them.

'He's right,' Karel said with relief. 'We have to get on. Take off your packs, all of you, and see what else you can fit in.'

But even when they had crammed in as much as they could and loaded extra on to the two remaining mules there was still a heap of things left on the ground. Without speaking, Octavio wrapped them in a groundsheet and began to lash the bundle to the top of his pack.

'It is too much,' said Karel. 'He cannot carry so much.'

'Do not stop him,' Agustin said. 'It is what he wishes. He is grieving for the death of the mule and he wants to carry its load.'

Karel shrugged. 'Very well. But he must not exhaust himself.'

Tying the last knot, Octavio slipped his arms through the straps of the rucksack. For a moment it looked as though he would not be able to rise with the weight. But he pressed both hands down on the ground and stood, a little unsteadily, settling it on his back. No one dared to speak to him. His face was grim and he seemed to stand in a pool of chilly silence. Looping Atoc's halter over his arm, he began to walk along the ledge, past the waterfall. Catching hold of the other mule, Agustin followed and, without a word, the procession moved off again.

Paula felt tears prickle in her eyes and she rubbed them away angrily. It would be disastrous if she started to cry. Instead, she lagged a little to let Finn catch her up.

52

'I don't want you to think I didn't realize,' she said awkwardly. 'That you saved my life just now. Thank you.'

Finn waved a hand. 'I'm just a natural hero. No need to make a big thing about it. But you can start a fan club if you like.'

His flippancy shocked her and she turned to stare at him. 'How can you *joke?* It died, Finn. The mule *died.* And Octavio's wretched.'

She could not believe that Finn was not upset. But his eyes slid away.

'No good looking on the black side,' he muttered. 'It was only a mule, wasn't it? I didn't come on this journey to mope over things like that.'

He began to walk faster, to escape from her, whistling jauntily between his teeth. Shaken, Paula plodded on, keeping her eyes turned away from the stream. Just in case it should be carrying a horrible pink froth as it gurgled its way down from the pool under the waterfall.

Chapter 5

When the stream of this valley flows into a larger stream,
the traveller will find a path on the other side of the bridge.

They toiled on along the ledge which sloped down-wards, bringing them back to the bed of the stream. Paula tried to concentrate on simple things. Like where to put her feet. But now that she had no mule to look after, there was room to think.

If only Karel had not insisted on untying the rope. Then the mule would have been safe. If only he had not got impatient and hit Atoc. Then the accident would not have happened. How could he — he, of all people — have made such stupid mistakes?

A horrible gulf of doubt opened in Paula's mind, more frightening than the steep valley that fell away under her feet. She tried to ignore it, but the further down the valley they went, the deeper it yawned. And her miserable thoughts clustered round it.

As though to match her mood, the valley began to grow tangled and shadowy. Small bushes clung to the slopes, gathering in tight thickets, and every now and again there were clumps of low trees. Passing close to one, she startled a flock of brown birds. They swirled up into the air, shrieking warning notes.

It was late evening when they reached the bottom of the valley they were descending. It merged with another one, coming in at an angle, and the stream they had been following plunged into a river about ten feet wide. At the sight of it, they all stopped. Jean gave a small, relieved smile and Finn yelled in triumph.

'Eureka! Just like the directions say.'

'You thought the river would have vanished, did you?' Karel chuckled. 'The rivers are about the only things we can be sure of. I wouldn't have come if there'd been nothing at all.'

'Expect me to believe that?' scoffed Finn. 'You'd have come however shaky the directions were. You know you would.'

Paula found herself tensing, waiting for Karel to explode. But he simply smiled a tired, tolerant smile and said, 'Perhaps.' Then he added, 'I was right about the bridge, though. There's no sign of it.'

'Oh, fiddlesticks.' Finn snapped his fingers. 'What's ten feet of water among friends? We can swim it if we have to.'

'It's more likely we'll have to wade.' Karel studied the water. 'Agustin, we must cross here. Tell your father.'

But Octavio shook his head, pointing at the darkening sky and then at the bundled tents which Atoc carried.

'It is late,' Agustin said. 'The mules are tired from carrying too much. We should camp here and cross in the morning.' Seeing Karel hesitate, he went on urgently, 'Please, Señor. For the sake of the mules. You have promised.'

Not just the mules, thought Paula. Her feet ached and all the muscles in her legs were so weary that they were shaking. *Please, Karel.*

It was Jean who settled it. Without saying anything. She simply started to unpack. 'Paula, you go and collect some firewood,' she said briskly. 'I want to get everything sorted out and the meal cooked before it's too dark to see properly.'

When she called out to say that she was ready, Finn looked round. 'What are Octavio and Agustin up to? Why don't they come and have something to eat?'

The two Indians were standing by the tethered mules, looking across the river. Immediately opposite, the far side of the main valley rose in a steep slope. But fifty yards to the left the slope was broken by a gigantic fault in the rock which had opened a huge cleft. The river turned and poured away through this gap, dropping out of sight in a great rush of water. Gazing through the opening, Paula could not see any more mountains. Instead, far in the distance, were the dark, clustered trees of the jungle roof thousands of feet below. Octavio was pointing down towards them and frowning.

'What are you doing?' called Karel. 'You should have some food.'

Agustin walked across. He looked troubled. 'My father says that there is a danger of mountain lions in this place. He wants to watch all night to guard the mules. But I tell him that he should sleep.'

'Right.' Karel nodded. 'Say to him that we will take turns to watch.'

Octavio did not seem to like the idea. Without raising his voice, he spoke more emphatically to Agustin. Karel stood up.

'It is not only tonight. There will be another night and another. Many more. Will he never sleep again? He must trust us to watch and we will wake him if a mountain lion comes.'

'*I'll* say,' muttered Finn. He raised his head and added, 'I promise to scream if I see a puma. My knees will shake and my teeth will rattle with fear. It is quite safe for Octavio to sleep.'

He mimed intense terror to show what he meant, jerking his plate of stew so that some of it slopped on to his knees. Agustin gave a quick gulp of laughter and Octavio nodded, smiling gently.

56

'Good thing I'm an idiot,' Finn said under his breath.

Jean glanced shrewdly at him. 'Nothing idiotic about you. You're as sharp as a sickle underneath all that clowning.'

'Exposed!' Finn flung an arm across his face. 'Leave me my defences! I feel naked without them.'

They all laughed, but the thought of pumas was still worrying and that night Paula slept uneasily. She was constantly aware of the great snowy peaks that towered behind them and the huge drop, beyond the far wall of the valley. Two or three times she dreamed of falling and woke with a jerk, trembling inside her sleeping-bag.

The third time, she found it hard to doze off again. Jean was curled up beside her, completely still, her head tucked into the angle of her elbow, but beyond her was an empty space where Karel had been lying. He must have woken and gone to take his turn at watching. Suddenly, Paula could not bear the thought of sleeping any more. Wriggling out of her sleeping-bag, she dragged it after her as she crawled through the door of the tent.

Karel was sitting by the fire, his face lit by the dull glow of the wood. He turned, alert at the sound of her feet, and held out a hand.

'What's the matter? Bad dreams?'

'Not really. But I can't sleep. Can I come and sit with you for a bit?'

He patted the stone beside him. 'Come and keep warm, then.'

She sat down, pulling the sleeping-bag round her shoulders, and snuggled up to him. He put an arm round her and she was wrapped by the warmth of his body and the heat from the fire. Turning her head, she glanced back up the valley, towards the mountains.

'Oh.' It was a disappointing sight. Beyond the narrow circle of firelight, everything else was completely black. They could have been sitting in the middle of the New Forest. Karel chuckled.

'Thought there'd be a great panorama, did you? Mountains looming against the sky and a faint gleam of snow? It's the night, you know.'

'But I thought there'd be *something*.'

'You're too civilized,' he teased. 'Can't imagine life without street lamps. When you get out in the wilds, you really understand about being afraid of the dark. It's always like this when there's no moon. An endless, terrifying blackness. Makes you realize that the world *is* huge, in spite of what people say.'

She looked up at him. 'But you're not frightened of it, are you?'

He grinned. 'Not please-Mummy-come-and-turn-on-the-light sort of frightened. No. But there's always a certain — oh, I don't know — a certain awe. Just at the immensity of it all. I quite like it, really.'

He sounded solemn and Paula asked, 'Is that why you do it? Come to places like this?'

'Great mountains and great thoughts, you mean?' He chuckled again, staring at the crackling twigs. 'You've been reading too many magazine articles. That's the sort of thing bright young reporters expect me to say.' He pulled a face. 'Still, I don't know. I suppose it's right in a way. I certainly look forward to nights like this when I'm back in England. But that's not *why* I come.'

'So why *do* you? I mean — do you know?'

He sat in silence for a moment. Then he moved his arm from around her, picked up a bundle of sticks and threw them on to the fire, sending up a stream of sparks that floated off into the darkness. 'Do you remember your grandmother?' he said slowly. 'My mother?'

'Only sort of.' Paula searched at the fringes of her memory. 'She used to sit in a chair in the corner. When I was small.'

He nodded. For a moment Paula thought that he was not going to say anything else, but suddenly he began to talk in a low, unhurried voice, still gazing into the fire.

'She wasn't always an elderly woman in a chair. When we first came to England just before the war, she was quite young. Very pretty and gay, with long, fair hair plaited up around her head, like a Polish girl in a picture. And she didn't speak a word of English. When my father joined the Air Force — quite a lot of exiled Poles did that — she was left by herself in London with me to look after. And I was only four. Not much of a companion.'

'She must have been very lonely.' Paula tried to imagine it.

'Oh, she could have coped all right. She was young and strong and clever. She'd have been O.K. if it hadn't been for the war. It was the air raids. They scared the wits out of her. I didn't understand what it was at the time, of course. I just remember —' he paused for a second '— I remember being woken, in the dark, scooped out of my bed and carried down to the cellar. She used to dump me on a bed in the corner and sit on the floor, hugging her knees. It was always the same. First she was very quiet. Then, gradually, she would start to shake as the bombing got going. By the end she'd be screaming, pressing her hands against her ears and rocking backwards and forwards.'

'How *awful*.' Paula remembered the old, blotched photograph of a little fair-haired boy with big eyes. She could see him, crouched on the bed in the corner, staring at his mother and listening to the screams that went on and on and on. 'You must have been terrified too.'

'I was in the beginning.' Karel stroked his beard and stretched out a foot to kick some burning branches back on to the fire. 'It was like a nightmare. And she never spoke about it. Never said anything to explain what was going on. Then — when I was about five — I made a great discovery. I found that I could *beat fear*. If I screwed up my mind, like clenching a fist, I could freeze the bit of me that was afraid and stay quite calm. And that was a sort of triumph. After a bit, I actually got to *enjoy* the wretched air raids. Just to have the satisfaction of knowing I could defeat the terror.' He grinned. 'I remember trying to tell my mother about it. But it wasn't any use, of course. There's no way a five-year-old can explain something like that. So we'd sit in the cellar, just the two of us, night after night. She'd be rocking and screaming and I'd be sitting bolt upright on the bed, grinning all over my face. Must have been a comic sight.'

Paula kept completely still, afraid that he was going to stop. He did pause for a while, and when he went on his face was troubled.

'It turned into a sort of obsession. *Winning*, I called it in my mind. I had to keep on *winning*, so that I wouldn't turn into a shaking creature like my mother, screaming in the dark. And when the war was over — I was about eleven by then — I found I couldn't stop. I had to go out and look for things that would frighten anyone else. Just to prove I could still *win*.'

'So you became an explorer?'

He grinned and ruffled her hair. 'Not straight away. I wish life were that simple. No, I nearly turned into a boring sort of thug. You know — taking dares and running stupid risks that put other people in danger. I might even have become a criminal, I suppose. Only —'

'Only what?' Paula wriggled round so that she could see his face better. 'What happened?'

'I met someone who actually *understood* what I was doing. And who showed me what a stupid way I was choosing. She dared me to go out and find a real test, somewhere really dangerous. So I went on that first expedition to the Himalayas. And that was how it all started. She changed my life.'

'Who was it?' whispered Paula.

'Who?' Karel looked surprised. 'It was Jean, of course.'

'*Jean?*' That was the last answer Paula had expected. She had always thought that Jean resented Karel's explorations. That she would have liked him to stay comfortably at home, like anyone else's husband.

'You two don't understand each other very well, do you?' Karel sounded both amused and sad. 'She —'

But whatever he had been going to say, he changed his mind. Putting his arm back round Paula's shoulders, he tapped the end of her nose with his other hand. 'Time you had another nap, Tabby. You look half asleep already. Go on, put your head on my shoulder. I'll wake you if there's a puma. So you don't miss any excitement.'

Paula leaned her head sideways and closed her eyes. But she did not stop thinking. *Jean* had changed Karel's life? She had always assumed that Jean was the dull one, carried along by Karel's enthusiasm but never quite taking off. There was something unnerving about discovering a different pattern under that familiar surface. For the first time, she started to wonder what really held her parents together.

She did not mean to go to sleep. She would sit quietly for ten minutes or so. Then, perhaps, she could persuade Karel to talk again. But the smell of the wood smoke and the rush of the water falling through the cleft drifted her into a real sleep and she did not wake again until Karel shook her.

'Come on. Time to open your eyes.'

'What?' She lifted her head. It was still dark, but the sky had lightened a little, and the shapes of the hills loomed clearly. 'What's happening?'

'Morning's happening.' Karel stood up and stretched. 'We must have breakfast and pack up. I want to start again as soon as it's properly light.'

It was nearly an hour before they were ready. By that time the sun was rising and wisps of mist had begun to float through the gap in the ridge opposite rising from the forest. Karel was in a brisk mood, fretting impatiently as he watched Octavio loading the mules.

61

'Get a move on. Here — I'll do your pack for you.' He gestured, to make his meaning clear. 'Give me the rope and I'll fix it.'

He crammed as much as possible into Octavio's rucksack and then made up the bundle that went on top, his hands moving quickly as he looped the rope that held it on. Still calling instructions to everyone else, he knotted the short ends of the rope roughly.

Finn took a step forwards. 'Hey, look, Karel. You've —'

'Leave it,' murmured Jean. 'He's got another one of his headaches. If you bother him now, he'll be in a temper all day.'

'But he —'

'*Leave* it.'

Finn frowned for a moment and then shrugged. 'Sorry. I forgot I was the village idiot.' But he did not sulk. Instead, he stepped up to the edge of the river. 'Shall I be the guinea-pig? Someone's got to go first and see how deep it is.'

'O.K.' Karel said. 'Want to leave your camera and stuff behind?'

'Not a chance. If someone's going to take them over the raging torrent, it's going to be me.' Finn patted his padded vest. Almost all his equipment was crammed into the two big front pockets. 'I can hold this up out of the way. And if it gets so deep I have to swim, I'll come back and think again. Right. Ready for the strip-tease. Are you going to blush, Paula?'

Grinning wickedly at her embarrassment, he slipped off his trousers, wrapping them round his neck like a scarf. His underpants were a brilliant fluorescent pink and, below them, his legs looked thin and white. He rubbed his hands vigorously up and down his thighs. 'Here goes, then. If I get swept away, you can have my clean pair of socks, Paula.'

He stepped into the water, howled dramatically as the cold reached him and began to walk across with slow, careful steps, keeping up a running commentary.

'There's a piranha fish nibbling my toes. Ouch! It's bitten one of them off. Now it's working its way up to my knees. I'll be a helpless cripple for ever.'

'Stop fooling about,' said Karel. 'Is the bottom safe?'

'Not bad. Lots of little stones, but quite firm.' Reaching the other side, Finn scrambled out and began to dance up and down, shivering.

Octavio went next. Catching hold of both the mules, he led them towards the river, clicking his tongue and signalling to everyone else to stand clear. The mules looked utterly disgusted, but they stepped out with perfect faith in Octavio, putting their feet delicately into the water and plodding across with their heads bent.

'Now us.' Karel looked at Jean. 'Want me to carry you?'

'Nonsense,' she said briskly. 'I'm no more feeble than the rest of you.' She had rolled her trousers up above her knees and she did not flinch as she stepped into the cold water. But by the time Finn pulled her up on to the opposite bank she was shaking.

It was not until they were all across that Finn said, 'Well?'

'Well what?' Karel looked up from lacing his boots.

'Well where's your path? We're supposed to find it when we get across the river, but there isn't any sign of it. We can't be meant to follow the river down. We'd break our necks.'

'Perhaps we have to go *up* first,' Jean said quickly. 'Over this hill. Then the path could go down the slope on the other side. Let's climb up and have a look from the top. If there's a clear view, we may be able to see it going down.'

'No rest for the wicked,' groaned Finn. 'Why did I ever leave England, with its nice, *little* hills? These mountains are great brutes.'

But he was exaggerating. The slope which faced them was no bigger than a good-sized English hill. It stretched along the side of the valley, broken only where the river plunged down to their left. They began to climb up through the trees, moving slowly because they had to choose a route that the mules could walk.

The top of the ridge was bare. Karel reached it first and they heard him shout, 'Well done, Jeanie! You were right.'

Scrambling up behind him, Paula felt her heart flip as she looked over the edge. The mountain fell away almost vertically. For hundreds of feet, only occasional stunted trees kept a precarious grip in its crevices. Then it plunged into the darkness of thick forest, wrapped in mist.

The path was a narrow, zigzag ledge, cut into the face of the rock. It ran downwards to the left a little way and then doubled back, a hundred feet lower. That was bad enough, but, immediately below them, as it ran back to the right, the ledge was broken. Only a very narrow rim of rock remained, poised above the dizzying drop. Paula gulped.

'Splendid,' Karel said, as though it were a three-lane motorway. 'We'll get down the mountain like lightning.'

The others were grinning with relief at having found the path. Paula bit her lip. Couldn't they see? That terrible gap, with an ugly scar of jagged rock below — and then nothing to guard you from the sickening fall into the black shadows of the forest. Why weren't they afraid? Or was she just a coward? Miserably she clenched her fists, willing herself not to make a fuss. She had to be able to get down that frightful path. *Had* to be able to cross the terrifying broken place.

Then she saw Octavio looking at her, his brown eyes kind. He smiled gently and spoke a few words.

'He asks if you are afraid of high places,' said Agustin.

She was startled, sure that she had not given any sign. 'Of course not,' she said quickly.

64

But Octavio was still watching her, nodding slowly. She remembered how quick he was to sense the mules' reactions. Now he was looking at her with the same steady, reassuring kindness. He handed the reins of both mules to Agustin and smiled again. Gesturing at the mountains above and at the forest below, he struck the palms of his hands together like cymbals, in a dismissive movement, as though to show that the drop and the threatening darkness below were of no account. Tapping his chest, he said something to her.

'He wants you to wait here,' Agustin said. 'To watch him. He will go first, to show you that there is nothing to be afraid of.'

With light, quick steps, Octavio ran along the sloping path to the left, his load bumping and swaying on his back. Then he swung round the curve where the path twisted back and they saw him coming along the lower section. The slope was so steep that he was close beneath them and they could see hardly anything except the top of his woollen cap, bright above the mist below, and the bundle on top of his rucksack, which bounced as he ran.

When he reached the broken place in the path, he stopped running and began to walk more carefully, edging close to the rock. Paula could see that he had been right. It was not nearly as difficult and frightening as it had looked. Coming almost to the end, he looked up and waved vigorously, as though to show that the crossing had been easy.

What happened next seemed to take place in agonizing slow motion. As Octavio waved, the bundle on top of his rucksack lurched and the knot that Karel had tied so hastily suddenly gave way.

The heavy load slid sideways, knocking him off balance. His fingers clawed at the rock wall beside him, but there was nothing to grip and he tipped over, his poncho swirling outwards in a billow of crimson.

For one appalling second, they could see him outlined against the open sky, his mouth wide and his arms flailing.

Then he crashed down over the edge of the precipice. There was the sound of branches cracking and stones rolling down the hillside and then the noise died away and they could hear nothing except the rushing of water and the howling of wind round the mountain top.

Cloud Forest

The ground tilts, treacherous, and the green, decaying
Woods drip, drip in a stealthy whisper
From the mist-wrapped trees and the snarled bark of the
    vines
In the twilight cloud forest.

Imprisoned in richness, the watchful eye chokes,
Cribbed into a compass of seven steps,
Feasted to sickness by the flaring, rainbow growth
Of the spawning cloud forest —

Feather-bedded by moss, festoons of lichen
And the soft crumble of rotting litter of wood
That cushions the stumbling slide of steps that shuffle
Through the drenched cloud forest.

And panic lurks in the shadowy darks, hidden
In knotted stems, behind the headlong fall
Of waters, rises in nightmare shapes cowled
In mist, couched on the rim of sight, winding
The nerves to an almost scream that strains at the taut
Hypnotized skin of silence spun in the head
By the deadly cloud forest.

Chapter 6

It is a hard path . . .

THE dust hung in a low cloud over the broken track, thickening the mist, and for an instant that seemed like an hour they all stood motionless. Then Agustin let go of the mules and began to run down the track, his feet scattering the stones. With a glance at each other, Karel and Finn started after him. Paula could hardly breathe. Spreading her fingers across her mouth, she whispered hysterically, '*I* did it, *I* did it, *I* — '

Jean slapped her face.

'Stop it!' Her voice was low and fierce. 'Stop it at once. That won't help anything. It would have been better if you hadn't behaved like a silly child, but it wasn't your fault. The knot came undone.'

Paula gulped. 'Karel's knot?' That seemed to make it worse, not better.

'It was a granny,' Jean said calmly. 'Finn tried to tell him, but I shut him up. And there's no point in going on about it now. We must do what we can.' She caught hold of the mules, who were snuffling nervously at the path, and handed one of the halters to Paula. 'Now pull yourself together and come on.'

They began to lead the mules along the path, looking down at the lower track. Agustin had fallen to his knees as he reached the gap and was peering over the edge. Karel came up behind him and caught his shoulders, pulling him to his feet and talking quickly. As the mules approached, he looked round.

'Bring them up against the rock here. We'll tie a rope to them and I'll go down.'

'But you're the heaviest —' began Finn.

'I'll go down.' Karel took the rope and began to knot it round the harness on the mules' shoulders, ignoring Finn's eyes as he tested the knots. 'The rest of you can keep hold of it and pay it out as I go.'

Slipping off his rucksack, he fastened the other end of the rope around his body and crawled to the edge of the path, lowering himself carefully over the side and climbing down with his face to the slope. Paula gripped the rope, her hands next to Finn's, and felt the rough surface burn her fingers as she let it go, inch by inch, keeping it taut.

Twenty feet below, Karel reached the rough bulge of rock that blotted out their view of the slope underneath. Slithering over it, he disappeared, moving down towards the gloom of the forest. All they could hear was the sound of his hands scrabbling at the face of the rock and the scrape of his boots on the stones.

'Watch the rope against that rock,' Jean said quietly. 'If it starts to fray, we'll have to warn him.'

Hand over hand the rope went down, until there was no more left. Then they could not do anything except watch as it sawed gently from side to side against the sharp edge of the bulge. Paula glanced carefully sideways at Agustin, but there was no expression on his face. It was as unwavering as the rock, his eyes fixed on the moving rope.

At last it went slightly loose and Jean nodded. 'He's coming up. Don't drag at the rope in case you knock him off balance. We just want to take up the slack.'

The ascent took longer, and there was time to imagine horrors before Karel's head appeared above the curve of rock. He hauled himself over it, scrambled the last few feet and climbed up on to the path.

'I can't reach him,' he said, in Spanish. 'It's virtually a precipice, for hundreds of feet, right down to the forest. And the path does not bend back as far as this again.'

'But you could see him?' said Finn.

Karel nodded. 'He is lying on a ledge among some trees. He —' He turned to Agustin. 'I am sorry. He is dead. There is no doubt. But I cannot get to him. I think he must stay there.'

Agustin stood quite still, his eyes glittering as he looked from face to face. Then he backed away from them along the path, inching past the broken section without even looking at his feet. When he reached the other side, he turned and ran down the sloping track until he came to a place where a great rock jutted out half-way across it. Rounding the rock, he crouched down behind it, totally hidden from them. Karel took a step forwards.

'Not yet,' said Jean. 'Leave him for a bit. Let him get used to the idea.'

Karel nodded and turned back to the others. Finn had begun to walk restlessly backwards and forwards along the path. At last he stopped beside the mules.

'Might as well be doing something useful,' he said roughly.

Without looking at any of them, he unlashed his tripod from Atoc's back and set it up, taking his camera out of his waistcoat.

'You're not going to take photographs? Now?' said Paula. Jean laid a hand on her arm.

'Let him deal with it in his own way,' she whispered. 'I don't think he finds things like this very — very bearable.' She herself was pale but controlled and she turned towards Karel. 'Was it very bad?'

'Bad enough. His neck was obviously broken and his head was — well, it wasn't a pretty sight.' Karel looked grave. 'To tell you the truth, I'm glad he's dead. If he'd just been injured, I don't know what we could have done. We'd need at least another fifty yards of rope to reach him.' His mouth twisted.

'Are *you* all right?' Jean looked anxiously at him.

'Of course I am.' He was almost snapping. 'Agustin's the one we ought to be worrying about. How long do you think we should leave him?'

He was still invisible, behind the rock, and they could not hear a sound. Jean nodded slowly. 'I'll go to him now. I think it's time.'

Carefully she edged along the path, past the broken place and down to the rock. As she came level with it, they saw her turn and look down at Agustin, speaking softly. She paused and at first nothing happened. Then he stood slowly, his eyes on her face.

She spoke again and, as she did so, reached out and touched his cheek. The movement seemed to break some kind of barrier. With a loud wail that erupted like a volcano of black misery, he hurled himself forwards at her, so that she staggered slightly and then wrapped her arms round him. He began to cry, with sobs that shook them both, laying his head on her shoulder. Jean's face was calm, but full of pity and she put her hand on his head, stroking it lightly.

It was a long time before he was soothed. His sobs echoed along the mountainside, mixing with the roar of the wind that tugged at his poncho and ruffled Jean's hair. When he finally raised his head, his face was swollen and streaked with dust and they could see him gasp for breath. Keeping an arm round him, Jean began to lead him back towards the others, talking quietly all the time.

Paula felt a quick, selfish stir of panic. What could she say? What could any of them say? The sound of that first, terrible cry was still in her ears and she shrank from the thought of what it represented. Finn, bent over his camera, actually moved further away and turned his back, as though Agustin's wretchedness were infectious.

But Agustin did not give any of them a chance to speak. He went straight to the mules and took hold of them.

'I was wrong to leave them,' he said in a dull voice. 'Now I must care for them. I take my father's promise on myself.'

'We will help you,' Karel said. 'The way is hard and —'

But before he could finish Jean interrupted him. 'No more travelling today. Beyond that rock there is a flat place. Room to make a camp. We will stop there for the rest of the day and talk about what to do next.'

She looked straight at Karel as she spoke, as though she were challenging him, and he frowned.

'No more travelling today,' she said again, firmly. She seemed very small and frail as she stood there on the path, with a smear of dirt across her cheek, but her back was rigid with determination. Karel lowered his eyes.

'Very well. If that is what you think. Finn, pack up your camera. The rest of you can help to unload the mules. We'll never get them along the narrow bit with all those bundles sticking out.'

Finn had stayed at a slight distance, keeping himself separate. Now he gave a brisk nod. 'O.K. chief. It won't take a minute.'

Avoiding Agustin's eyes, he began to unfasten his camera from the tripod while the rest of them fumbled with ropes and straps, lifting off the baggage and heaping it in a pile on the path. Then Agustin caught hold of Atoc's halter.

'I shall take both mules,' he said, still in the same, dead voice. 'They will trust me.'

Karel stirred impatiently, but Jean murmured, 'Let him do it.'

So they waited while Agustin coaxed Atoc past the rim of rock. The mule inched along, its feet moving cautiously and its shoulder rubbing against the cliff face. Jean crossed after them, ready to take the halter while Agustin went back for the other mule.

It was only about a hundred yards down the path that the slope curved inwards, leaving a small half circle of flat ground, but it took them well over half an hour to carry all the baggage down and stack it together. By the time they had finished, Paula was shaking with exhaustion, but Karel did not allow them any rest. He looked quickly round the space, making up his mind, and then began to give orders.

'Right. Agustin — tether the mules over there and give them something to eat. We'll pitch the tents, Jean. One here and one there. That should leave us room for a fire in between. Finn and Tabby can start collecting firewood.'

The low, tough bushes that burnt with a resinous smoke clustered thickly around the path. Stooping to break off dry branches, Paula thought miserably about their ruined journey. When they set out, it had been a golden dream, but now there was a terrible stain of blood across the gold. The dream had been shattered by Octavio's horrifying death, and there was nothing to look forward to except the slow trek back along the way they had come, with the prospect of difficult questions at the end.

But even while she was thinking, she hated her own thoughts. It seemed wicked to be miserable that the expedition was over. Her misery ought to have been for Octavio's death and Agustin's unhappiness.

She glanced across at Agustin. He was standing by the mules, with his back turned to everyone else and his face buried in Atoc's mane. Suddenly, Paula understood just how isolated he was. He was alone in a pit of misery, with four strangers who did not know what to say. But suppose it had been Karel lying dead? Imagining it, even for a second, she felt a dark flood of panic. Dropping her armful of branches, she walked over to Agustin.

'Agustin, I —' But the words vanished. She was left twisting her hands together and looking foolish.

He nodded slowly. 'I know. You want to tell me that you are sad.'

She twisted her fingers harder. 'He was a good man, your father.'

Agustin nodded again. 'He was a good man, and he is dead. And I have wept. I shall not forget him, but now is the time for work. I must do the things that he would have done. Perhaps it will be easier not to speak about him too much.'

'I'm sorry,' Paula said uselessly. *Wrong again*, she was thinking. *Stupid, clumsy girl. You always do the wrong thing.*

But Agustin was smiling at her, almost with his father's smile. 'You were kind to come to me. It is good to have a friend.'

His eyes rested on her face for a moment and then he turned away to take the halters off the mules. Paula, who had meant to comfort him, found that she was comforted herself. She went back to her task of gathering wood, not stopping until she had heaped up a great mound.

Finn signalled to her. Typically, he did not say anything about what had happened. He did not even meet her eyes. With a brisk gesture, he pointed at the space between the tents.

'Let's go and get a fire started, before Karel shouts at us. We must all be starving, even if we don't feel like it. It's time we had some food.'

Jean had already gone clambering over the rocks to look for water. Now she staggered back with a big billycan full of it, ready to put over the fire.

As soon as it boiled, she glanced up at Finn: 'Fetch some rice, will you? And some of those packets of dried vegetables. We'll throw them all in together today. I don't think it's a time for fancy cooking.'

'Right.' Finn rummaged in one of the bags and pulled out the rice. Not bothering to measure, he tipped a stream of it into the boiling water. At that moment, Karel looked round.

'Go easy. You know we haven't got enough to waste.'

'There's plenty now.' Finn waved a hand casually. 'It'll last us five times over.'

Karel put down the stone he had been using to hammer in the last tent peg. 'What do you mean?' he said slowly.

'Well, we brought enough supplies for weeks.' Finn looked up, as though Karel were being stupid. 'Because we didn't know how long the journey was going to last. But it'll only take us a few days to get back to the Land Rover. So we can stop counting every grain of rice.'

Karel straightened, his hands on his hips. 'What do you mean — *get back to the Land Rover*? What are you talking about?'

This time there was no mistaking the dangerous edge to his voice. Everyone turned and looked at him, even Agustin, over by the mules. Finn was completely still, the open packet of rice clutched in his hand.

'I'm talking about the journey back, Karel,' he said. 'Now that we're going to abandon the expedition.' When Karel did not answer, he added, 'We've *got* to abandon the expedition.'

'Oh no we haven't,' said Karel. 'We're going on.'

Chapter 7

Very slowly, Finn fastened the neck of the packet of rice and put it down on the ground. Then he said, his voice just loud enough to be heard, 'All through this journey, Karel Staszic, you've been in a hurry. You've been making decisions — not always very good decisions — and you've been racing us along too fast. I don't know why you're so desperate, but even you must recognize *facts*. After what's happened, we can't possibly go on.'

'On the contrary,' said Karel, equally cold and calm, 'I'm the only person who *does* see facts. We've still got enough time and enough resources to finish the expedition — but only just. If we go back now, we'll get involved with official questions and enquiries. Everyone will find out what we're doing. Even if the Bolivian government lets us start again — and that's not at all certain — we'll be at a disadvantage, scrabbling round for more money. And by the time we can get going, Peter Laban will have made his research public and there'll be at least one other expedition. Probably two or three.' He hesitated for a moment, and then added, 'And the Kallawaya will be wise to us as well. Which is what I've been trying to avoid all this time. They could be the worst enemies of all.' He looked Finn briskly up and down. 'It's now or never. We *must* go on.'

79

Finn folded his arms. 'I think we should go back.'

'You think? *You* think?' Karel raised his voice, growing angry. 'Who are you, anyway? A jumped-up schoolboy! I'm the leader of this expedition, and I'll decide what happens.'

'Not this time,' said Finn. He was still speaking slowly, but he was making an obvious effort to control himself. 'I haven't challenged you before, even when I should have done, because I didn't think it was important. But this time it *is* important. You could be taking us into danger. You could even be risking our lives. I don't think you have the right to take that decision on your own.'

Karel stepped closer. 'You're questioning my authority?'

'Yes.' Finn did not waver. 'I'm questioning your authority.'

They stood facing each other, both of them motionless and obstinate. Karel towered like a great golden lion. Finn, by contrast, looked almost frivolous, with the flaps of his woollen cap framing his lean face. But there was nothing frivolous about his expression. It was just as determined as Karel's.

Jean interrupted, deliberately breaking the confrontation by catching at Karel's shoulders and pulling him round to look at her. 'I don't think any of us are in a state to discuss things at the moment. We're shaken and hungry and tired. Let's get settled and have a meal. Then we can discuss things sensibly.'

'And *vote*,' said Finn.

'All right!' Karel roared. 'That's what we'll do then, Mr Clever. We'll vote. It's time you were cut down to size. Get to work, everyone, so that we can have our meal and clear this nonsense out of the way.'

He shook his head irritably from side to side and, with an anxious glance at him, Jean turned away towards the baggage, beginning to rummage in the medicine chest.

80

Another headache, thought Paula. Until then, she had been bewildered by the argument, not sure which side to take, but now she felt a burst of rage. Karel was obviously in pain. His face was grey and two deep furrows ran between his eyebrows. How *dared* Finn force a quarrel on him after all he had been through already that day? Abruptly, she walked across to the pot of water which was boiling hard, the sticky yellow froth from the rice oozing over the edge and threatening to put out the fire. She seized a spoon and stirred the water vigorously, scraping at the rice which was stuck to the bottom of the pan.

'I'll help you.' Finn came over to the fire and picked up the bag of dried vegetables, but Paula ignored him and they prepared the meal in silence, without looking at each other.

By the time they had eaten and cleared the meal away, it was almost dark. They settled in a circle round the fire, listening to it crackle and splutter. Always before, their camps had been peaceful, surrounded by the massive bareness of the mountains. But now, only a few hundred feet below, was the dense, black tangle of the forest. From beneath its roof rose disturbing, unfamiliar noises. Birds screeched harshly and, every now and again, the air was cut by a strange, unearthly cry, rising hysterically up the scale.

'Howler monkeys,' Karel said absently. Now that they were ready to start talking, he seemed almost vague, poking at the fire with a stick and staring into the leaping flames. In the end, it was Finn who started the discussion.

'You should explain to Agustin first,' he said. 'Tell him what it's all about. He ought to have a vote, like the rest of us, and he can't vote unless he knows the purpose of the expedition.'

Karel wavered for a brief moment and then nodded. He leaned forward, his face bright in the firelight. 'Listen, Agustin. We are on our way to find a lost city of the Incas.

A city that was prepared for Atahualpa, before the Spaniards murdered him. One of the Spanish soldiers found out the way to that city and we have a copy of what he wrote down. Can you read Spanish?'

He took the much-folded sheet of paper from his pocket and Agustin reached out a hand for it. He read it slowly, his lips moving and his finger running along underneath the words. Then he passed it back. He did not say anything, but leaned his chin on his knees, watching Karel and Finn across the flames.

'So.' Karel refolded the paper and drew a deep breath. 'Now Finn and I will each say what we think. Then we vote. One vote each. Agreed?'

Finn nodded, without speaking.

'We must also promise,' Karel said, 'to stand by what is decided. And if we decide to go on, I am still the leader. Still in charge of what will happen. Agreed?'

Three of them nodded at once. After a fractional pause, Finn bent his head as well. 'We have to agree,' he said. 'Splitting the expedition would be the worst thing of all.'

'Very well.' Karel's manner was formal, as though they were sitting in an official meeting. 'You speak first, Finn. Tell us why we should go back.' He settled himself cross-legged and waited.

Finn paused, gathering his thoughts, and then began slowly. 'When we started this journey, we knew we were taking a gamble. We had hardly enough money to set up the expedition and only that paper — the one you have just read, Agustin — to guide us. But I believed the chances were in our favour. Just about. If I had not thought that, I should not have agreed to come. The first doubt I had was when Karel chose Octavio and Agustin to guide us.'

He raised his head and looked apologetically at Agustin.

'I liked you both and I trusted you. You must understand that. But you are only a boy, and your father does not speak — did not speak Spanish. I thought it was unwise to bring you. But still our chances seemed good.'

His mouth twisted thoughtfully, as though he were doing sums in his head. Then he said, a little more briskly, 'But now things have changed. Yesterday we lost one of our mules. Today we have lost part of our supplies and our only adult guide. If we go on, we shall have to rely on Agustin to deal with the Indians we meet.' Again he glanced apologetically across the fire. 'You are clever and sensible, Agustin, but you are not a man. And you must be hurt and bewildered by your father's death. We should be putting too much on you.'

Agustin gave no sign of agreement or disagreement and, after a brief pause, Finn summed up. 'I believe that these things have turned the balance of chance against us. If we go on, we face hardship — possibly even another death. We must go back.'

His eyes flicked from face to face as he tried to assess the effect of his words. Jean and Agustin were both quite still, their faces patched with dark shadows, and Paula looked down quickly at the ground, not wanting to show that she had been impressed by his arguments. There was a horrible, cold logic about them. Everything he said had been licking at the edges of her mind before, supporting her instinctive feeling that the expedition was over. Even while she waited anxiously to hear what Karel would say, she could feel her hopes sinking and dying.

Karel sat for a second tapping his fingers together and then, unexpectedly, he laughed. 'What a cold fish you are, Finn,' he said, the words sounding queer in Spanish. '*The balance of chance.* You sound like a business man with a thousand pounds to invest. If I had lived my life by the balance of chance, I might have been a millionaire by now. But I'm not. Because I chose something else.'

He leaned forward to put another handful of sticks on the fire and the thick, resinous smoke stung Paula's nostrils. When he spoke again, his voice was soft. 'I chose dreams. Because we are nothing without our dreams. Only misers, counting grimy piles of coins in a dusty room. My gold is not like that. Not heaps of dead metal stamped out by a machine. My gold is down in the jungle, where it has hidden for hundreds of years. There may not be anything there that can be counted by a miser with his heart set on money, but it is gold to me, because it bears the stamp of a great empire that was wronged and thrust into the shadows centuries ago. I *know* it is there, and I am determined to bring it into the light again.'

The flames gleamed on his face, touching his hair and beard with a rosy glow. 'I don't think any of us will die — that's melodramatic nonsense, Finn. But I expect there will be hardships. They will be worthwhile because of the importance of what we are looking for. It is in the nature of a dream that you give yourself to it, totally and without counting the cost. This dream has been the centre of my life for twenty years. I *must* go on.'

As he spoke, his voice had grown quieter and quieter, until he was almost talking to himself. Now, as he stopped, Paula felt a flicker of panic. She knew what he meant. But she had wanted him to answer all Finn's arguments. To squash cold logic with cold logic. Instead, he had presented them with a picture.

On one side of the picture was Finn, like a shabby, black-coated miser, his hand on a neat pile of coins, meticulously counted. The room he stood in might be dingy, but the gold under his hand was real.

On the other side of the picture was Karel himself, huge and splendid, like a giant golden image set on a mountain top, gleaming in the sunlight. But the sun was in her eyes, and she could not tell if the gold were genuine or only a mirage that would dissolve when the shadows came.

Suddenly, in her mind, the golden image began to tilt horribly, tottering over a black precipice. Because she knew that Karel might be wrong. All her life she had accepted, without question, that he was the best and the strongest and the wisest. But now —

The thought was unbearable. To squash it back, she said quickly, without giving herself any more time to decide, 'I think we ought to go on.'

Karel squeezed her hand so roughly that he hurt it. For the first time she realized how tense he was, waiting for the result of the vote. But he did not say anything to her. Instead, he turned to Agustin.

'What about you? You must understand my dream. Because it is also the dream of your people. Do you want their glory to stay hidden in the jungle for ever?'

Agustin shrugged. 'A dream is of the future,' he said. 'But these things you have spoken about — they are of the past. What do they matter to me? The White Faces have taught me to speak Spanish. They will teach my children to work in factories and live in towns. Soon there will be no more Indians. Why should I give my heart to what will be lost? I think we should go back.'

'Two all,' said Karel. 'Evens.' Suddenly he gave a huge, exuberant laugh, like a gambler making the final throw. 'There you are, Jeanie. You're holding my life in your hands again. Tell us what we're going to do.'

Paula felt a quick, traitorous stab of relief. Because she knew what her mother would say. Jean was one of Finn's sort, cold and calculating. There were no dreams for her, no leaps into the unknown. She was the one who paid the bills, the one who let nothing go, not even a smile, unless she had a good reason. She was sure to choose the sensible, safe course. They would go back.

Jean lifted her head and stared for a long time at Karel's face. Then she smiled a slow, sad smile.

'We'll go on,' she said.

'What?' Finn had clearly been thinking the same as Paula. Now his mouth dropped open and he gazed at Jean. 'I thought you were a sensible woman. How can you? Think about it.'

So you had that all worked out as well, thought Paula. *Even before you asked for a vote. You thought you were sure to win.*

Jean glanced at Finn, as though she knew exactly what was going on in his mind. 'I have thought about it. It won't make any difference to Octavio if we go on. It's too late for that. And we probably have enough supplies left. More or less.' She turned to Karel, speaking in a queer, tense voice. 'And it's now or never, Karel. If we go back, we shall never come again. And you will have deserted your dream. So I vote for going on.'

Karel flung his arms above his head with a great crow of triumph. 'The dreamers have won over the misers! We are going down into the forest!' He held out his hand. 'Come on, Finn. Shake on it. No hard feelings?'

Finn got to his feet and backed away from the fire. 'Don't worry,' he said evenly. 'I'll keep my promise and come with you. But if this journey's going on, it'll take all we've got. I need to think about that.'

Turning away, he strode off into the darkness outside the firelight and they heard his feet scatter the loose stones as he walked down the path. Paula snorted in disgust.

'What a rotten loser! He ought to —'

'Leave him alone!' Jean said sharply. 'He's gone to face it by himself. Poor boy. It was a cruel thing to do to him.'

'Then why did you do it?' said Paula annoyed. 'No one expected you to.'

Jean's mouth pinched tight. 'I had my reasons. And they don't concern you.'

She gazed after Finn as though her sympathy was with him and not with the little group around the fire.

Chapter 8

. . . and it goes down through the forest.

'Wakey wakey, ladies. Rise and shine.' Finn
scratched at the door of their tent and put his head through
without waiting for an answer. 'We'll never catch Karel up
if you don't get out of bed.'

'What?' Jean sat up, jerking out of her sleep. In the dim
light, her face looked pale above her thick green jumper.
'What are you talking about, Finn?'

'He's started already.' Finn laughed down at her. 'Don't
panic. He's just gone on ahead.'

'By *himself*?' Paula struggled up sleepily, hardly
understanding what he was saying. 'Why?'

Finn shrugged. 'Dunno. He said he wanted to clear his
head. But I think he was panting to sort out that business
about *the great huaca.*'

'But it's barely light.' Paula began to wriggle out of her
sleeping-bag. Beside her, Jean was sitting quite still,
gathering her wits. When she spoke, she was cool and
practical.

'Did he have any food with him?'

'Might have done.' Finn sounded unconcerned. 'If there
was any in his pack. That's all he took. Oh, and one of the
machetes. You know — Intrepid Explorer Cuts His Way
Through the Jungle. That sort of stuff.'

'And he's just gone?'

'Oh no,' Finn said cheerily. 'He went about half an hour ago.'

'Half an *hour*?' Paula gasped. 'Why didn't you wake us? Or try to stop him?'

'Me?' With an elaborate shudder, Finn flung his arms round his body, hugging himself. 'That would have been as much as my life was worth. He's the leader, remember, the one who gives the orders.'

'Don't be silly, Finn.' Jean was pushing her sleeping-bag off now and reaching for her boots. 'Why don't you stop fooling about and tell us exactly what he said?'

'Right, missus.' He saluted smartly. 'It was like this. I woke up early. I didn't sleep very well and I was cold. So I thought I'd get up and plan out a few pictures. Dawn Over the Forest Slopes and all that. Classy stuff. I'd hardly set the camera up when Karel came crawling out of your tent.'

'He was —' Jean hesitated. 'He was all right? Not upset or anything?'

'He was brilliant. Oh, I think he'd got one of his headaches, but he was in a good mood all the same. Made some choice remarks.' Finn looked slyly at Jean. 'About wives who slept like pigs when it was daylight. Then he said he was off to see what was down the path. I don't think he could have waited another second. He went plunging away like — like a golden angel.'

'So why didn't you wake us?' Jean said coldly. 'Straight away?'

'Just obeying orders.' Finn was full of injured innocence. 'He said to let you sleep on a bit, but not more than an hour. So I did what I was told. I'm bored with being chewed up for rocking the boat.'

Jean laced up her second boot and began to organize him. 'Right. Get out there and wake Agustin, then. You two can start to load the mules. There's a bit of cold rice and stuff left from last night. We won't bother to heat it up

— it'll take too long. Paula and I will start on the tents in a minute.'

Finn touched his forehead and disappeared. With a frown, Jean pulled on her anorak. 'As long as we're not too far behind. I hope Karel's all right.'

'All right?' Paula looked up from rolling her sleeping-bag. 'Why shouldn't he be all right? He's used to mountains and forests.'

Jean did not bother to explain. She crawled out of the tent, stretched briefly and hurried over towards the mules. Paula scrambled after her.

The air was cold and clear outside, still pink with the light of dawn, and the mountain peaks behind them loomed against the sky. Paula was not interested in them. She peered down the slope, hoping to see some sign of Karel on a lower section of the path.

But it was not easy to see anything clearly. Below, mist had already started to form, crawling up the mountainside and curling round the stunted trees that marked the beginning of the forest. The forest itself was hidden in thick cloud which blanketed the tree-tops and swirled wispily in the breeze.

She did not have long to stare. After a few seconds, Jean called impatiently.

'Don't dally about. Come and help me get the tents down so that we can pack them away.' Her voice was calm, but she was moving very fast, knocking out the tent pegs and looping up the guy ropes with efficient speed.

It took them nearly half an hour to pack up the campsite and they left it without any ceremony, still chewing the last sticky grains of the cold rice. Paula led the way. Finn and Agustin followed with the mules and Jean came last, the brisk sound of her boots on the stones hurrying them more effectively than anything she could have said.

They went from the sunshine into the shadows. Gradually, as they travelled down the slope, trees rose around them, choked with creepers and muffled by swirls of mist.

By the time they had been walking for two hours, it was impossible to see more than a few feet into the forest which closed them in.

'Aha!' Finn stopped abruptly, his boots squelching in a cushion of red moss. 'Our leader has passed this way!' He waved his hand at a giant fan of ferns that had once grown across the path. It had been hacked down by a machete and trampled into the ground. 'Hearken, O fellow-travellers. Can you hear the sound of his axe?'

Paula strained her ears. But there was nothing except the buzzing of insects and the incessant noise of water, dripping from the branches and trickling over rocks.

'Perhaps he's been gobbled up by a man-eating orchid,' Finn said with enthusiasm.

'Ha, ha.' Sourly, Paula pushed at an encroaching branch, flicking a spray of droplets over herself. The forest was beginning to oppress her. So much suffocating colour. Plants scrambling one upon another, fighting for every inch of ground and growing, leechlike, out of the trunks of the trees. And everywhere the ghostly gloom of the mist. Hour after hour after hour. But no Karel.

There were plenty of signs that he had passed that way. Again and again, they saw mangled branches, their ends raw where the machete had chopped at them. And where the earth had overlaid the stones of the path, his footprints were clear in the damp soil. Where *was* he? Paula hurried on desperately.

'We're not all long-distance runners,' Finn hissed in her ear. 'Slow down a bit.'

Paula glanced over her shoulder and saw that Jean was missing.

'It's all right,' Finn said. 'She's back round the bend. Stopped to tie up her bootlace. What's the matter? Did you think you'd lost both parents?'

'Karel's not lost!' Paula snapped. 'He's bound to wait for us at the end of the path. He wouldn't be stupid enough to — '

'To go on alone?' Finn cocked his head at her as though he were going to tease. Then he changed his mind and riffled the mule's ears. 'Aren't you beginning to wonder about him, Paula?'

'Why?' She stopped walking. 'What do you mean?'

'Well, it's a bit queer, isn't it? This going on alone, after he insisted we should all stick together. And there have been other things. Things that weren't quite —' He turned to Agustin, who had come up behind. 'You have seen it too? Karel is behaving strangely?'

'You are all strange,' Agustin said non-committally. 'All foreigners are strange.'

Paula did not realize that it was a joke, but Finn obviously understood Agustin better. He laughed and thumbed his nose at him.

'Rude boy! You are a foreigner to us, remember. But do we insult you?'

'No, you are most kind to me. As if I were a small baby.' Agustin grinned suddenly, the sorrow lifting from his face for the first time since he had seen his father give that last, fatal wave. But almost immediately he was serious again. 'Still, you are right. The *patron* is different from the rest of you. More — more fierce. I do not understand why he wanted to continue this journey. Nor why he ran off before we woke. Sometimes he makes me feel afraid.'

'You see, Paula?' Finn was insistent. 'It's not in my imagination. Agustin has noticed it too.'

'You just don't understand Karel!' Paula said, in a fury. '*I* can understand why he went on ahead. I expect he wanted a rest from you. You're always arguing and playing the fool and —'

She choked the words back, frightened that she might say something unforgivable. It was not Finn's fault that Karel had left her behind, and she knew that part of her rage came from a stupid, childish feeling of disappointment. Because Karel could so easily have woken her and taken her with him. To stop herself saying any more, she turned and ran on down the path.

But Finn did not let her escape. Forcing his mule to a bumpy trot, he ran after her and caught at her sleeve. 'Hey! What's all the temper about? I was trying to have a serious conversation and you just exploded. I thought you were going to bite me.'

'It *wasn't* a serious conversation!' Paula raged. 'It was just more of your nasty sniping at Karel. How could you? In front of —'

'In front of the servants?' Finn said. His voice was quiet and dangerous, and Paula hung her head, ashamed, because that was almost what she had been going to say. Above them, a parrot whirled up into the trees, its raucous squawk like a mocking laugh.

Finn took her elbow and began to lead her on, sounding more friendly. 'Look — I didn't say those things just to upset you. Even you must see that Karel hasn't been completely right about everything. Can you put your hand on your heart and say that you're utterly happy with all the decisions he's made?'

'I don't pretend to be an expert,' Paula said sulkily. 'Not like you. You work things out as though they were sums. But Karel's not like that. He's always been brave and daring. If you don't want to share that, why are you here?'

'Oh, it'll be good for my career,' Finn said lightly.

But Paula looked scornful and he suddenly stopped joking. 'No, it's not just that. Not any more. I did a lot of thinking after that vote last night, and I realized this isn't just an *expedition* for Karel. It's a crusade — an assault on darkness and ignorance, to let the light in. And that's something worth sharing. If I can do it in pictures — the way he does it in words — then I'll really have gained something. Not money or fame, but something real, for *myself*.' He laughed, as though he were embarrassed. 'It's silly, but finding that city of yours seems the most important thing in the world. I'm just as crazy as the rest of you.'

92

He had been staring at the ground as he spoke, but suddenly he looked up and saw Paula's puzzled face. Tapping the end of her nose with one finger, he grinned. 'Stop fretting, will you? I don't want to quarrel with Karel. I'm his Number One Fan. Remember?'

'Then how can you —?' Paula began. And stopped. Because they had come round another bend in the path and there was Karel himself, ten yards in front.

For a moment, idiotically, she was not sure it was really him. While she was talking to Finn about him, she had been imagining him huge and bright. The figure hunched on the path seemed too small.

He was sitting on the ground, his legs stretched out in front of him and his head turned away as he gazed down at something. Immediately above him, the trees thinned slightly and a greenish light filtered down through the leaves on to his head.

Paula started forwards at a run and heard Finn say quietly, 'Don't make him jump.'

But Karel did not jump. He did not look up as she reached him, even though her shadow fell across his face.

'Hallo,' she said.

'Tabby!' He sounded delighted, but surprised. And a little distant, as though he were seeing her from a long way away. With one hand, he patted the ground beside him. 'Look what I've found. Isn't it beautiful?'

She crouched down and looked. Just off the path, pushing up through the moss, was a strange plant. At its centre was a spike of pale yellow flowers, each one tightly closed. Out from the spike spread a whorl of very narrow wine-coloured petals, like the spokes of a wheel. They tapered to a fine point at the end and from each spoke hung a line of dewdrops, crystal clear and shivering slightly in the breeze. Paula had spent so long peering into the mist, straining her eyes to make out indistinct shapes, that this flower seemed unnaturally sharp. It was etched against the blurred background of the moss like some giant, predatory spider.

'Beautiful,' said Karel again, in a drowsy voice. He reached out and snapped the stem, breaking off the flower head and dropping it on to the ground.

'Oh!' said Paula. 'Why did you do that? You've spoilt it.'

'No, no. It'll grow again.' He closed his eyes and murmured, in the same sleepy way, 'The forest's persistent. Think what it must have seemed like to the Incas, after all those bare mountains like the ones we've come over. The mountains were their world, but there was always this, lurking at the foot of them. And they couldn't tame it.'

He leaned his head back against a tree trunk and the pale green light softened the sharp angles of his face. 'That must be why they loved order so much. And they did stamp their order on the mountains. Roads from end to end of the kingdom. Hillsides terraced to grow more food. Even poverty conquered. Imagine that. Up there — in all that cold and wind and thin soil — no one starved to death. Not one. The empire cared for them.'

He opened his eyes and spoke with a stronger emphasis. 'People will try to tell you that the Incas were rigid and soulless. But don't you believe a word of it. They knew what would happen if they let go, because there was always this to remind them.' He waved a hand at the forest around them. It knocked against a bush, dislodging a shower of tiny insects which buzzed angrily. Paula felt a sharp stab in her leg, as though something had bitten her, but she did not even wince, bound into stillness by Karel's dreamy voice.

'It was a triumph,' he was murmuring. 'A triumph of reason and order, two and a half miles up in the sky.'

'A — lle —lu —ia!' said a voice above their heads.

Paula looked up. The others had arrived and were standing in a half circle on the path. It was Finn who had spoken, mocking. Paula bunched her fists and glared up at him, but Karel was not disturbed. He smiled as though Finn had said something funny. 'It amuses you? *You*, of all people?'

'Karel.' Jean squatted down and touched his hand. 'What are you doing?'

He smiled again and closed his eyes. 'I was tired, Jeanie. Exhausted to death. I thought I'd sit down and wait for you.'

'And how long have you been there?' She was half scolding, half joking. 'Look at you. You're sitting on the bare earth. Your clothes will be wet.'

'I won't get ill,' said Karel lazily. 'I'm never ill.' He chuckled. 'Never ill, am I, Jeanie?'

The mules began to stamp restlessly. They did not like the forest with its whispering dampness and its swirls of mist. Agustin stroked their necks and muttered to Finn, 'Why do we not go on? Is the *patron* hurt?'

'Tired,' Finn said.

Agustin raised his eyebrows. 'We are all tired. But this is not a good place to stop. There is no flat ground for tents and the trees are too thick to sling our hammocks. I do not want to be in a place like this when it is dark. We should go on.'

Paula tried not to listen to him, but she knew that he was right. They ought to be covering as much distance as they could, trying to get down off the slope before it was dark. But Karel was still smiling in the sun.

'Karel.' Jean shook him. 'Don't you remember? We were aiming to get all the way down this path today. To find the great *huaca*.'

He sat motionless, without opening his eyes, and she spoke louder. 'Karel, the *huaca*. We have to find out what it is.'

Suddenly, in a single movement, he stood up and shook himself. 'The *huaca*? Haven't you worked that out yet? What were you doing all the time you were coming down the path? Singing hymns? It's obvious what the *huaca* is if

95

you use your brains. I realized hours ago. Now come on, or we'll get caught by the dark.'

He strode off briskly down the path, leaving them all staring after him.

Chapter 9

*At the end of the path, the ignorant despair and turn back,
but the wise should seek the guiding-sign of the Lord Illapa,
which is the sound of the great huaca.*

By late afternoon, the mist had cleared and the damp
heat was almost unbearable. Stopping while Finn and
Karel sliced away at yet another tangled barrier of creepers, Paula took off her jumper and knotted it round her
waist. At once, small black insects settled on her arms and
she flapped them away, rubbing at the bites. But the most
irritating bite was the one on her leg, that she had felt
when she was crouched beside Karel. It itched infuriat-
ingly and she scratched at it through her trousers.

The further they went, the more exuberant Karel
became. Whenever he paused from swinging his machete,
he cocked his head to one side, listening and smiling. But
he did not say anything.

The noise had been in Paula's ears for half an hour or
more before it made any impression on her brain. At first
it was only a whisper, one among many sounds, but
gradually it swelled to a steady, insistent roar.

It was not until they came to the end of the path that she
realized what it meant. The track stopped abruptly,
widening to a circle of stones set in a platform of ground.
Karel stopped in the middle of the clearing and looked
round at them all.

'Well?' he said.

'Of course!' Paula saw her sudden understanding mirrored on the others' faces. 'The *huaca*. It's a waterfall!'

'The Lord Illapa,' Karel said. 'The god of thunder and rain. Of water that falls from above with a huge noise. His guiding mark had to be a waterfall. It must drop straight into the river that we've got to follow. But, all the same, I hadn't expected as much noise as this.'

They stood for a moment, listening to the thunderous crash of the hidden water. It must still be several hundred feet below them, Paula guessed, but it was already loud enough to drown out the small noises of the forest.

'It must be massive,' said Finn. His eyes were narrowed and Paula could see that he was already thinking of his photographs.

Agustin looked awed, his eyes vague and his mouth half open. 'It is a mighty *huaca* indeed,' he said.

Jean was looking around. Behind them, the path stretched diagonally up the slope, but on every other side they were hemmed in by a close web of branches and leaves. 'It may be a fantastic sight,' she said, in a down-to-earth voice, 'but how do we get to see it? There's no sign of any way through this lot.'

'We'll have to cut our way through,' Karel said impatiently. 'Didn't you expect it? It's quite clear from the directions. The path was made as far as this — cut into the hillside and cobbled. But the bit below was obviously left as a bare track on purpose. So that the forest would grow back and hide the way. There's only the noise to guide us now, until we can get down to the river.' He swung the machete loosely in his fingers and took a step towards the green wall in front of them.

'We can't start on it today.' Finn sounded astonished. 'It'll be dark in an hour or so. We'd be mad to get ourselves stuck in the middle of that lot.'

'So we waste time, do we?' Karel turned on him furiously. 'That's all you ever think of, Finn Benjamin. Delay, delay, delay! If you'd had your way, we'd still be stuck out on top of the mountains, admiring the view.'

'Karel.' Jean's voice was very quiet. 'We can't start down until tomorrow.'

'You're all crazy!' Karel yelled. He swung the machete in a great arc around his head, slashing into the green. A shower of little twigs fell into his hair. 'We've actually got here. We've cracked the most difficult puzzle in the directions. And now you want to stop! Why don't you get out the cups and have a tea-party? You might just as well. It's like travelling with a crowd of old women!'

His voice rose and he whirled the machete as the words poured out of him. Jean gave a quick, warning glance at the others and then folded her arms, as though she were waiting for him to wear himself out.

As though he were a toddler having a tantrum, Paula thought irritably. And then winced away from the idea, because it was too near the truth. Karel, striding up and down and bellowing at them, looked just like an angry child, shouting for something that he could not have. She had never seen him behave like that before and even she could see that what he was asking them to do was stupid. Suddenly she could not bear it any longer.

'Stop it! Please stop it!' She pressed her hands against her ears. 'It's awful!'

Her words seemed to push him over some kind of edge. 'You as well!' he shouted. He swung the machete again and let it go. It flew into the trees and bounced off the thick stem of a creeper, falling to the ground. As it dropped, Karel turned away and leaned his head against a tree trunk, with his back to them. Even the noise of the waterfall seemed quiet after the storm of his voice.

Finn took a step forwards, but Jean caught his wrist. 'Not yet,' she muttered.

They waited for a moment, gazing down at the ground so that they should not have to look at each other. Then the line of Karel's back relaxed, his shoulders humped forwards. Jean walked across to him and touched his arm.

'It's too overgrown for the tents,' she said briskly. 'We'll have to use the covered hammocks.'

He nodded, without turning, and Jean signalled to Finn and Agustin to begin unloading the mules. As Paula moved across to help them, she heard Karel murmur, 'My head's splitting, and if I move, I'll throw up.'

Jean winced visibly, but her voice gave no sign of it. She stroked his back firmly and steadily and said, 'I'll look after that. I'll make it go away. Then you can get some sleep.'

In the morning, it was as though it had never happened. Karel woke them all, walking between the hammocks and setting them swinging.

'Come on, you lazy lumps,' he said cheerfully. 'I've made the breakfast already. This is a luxury hotel, you know. Four stars and three knives and forks. On your feet.'

The mist was already thick on the ground, licking its way up the trunks of the trees. Paula pushed back the mosquito netting that shrouded her hammock and swung her legs out. As she slithered down, the cloth of her trousers rubbed against her skin, just above the ankle, and a wriggle of pain ran up towards her knee. Just where she had been bitten the day before.

She would have rolled up her trouser leg to look at it, but there was no chance. Karel caught at her hand and pulled her across to the fire he had made.

'There you are. Lovely breakfast. Gollup it down and we can get going.'

For an hour it was like that. She ate quickly and then started to work hard, with no time to think of anything except rolling up bundles and fastening straps. The whole mood of the camp was one of frantic excitement, as though none of them could wait to start breaking a way out of the forest.

Finn danced around with his little hand camera, racing to take pictures before the mist grew too thick.

'Just one more, guv'nor. Just one more,' he kept pleading. 'Got to get my holiday snaps. I've promised to show them to the Mothers' Union when I get home.'

Karel played up to him, striking ridiculous poses. 'How about this one, Finn? Intrepid Explorer Faces Savage Jungle?' He lifted the machete above his head and bared his teeth in an expression of grim determination.

'Great, great.' Finn pranced and snapped. 'Pity you didn't bring your pith helmet with you. That's what the public wants. Haven't you got any idea how to *advertize* yourself?'

Agustin, Jean and Paula were left to load the mules by themselves, laughing too hard to concentrate. So it was not until they were ready to start that Paula was able to rest for a moment. She pulled up her right trouser leg and rolled her sock down below her ankle.

There on her leg, where she had been bitten, was a large lump, as big as the bowl of a teaspoon. The skin stretched over it was shiny and red and when she touched it carefully, with one finger, it felt hot.

'I think someone should look at this,' she said quietly, praying that Karel would not rage at her for delaying them.

He sauntered across and looked casually down at it. 'Oh, that's all right. I thought it must be a snake bite from the way you were carrying on. You'll have to get used to being nibbled by insects.'

'But it hurts.'

'What a fusser you are.' He tugged her ear gently. 'Jean! Have you got any antihistamine? Paula's having a little moan.'

That meant unstrapping Atoc's bundles again to reach the medicine chest. But even then Karel was not annoyed. He started to show Finn and Agustin the best way of using a machete, teasing them about their clumsiness and demonstrating the even, economical movement that cut the largest swathe.

Jean frowned as she ran a cool hand over Paula's leg. 'I'm not sure —' she began. But Karel strolled across to them.

'Still at it? Don't encourage her. She'll be wearing splints and asking for a crutch before you can turn round. Eh, Tabby?' He grinned, and there was nothing for Paula to do except grin back. 'There, you see. It's not so bad. We'll see much worse before we're through. Now slap a bit of ointment on it and get packed up. We're going to start making a track.'

As the steady sound of chopping began, Jean rubbed some antihistamine into the bite, ignoring Paula's sharply-drawn breath, 'Right. Now pull up your sock. But keep an eye on it. It doesn't look brilliant.'

She screwed the cap back on to the tube and threw it into the medicine box. By the time Paula had rolled up her sock, lifting it very carefully over the soreness, Atoc was loaded again and Jean was pointing at the other mule.

'You take that one. Old Atoc looks as though he wants to take a nip at someone. I'd better keep him in order. The others have got enough to do without being worried by the mules.'

The other three had developed a sort of game. Karel was leading the way into the thick undergrowth, making the preliminary slashes and leaving Finn and Agustin to widen the path. He worked steadily, taunting them, in a constant stream of cheerful Spanish abuse, for their inefficiency. Finn played up to him, whining like a little boy.

'I'm trying, sir. Honest. I'm doing my best, sir. Do I get an A for effort?'

Agustin worked quietly, watching the other two with an amused grin. He had been the clumsiest to start with, but he picked up the knack of using the machete much faster than Finn did. Soon he was easily keeping pace with Karel.

The slope was so steep that Karel was forced to copy the earlier path, cutting his way in a zigzag. But it was very

102

slow. The machetes hacked and sliced endlessly, spattering everyone with insects, dead leaves and bits of bark as they disturbed the branches. And for every hundred strokes, they moved only a few feet forward. Time seemed to have lost its meaning. All the while, Jean was watching Karel anxiously. As the hours dragged on, Finn and Agustin looked weary, but he was obviously tiring faster than either of them. Once Jean stopped, digging her toes into the soggy litter of wet leaves on the ground.

'Karel!' she shouted, above the drumming of the waterfall. 'Why don't you stop? Let me take a turn?'

But he only grunted and shook his head. Jean ran a hand through her hair.

'Why won't he let me *help* him?' she muttered.

She sounded almost ready to cry, and Paula could understand it. The sight of the raw, spreading blisters on Karel's hands made her feel sick and it frightened her to see him drooping with exhaustion. *It's not right. It can't be. He's so strong.* The words hammered in her head and she glared round at the trees, hating them.

Glancing at her watch, she saw that they had been battering their way into the forest for three hours. But it might just as well have been three days, or three weeks. Life had narrowed to a small patch of trampled leaves in the centre of an infinite, suffocating jungle. Behind them, the plants sprang up again, shutting them in completely. She braced herself sideways against the slope of the ground and tried to calm her mule, which was twitching its ears nervously.

Suddenly, Karel gave a loud shout of triumph. Abandoning his sensible zigzag path, he swung his machete hard to the left, aiming directly down the slope.

'Hey!' Finn's head jerked up as he yelled. Then he saw it too. They all saw it. The gleam of water no more than twenty feet below. The river.

He and Agustin copied Karel, beginning to hack wildly downwards, forgetting their exhaustion and laughing like children at the sight of the open space below and the glitter of sunlight on the water.

The path they cut was almost impossibly precipitous. Jean and Paula raised their eyebrows at each other and gripped the mules' harness tightly, leaning backwards with their whole weight in an attempt to prevent the animals from sliding forwards and crashing into the three in front. As her muscles tensed, Paula felt pains shooting up her right leg from the ankle, but she ignored them, as desperate as everyone else to be out of the dense, choking greenness.

Then, ahead, there was a slither of earth. First Karel, then Agustin, then Finn leaped forwards through the last few inches of the barrier of bushes. They dropped their arms and stood completely still, the sunlight startlingly bright on their heads.

The mules, too, had seen the light. They lurched ahead, their sliding feet cutting grooves into the soft earth.

'Watch out!' shrieked Jean. 'We can't hold —'

Unable to keep their balance, the mules slipped down the last foot of the slope, straining at the straps, and Paula and Jean tumbled out of the darkness.

'Well?' shouted Karel, his voice hardly audible above the noise of the waterfall. 'Was it worth it?'

Light blazed at them off the river, hurting their eyes. Opposite, across the water, the forest ran wild up the hillside, the colours of the flowers exploding through the green canopy. In the smooth water in front and to their left, that colour was reflected in a strip of brightness that curved away round the shoulder of the hill.

But to the right there was a constant thunder that shattered the serenity. A pillar of water crashed white for two hundred feet down a shallow cleft into a black pool. Over it, in the huge spray it threw up, trembled a rainbow.

'The great *huaca!*' shouted Karel.

Agustin's mouth was trembling, almost as though he were afraid, and his eyes were fixed on the waterfall, wide with awe.

104

It was Finn who moved first. He began to rummage in the pockets of his waistcoat, pulling out his camera and frowning at the waterfall as though it were a complicated puzzle that he had to solve. But his hands were shaking. *Perhaps he does care*, Paula thought. *Underneath*.

Before he could take a single shot, Karel caught hold of the mules and dragged them backwards towards the trees, gesturing frantically to the others to follow him. When Paula looked round enquiringly, he pushed her hard, so that she staggered back into the darkness. All the delight had gone out of his face. He looked grey and haggard and he did not give anyone a chance to think until they were all under the trees, hidden behind a narrow band of bushes. Then he pointed to the right, up the river.

A small boat had come into view. At first they could see it only vaguely, a blob of yellow bobbing beyond the great turbulence that swirled out from the foot of the waterfall. But as it passed the cleft, hugging the far bank where the water was calmer, they could see that it held three figures.

In the back, crouched over the outboard motor, were two Indians. Their hair was long, bound back by a strip of cloth about their foreheads. Their faces were daubed with lines of black and red and they wore nothing except a narrow garment knotted round their hips.

In the front of the boat, utterly still, sat another figure. He also was an Indian, but his face was unmarked. His loose black shirt and trousers made a scar of darkness against the brilliance all around, the sombre colour broken only by two bags he wore hanging from his shoulders. Their crimson cloth was intricately patterned with yellow and orange. Incongruously, he was wearing an ordinary brown trilby hat, and on his shoulder, its tail waving from side to side, crouched a small monkey. Its head darted nervously as it surveyed the river.

Crouched in the shadows, the watchers heard, for a second or two, the steady put-put of the boat's engine as it drew level with them, its bows sending out a diagonal wave on either side. Then the noise was swallowed up again in the roar from the waterfall as the boat moved on, its yellow paint brilliant against the surface of the river.

The two Indians in the stern were gazing back at the waterfall, their hands raised in a curious, submissive gesture, but the man in the front did not move at all except to lift one hand and stroke the monkey on his shoulder. Then the boat rounded the curve in the river and disappeared past the side of the hill.

Paula felt Agustin stir beside her and, glancing at him, she saw his lips shape a word, although she could not hear his voice.

'Kallawaya!'

Chapter 10

It is necessary to travel downstream for many days . . .

'You are sure?' Karel gripped Agustin's arm. 'That it was a Kallawaya?'

Agustin nodded and the others leaned closer, their heads almost touching, to hear what he said.

'The bags he wore on his shoulders. They use those to carry their medicines. And the hat.' He sketched its shape in the air. 'All of the Kallawaya of importance wear such hats. From La Paz.'

Karel narrowed his eyes. 'It is worse than I thought. They are very close. I had hoped they would lose us while we were in the forest.'

'What?' Finn sounded amused. 'You think we are being followed?'

'Of course we are. Did you think we could cross the mountains without being noticed?' Karel looked scornfully at him. 'Remember the people in the fields? The boys with the llamas? The old man with the mule? All along the way, there were people to watch us.'

Paula felt a slow, cold shudder run up her spine. Had it really been like that? It seemed impossible, but Karel looked very sure. And he was right about the people they had met. It would not have taken much watching to keep track of them on the bare mountain slopes. Once they were in the forest it might have been harder. But who was to say that there had not been figures crouched just off the track, observing them? She glanced round nervously, half expecting to see bright eyes gleaming in the darkness of the undergrowth.

Finn did not look convinced. He laughed softly. 'You've been reading too many thrillers, Karel. Why should they bother?'

'Why should they *bother*?' Karel stared at him. 'Have you forgotten what we are looking for? Diego's Indian still had enough spirit left, even when he was being tortured, to talk about *the secret city of the East from whence our Lord shall rise again*. People don't give up that kind of thing without a struggle.'

Agustin looked puzzled. 'You think that the Kallawaya are still guarding that city? Because of the Inca?'

'Why not?' Karel's look was a challenge. 'The Indian rebels of the eighteenth century cared enough to take the name of the last Inca. If the memory was so strong then, why should it be dead now?'

'But the Kallawaya are not Inca,' said Agustin. 'They are a people of before. Older than the Inca.'

'They were doctors to the Inca,' Karel said impatiently. 'And the Incas were the great glory of this land. Would it be wonderful if the Kallawaya waited for the return of that glory?'

'Perhaps not. It may be as you say.' But Agustin sounded merely polite. Karel ignored him. Pulling the big map out of his pocket, he unfolded it and bent it back to show a square of white streaked with blue.

'We're here. Somewhere along this river.' He ran his finger down a wriggling line. 'We have to go downstream, but it won't be easy.' He gestured across the river, at the tangled growth on the opposite bank. 'It could take weeks. And, if the Kallawaya are close on our tails, that might mean disaster.'

108

Jean leaned forward. 'We've got to get a boat from somewhere,' she said quickly. 'We can't afford to take weeks.'

She sounded urgent, almost panicky. Paula frowned. What was going on in Jean's head, underneath her coldness? Last time she panicked, Karel had been in the Middle East and a war had broken out there. For three days, until news had come, she had sat in a corner, rigid and speechless. But then it had made sense. Why should she panic now?

Karel had not noticed it, hearing only what was said, and he nodded with approval. 'Exactly. A boat. And I think I know where we can get one.' He pointed at the map again, indicating a small black square beside the river. 'That should be a village. We can't be certain it's there. The map is not that reliable. But if it is, the people will surely have boats. We could hire one or two and lay a false trail, both at the same time. Agustin —'

'Señor?'

'When we reach this village, we shall ask the villagers to keep our mules for us and lend us boats.'

Agustin jerked upright. 'I must not leave the mules. My father promised that they should be safe. I must keep his promise.'

Karel's mouth tightened. 'You will do as I say.'

Agustin glanced sideways at Finn, as though he were asking a question, and Karel slammed a fist into the palm of his other hand. 'You will do as *I* say,' he repeated.

'You have to obey,' Finn said quietly. 'You have no choice. We can't leave you behind alone.'

Slowly Agustin nodded, as though the movement caused him physical pain. Then he scrambled up and walked closer to the mules, burying his face in Atoc's neck. Karel glared at Finn, with no sign of gratitude.

'I didn't need your help. What are you doing? Setting yourself up as an authority?'

'Me? Would I dare?' Finn said lightly. He looked amused, but Paula noticed, when they came out of the trees and began to struggle along the river bank, that he had taken the other halter and was walking close to Agustin. The two of them talked in low voices, glancing from time to time at Karel, with troubled faces.

She felt terrifyingly exposed as they toiled along. Often the forest grew down to the water and they had to cut their way, tripping over tree roots and wincing as branches whipped back into their faces. But always they were visible, with the broad openness of the river on their right.

Once they had left the waterfall behind, the valley was silent and the noise they made, as they crunched the broken stems underfoot, seemed to echo like the blaring of trumpets. Paula wished she could have been scornful of the idea of watchers, as Finn was. But she kept glancing round nervously. Karel was so *certain* — and it would have been easy to follow them.

Although Karel tried to hurry them along, they did not reach the village that day. The journey grew harder and harder, until they were travelling at only half a mile an hour, and in the end darkness forced them to stop. Paula ate her meal and collapsed into her hammock in disappointed exhaustion, too tired even to look at her throbbing, painful leg.

It was an effort to start out again in the morning. All of them ached from the slow, tough struggle down through the forest the day before, and the trees along the river bank seemed to have grown denser, more thickly interwoven with creepers. Yesterday they had looked ahead, straining their eyes to catch the first glimpse of the village, but now they walked with their eyes on the ground, needing all their energies to concentrate on not stumbling.

So it was a surprise when, late in the afternoon, Agustin stopped suddenly and pointed.

'Look there! The village!'

They had just come round a bend in the river and, ahead of them, a stream flowed down the slope, plunging across their path and into the river. On the opposite bank, there was a flat stretch of ground where the forest had been chopped back to make a rough clearing, dotted with blackened treestumps. In the centre of the clearing, a cluster of small round huts encircled an open space. On the other side of the river.

Paula felt herself wilt with exhaustion. 'What do we do?' she muttered. 'Swim?'

'That's *enough*,' said Jean, with unnecessary violence. 'We're all tired. If you moan, you'll make us feel worse.'

'But I wasn't — ' Paula protested. Karel put an arm round her shoulders.

'It's O.K. Tabby. Keep your claws in. No one said you were.'

The sight of the village seemed to have stirred him out of the stupor in which he had been walking. As he squeezed her shoulders, Paula could feel his excitement. 'Look.' He pointed across the river.

Drawn by the noise of voices, people had begun to crawl out of the huts and emerge from the trees. They gathered on the bank in a little group, gazing over the water. Like the Indians in the Kallawaya's boat, they were wearing very little clothing and they had long hair, tied back. Three or four old men shuffled together, glancing at each other, and women clutched babies on their hips and signalled to older children to come close. All of them were staring with frank curiosity, neither friendly nor hostile.

'Go on, Agustin.' Karel pushed him to the front. 'Speak to them. Ask how we can cross the river.'

Agustin hesitated for a minute, as though he were choosing his words. Then he raised his voice and began to shout across the water. But there was no sign of any response.

'What's the matter?' Karel said quickly. 'They don't understand?'

'I think they do not speak Aymara. I will try in Quechua,' Agustin said. 'Be patient, Señor.'

He began to speak again, more slowly this time, as though the words were less familiar. And he gestured at the water and repeated the same things two or three times. Gradually, one of the old men began to nod. He shouted back in a harsh, cracked voice, the words barely carrying over the river. Then he raised a hand and signalled to some of the older boys. They ran back to the clearing and began to drag a couple of small canoes from behind one of the huts.

'They will bring us across.' Agustin turned to explain. 'The people and the baggage. But the mules must swim.'

He started to undo the fastenings round the loads and Paula moved across to help him.

'Will they be able to swim?' she said. 'Have they done it before?'

'They are from the mountains.' Agustin shrugged. 'Like me. I do not think they have ever seen so much water before. But I think it will be possible.' He glanced over his shoulder, towards the rough water where the stream ran into the river. 'I do not think there are any piranha fish in this river to eat them.'

Paula looked quickly at him, but she could not tell whether he was joking.

The canoes were approaching the bank now, driven vigorously through the water by wooden paddles. Karel started to give orders.

'Jean, you go in that one, with Finn and Tabby. I'll take the baggage in the other one. Agustin can deal with the mules.'

When they had loaded the bundles, Paula climbed carefully into the small, rocking boat. As they pushed off from the bank, she looked back to see what Agustin was doing. He had jumped on to Atoc's back and picked up the halter of the other mule, urging them both forward to the river.

112

Atoc, as usual, was making his displeasure clear. He whinnied, baring his teeth, and moving cautiously towards the slope of mud that led into the water. As he stepped in, he gave a long, convulsive shudder, almost dislodging Agustin.

'What happens if he falls off?' Paula whispered to Jean. 'Do you think he can swim?'

'Don't suppose so,' Jean said calmly. 'How could he ever have learnt? Ssh, now. Don't distract him. He's managing very well.'

Gripping hard with his knees, Agustin had recovered his seat. Now he dug his heels in hard, leaning over to whisper in Atoc's twitching ears.

Step by step, the two mules inched out into the water. It rose around their chests, covering the lower part of Agustin's legs. Suddenly Karel turned round in the second canoe.

'Get going!' he yelled. 'Come on, boy. Make them swim!'

The unexpected noise startled the mules and they both stopped dead, planting their feet wide apart, their ears laid back. Paula saw Agustin clutch quickly at Atoc's mane.

'Come on!' bellowed Karel. 'Keep it going!'

'Why doesn't he stop?' murmured Finn. 'He's making it worse. He'll frighten them and —'

'Just be quiet,' said Jean. 'Don't add to it.'

Agustin had ignored the noise. They could hear the steady mutter of his voice as he whispered reassurances. All at once, with a great jerk of his head, Atoc began to swim, dragging on the halter so that the other mule had to copy him. Although the river seemed smooth, the current was running strongly. It broke in a wave against the animals' shoulders, sending out strong ripples that rocked the little canoes.

Rising almost to his feet, Karel waved his arms about wildly. 'There you are! I said you could do it!'

113

'The *idiot!*' muttered Finn. He had seen the mules falter, put off by the sound of Karel's voice. Agustin had slipped sideways, flinging one arm round Atoc's neck to keep his balance. Even the boys paddling the canoes looked disturbed, whispering to each other as Karel's waving arms set the boat rocking. Only Karel himself seemed unaware of the effect he was having. He went on waving and shouting.

'That's wonderful, boy! Don't be afraid!'

'He's got to *stop* it!' Finn knelt up in the boat, getting ready to yell at him, but Jean clamped her fingers round his wrist.

'Be *quiet*, will you? You can't do anything except make it worse.'

Paula stared at Karel, unable to understand what had happened to him. It was as though his excitement had grown so great that it was overflowing uncontrollably into noise and movement.

Agustin was the only person not looking at him. All his attention was focused on the mules. Paula could see the muscles in his face clenched tight with the effort of urging them on.

At last, the canoes reached the bank. Karel, distracted, stopped shouting as he climbed out and Agustin chose that moment to steer the mules to the right, to where they could scramble up a muddy slope and on to firm ground. Slipping off Atoc's back in a single movement, he lay face down on the earth, shaking slightly.

'He was tremendous!' Karel looked round at the others. 'Really kept his head.'

'No thanks to you,' Finn said coldly.

But even that did not seem to squash Karel's hectic enthusiasm. Striding across to Agustin, he pulled him to his feet.

'Well done. Now you must try to make the villagers understand about the boats.'

114

'For heaven's sake!' Finn exploded. 'Can't you see he's shattered? He deserves a breathing space.'

But Agustin raised his head wearily, catching the sense of the words. 'It is best I talk to these people now. They want very much to know who we are and why we have come across the river.'

The little group of Indians had split up. The women and children were clustered round Jean and Paula, gazing at them. One of the children put a hand up to touch Paula's fair hair and then snatched it away nervously. The men, less obviously inquisitive, had moved into a half circle behind Karel, their arms folded.

Agustin turned to Karel. 'What shall I say, Señor?'

'Ask them first about the Kallawaya,' Karel said. 'Say that we saw him up river and we wonder whether he has passed this way.'

Agustin began to speak slowly and carefully, addressing himself to the old man who had replied before. After a moment, the man nodded and answered, gesturing up the river.

'Yesterday,' said Agustin. 'He came yesterday. The old man asks if you want to find him.'

'Tell him no. Tell him —' Karel grinned suddenly '— that we are going right down this river, until it flows into the River Beni. And we want to hire the boats and leave the mules. Say that we will give them money.' He chuckled and murmured to Jean, in English, 'That should put them off the scent. If they think we're going all the way down the river.'

But when Agustin translated the message, the old man frowned and shook his head decisively. Then he reached out and took hold of Karel's shirt, rubbing the cloth between his thumb and forefinger. Agustin looked faintly scornful.

'These are ignorant people, Señor. They have no use for money. But I think they would be pleased if you gave

115

them shirts. If you do that, they will lend us two boats and a guide.'

'They can have clothes,' Karel said. 'We can make the rest of the journey in what we're wearing, even if we stink by the end. But no guide. We will travel alone.'

It was obviously not a welcome reply. The old man turned his back and walked a few steps away, folding his arms obstinately.

'These people are *impossible*,' Karel fumed. 'It's a simple enough request. Why does he have to make difficulties?'

'Don't be in such a hurry,' Jean said quietly. 'Remember we're strange to them.' She smiled at a woman who was fingering her shirt cuffs and undid the button for her to see. 'Let Agustin deal with them. He'll do much better if you don't rush him.'

Agustin had followed the old man and was talking softly and respectfully to him. The old man turned round, but his face was still hostile. Paula heard a wheedling note come into Agustin's voice and saw him point at Karel.

The effect was extraordinary. The old man looked Karel up and down, his face twisting into a scowl. Then he caught Agustin's face between both hands, muttering urgently.

'Oh, what's he *saying*?' Paula whispered to Finn. 'It's maddening not being able to understand.'

'Just giving him the weather forecast, I expect,' said Finn in a flippant voice. But he was watching the old man closely and, under his breath, he added, 'Looks as though there's going to be a storm.'

Agustin spoke again, obviously pleading, and the old man's face changed. With great solemnity, he nodded and said something that made Agustin look pleased and embarrassed. Paula chewed at the side of her finger, bubbling with frustration.

But when Agustin returned to them, she was none the wiser. He seemed almost aggressively businesslike, and all he said was, 'It is arranged. There will be no guide. I have promised them three of the Señor's shirts and two blankets.'

'Cheeky devil,' Karel said cheerfully.

'And that we will sleep here tonight and leave in the morning.'

'Not so good.' Karel frowned. 'Not safe. I want to get away from where we can be watched.'

'Tomorrow.' Agustin was firm. 'It is necessary for us to stay one night before they will trust us with their boats. I am sorry, Señor. There was no other way.'

'I think you have done very well,' Jean said quickly. 'It is not easy to be a boy and talk to the head of a village. Now perhaps we should find some food to share with these people.' Linking her arm through Karel's, she led him away towards the baggage.

Paula looked curiously at Agustin. 'You have not said everything. What did you say to the old man? When you pointed at Karel?'

'I told him that the Señor was an important man. Famous in his own country. And that great good would come of this journey.'

'He did not believe you?' Paula remembered the old man's sharp glance and the urgency with which he had spoken. 'What did he say?'

Agustin looked embarrassed again. 'He is an ignorant man. He makes much of little things.'

Finn chuckled suddenly. 'I can guess one thing he said. When you blushed. He told you that you were brave to bring the mules across the river, and that he would trust his boats to you.'

Agustin grinned. 'He is a foolish old man.'

'I think perhaps,' Finn said slowly, 'that he is a very wise old man. Who sees things we have ignored. Maybe we should listen to him.'

Paula did not know what he meant, but Agustin looked up quickly. As his eyes met Finn's, Paula saw understanding leap between them. A shared knowledge that excluded

117

her. She felt, uneasily, that Finn had guessed something she had been too stupid to see.

But immediately, as though he wanted to distract her, Finn made one of his grand, extravagant gestures. 'Tomorrow we set sail! Oh joy! No more horrible trees to fight. No more beastly creepers wrapping themselves round my neck.'

'You are feeble like a grandfather,' Agustin said mockingly. 'Perhaps I should have carried you on my back.'

'Perhaps you should treat me with more respect.' Finn bared his teeth ferociously. 'In case I beat you with a rope.'

They both started to giggle, like little boys, and Paula put her hands on her hips and mimed disapproval. But she sensed that the performance was put on for her benefit. Whatever it was that they knew and she did not, it linked them in a private alliance, setting them apart from the rest of the expedition.

Suddenly her disapproval was real. They had no right to do that, *whatever* they knew. They should all stick together. The important thing was to force their way on and find the city. It was worth stamping on all their doubts, ignoring all their problems, if that was the only way they could come to the end of their journey. To the lost city that waited for the return of the Inca.

Chapter 11

. . . bearing the sorrows of the journey . . .

In the early morning the mist drifted lazily over the surface of the river, blurring the far bank and rising round the two boats that floated on the surface of the water. Although it was only just light, the baggage they were taking with them was already loaded. The rest, wrapped in bundles in the groundsheets, had been stowed carefully in one of the huts.

His face chalky and drawn, Karel was striding up and down the bank in a ferocious temper.

'Why doesn't someone go and tell that boy to stop fooling about? We ought to have started ten minutes ago.' He glanced irritably at Agustin who was standing by the tethered mules. 'Tabby, go and fetch him. We can't wait all day.'

Reluctantly, Paula began to walk between the huts. For some reason she felt very tired. Every step seemed an effort and when she reached Agustin her legs ached.

He looked round and smiled. 'I am telling the bad Atoc that he must be good until I come back. To save his teeth for *my* fingers.' He sounded flippant, but his hand lingered on the mule's nose.

'I'm sorry,' Paula said gently. 'We must go now.'

He nodded in a matter-of-fact way, but as they walked over to the others he kept looking back to where the mules stood, tossing their heads to drive off the flies that had already begun to cluster on their faces.

Finn gave him a sharp, shrewd glance and said, 'Paula and I will paddle. You go up at the front of the boat.'

Karel, already aboard, was signalling impatiently. Paula scrambled into the second boat, pulling at her trouser leg as she settled herself, so that it would not rub the skin. When she looked at her leg that morning, the huge, angry swelling had frightened her. But Jean had been busy soothing Karel. Quietly, Paula had found the antihistamine herself and smeared some on, but it had not helped. All she could do was try to ignore the pain.

They pushed off into the current, the wet dip, dip of the paddles eerily quiet after all their crashing through the trees. The villagers had gathered on the bank to see them go. They stood in a line, shoulder to shoulder, without any expression on their faces. When the boats reached the first bend in the river, Paula turned to wave goodbye and she saw the old headman's scrawny arm raised in reply, the fingers spread wide. Then the boats slid on and the village disappeared round the curve, melting into the dark pattern of the forest.

'Do you really think they'll give us away?' she said to Finn. 'Send messages to say where we've gone?'

'Send messages where?' Finn gave her a sidelong glance, the corner of his mouth twitching.

'To the Kallawaya, of course.'

His smile grew. 'You really believe it? All that rubbish?'

'It's not rubbish,' she said stiffly. 'You're only saying that because you want to be cleverer than Karel.'

Finn scowled. 'Why don't you just stop being an adoring daughter and *think*? Do you imagine the Kallawaya have got time to come snooping after us? If I really believed they cared that much about this city —' He hesitated.

120

'Yes?' Paula said coldly.

He dipped his paddle, without looking at her. 'I'd jump straight out of this boat and swim back to England. Because it's *theirs*. The Indians have had enough stolen from them already.'

Paula could not make herself disagree. 'But you don't think they *do* care?' she said in a small voice.

'Of course not.' Finn spoke louder, so that his words carried down the boat. 'Agustin when you dream while you are awake, what do you dream of?'

Agustin laughed from the front of the boat. 'I dream of engines. Spanners and oil and pistons. Beautiful dreams.'

Finn nodded. 'And what about the past? The time of the Incas and before? Do you care about that?'

He asked confidently, as though he knew the answer, but Agustin wavered, trailing his fingers in the water, so that little ripples ran outwards, breaking the wake of the boat. When at last he answered, he sounded embarrassed.

'If you had asked me that when we were in the mountains, I should have known what to say. That the modern things were the things of the city and that the things of the Indian were best forgotten. But now?' He shook his head. 'Now I am not certain. The old man in that village was not ignorant. In five minutes, he saw what none of us was wise enough to see. Perhaps there is knowledge that is being lost.'

'What did he say?' asked Paula. But there was part of her that did not want to know, that was relieved when Agustin glanced at Finn and Finn shook his head, almost imperceptibly.

'I think the forest is getting into our heads,' Agustin said with a grin. 'It is a tangled place, and it makes us talk of the tangles in our minds.'

He waved a hand at the bank. They were passing a group of flowering trees which hung out over the water, the smooth surface reflecting their heavy swags of creamy-white blossom. One of the trees on the edge had tilted over at a great angle, the earth washed away from round its roots. But it was laced and looped with so many creepers that it could not fall completely. Its few remaining roots held and it blossomed with the rest.

'It is very beautiful.' Paula said.

'It is very wild.' Agustin shrugged. 'The forest sucks up the water and the water eats at the forest. It is a struggle that does not change.'

Paula nodded, but she was hardly attending to him. There was too much to think about. Until then, she had believed Karel's fears about the Kallawaya. Had thought that Finn was being irresponsible to dismiss them. But now she was almost persuaded the other way. Could everything be as dramatic, as *organized* as Karel claimed? Ever since they started the journey, he had seemed somehow — too much. Too angry, too excited, too peaceful. Was he exaggerating about this as well?

And all the time, at the back of her mind, a nasty little voice was whispering, *You're feeble. You haven't got any opinions of your own. You change every time you talk to someone different.*

She frowned and worried and dipped her paddle in and out of the water.

They camped that night at a bend in the river. It curved away to the right and on that side the current had eaten away at the bank. It rose sheer for twenty feet, a wall of mud and stones out of which tree roots dangled uselessly.

On the left hand side, giving back what was taken, the river had deposited a wide spread of silt, so that the ground shelved gently up from the water's edge. Karel waved a hand to indicate that they should land there and pull up their boats.

As Paula stepped out, putting her weight on her right leg, it gave way and she fell to her knees in the mud. Jean looked round quickly.

'Pins and needles? Or is it that bite?'

122

'Bit of both, I think.' Paula planted her hands on the sticky ground to lever herself up. 'Could you have a look at it? Later on?'

'When we've fixed the camp. Don't let me forget.'

It seemed a long time to Paula. Trying not to limp, she helped the others sling the hammocks and collect firewood. At first, Karel protested at the idea of a fire.

'It's insane! Advertizing ourselves to everyone for miles around. We'll have to make do with water-purifying tablets.'

But Jean was obstinate. 'As soon as it gets dark, it's going to be cold. We need hot food — soup and rice. When we go to bed I'll rake the fire out.'

Karel shrugged, losing interest, and began to wander round from tree to tree while she prepared the meal, stopping to scrape absentmindedly at a huge orange gall that swelled out from one of the trunks.

When Paula finally sat down and pulled up her trouser leg to show the swelling, he gave it an aimless stare. But Jean frowned, feeling gently round the edges of the lump. When Finn and Agustin moved closer to look at it, Karel flapped his hand at them.

'For Heaven's sake! Are we going to spend every evening fussing over Paula's leg?'

Paula bit her lip, and Jean said quietly, 'I don't think it's very good, Karel.'

'Oh, I expect she's been scratching it. Give her some antibiotics. That should settle it.' As Jean reached for the medicine chest he added, in a lower voice, 'You might give me something as well.'

'Still?' Jean glanced up at him. 'Hasn't it cleared today?'

Karel snatched the box out of her hand, spilling tubes and packets on to the ground. 'Don't twitter. It's only a headache. Just shove some pills into Paula and let's eat, so we can put the fire out.'

He wrenched the top off a bottle, gulped a couple of pills and strode off into the trees.

'It's not fair,' muttered Paula. 'I wasn't complaining.'

'He's in pain,' Jean said calmly. 'People do funny things when they're hurt. Now take these and come and have some food.'

But she was distracted for the rest of the evening, watching Karel secretly while they ate. Every time he spoke she tensed.

By the time they had finished the meal it was almost dark. Karel got to his feet and kicked the fire apart, stamping on the embers as the glow died out of them.

'Time we all went to bed. I want to start early in the morning, and I don't suppose we'll be able to shift Finn until he's taken his three hundred photographs.'

'Art is a hard taskmaster!' Finn pressed a hand to his chest. But even he was too subdued to continue the joke and he got up without another word and helped Jean to clear the meal, packing away the extra food she had saved for breakfast.

When she climbed into her hammock, Paula fell asleep almost immediately. She was so tired that the noises of the forest were soothing instead of disturbing and even the eerie cries of the monkeys faded into the background. She slept heavily.

But after a few hours she was woken by the pain in her leg. It had begun to throb, with a slow, steady beat, and she turned over to her other side, to try and make it more comfortable, closing her eyes. But before she had time to draw another breath, she heard something that jerked her wide awake.

Footsteps.

Slow, soft footsteps were padding round between the hammocks, rustling the dead leaves on the ground. From low down, she heard the noise of someone, or something, brushing against the trunk of the tree at her head.

Too terrified to sit up, she tried to peer through the mosquito net. She had hardly made a sound, but from close beside her she heard Karel murmur, 'Ssh.'

Then she realized that all the others were awake as well. No one spoke, but their breathing was tense and irregular, barely audible. And still the footsteps shuffled up and down in the dark. Once, something touched the underside of her hammock and she wrapped her arms round her body, too frightened even to scream, screwing her eyes up tightly and trying to control the shudders that ran through her.

All at once, the steps quickened. There was a sudden rustling in the bushes and then, for a moment, utter silence. It was only when a bird called, far overhead, that Paula realized how every sound had stopped before, as though the whole forest were gripped by the same, paralysing fear that she had felt.

'Go to sleep, everyone.' Karel's voice came softly through the darkness. 'I'll stay awake for the rest of the night.'

'Karel, you can't.' That was Jean. 'You'll be exhausted in the morning.'

'Go to sleep.' It was the familiar, confident voice. The voice of Paula's childhood. Letting herself believe that things were still like that, she drifted off into sleep.

She was woken by the sound of a furious argument. Karel was shouting at Finn and Agustin.

'If you don't know what happened last night, you must be even more stupid than I thought!'

Poking her head between the swathes of netting, she looked out. Karel was standing with his back to her, his arms folded. Finn, facing him, looked profoundly uncomfortable. Only Agustin was calm.

'It was a cat, Señor. A big cat. They come to the mountains as well. I have seen them.'

'A cat!' Karel said. 'Why should a puma want to come exploring our camp? I tell you I *know* what it was. Or *who* it was.'

125

'You can see a Kallawaya up every tree,' muttered Finn. 'How many of them do you think there are? Millions?'

Agustin looked sharply at him, warning. Then, in a low soothing voice, almost as though he were talking to one of the mules, he said, 'It was a puma. I smelt the cat smell, very strong, very close.'

Karel lifted his head. 'Can you be deceived so easily? You know the Kallawaya have all kinds of herbs. Do you think they could not make themselves smell like pumas?'

Paula saw Finn wince, his face growing very pale. But Agustin was still watching him and he made an obvious effort to control himself. 'Look, Karel, *you* may be sure of what you think, but we need to be persuaded. We all know that there was something round the camp last night. We should stop guessing and look for evidence. See if there are any footprints.'

'You think there would be footprints?' Karel laughed. 'Anyway, I'm not guessing. I have my evidence. I saw them.'

For a moment, Finn and Agustin were clearly shaken. Then Agustin said, still in the same gentle voice, 'Please tell us what you saw.'

'I saw two men,' Karel sounded almost triumphant, 'with hats like the Kallawaya wore in the boat. Black figures with cunning faces, creeping round and round the camp.'

Paula was suddenly cold with terror. But Finn snorted. 'You couldn't have seen that. It was too dark. Much too dark to see the expression on a face.'

The effect on Karel was strange. For a moment he stared at Finn and then he nodded. 'Yes,' he said slowly. 'You would say that. It all points to the same thing. All your behaviour, ever since the journey began. I know what you're trying to do, Finn Benjamin.'

Before anyone could react, Jean came slipping out of her hammock and hurrying towards them. 'What's the use of arguing?' She shook Karel's arm to distract him. 'It doesn't

126

matter what anyone thinks. What are we going to *do*?'

It worked. Karel turned away from Finn and began to give orders. But as Paula heaved herself to the ground the forest swam round her in a nightmare. Puma or Kallawaya? Finn and Agustin or Karel? What was real and what was imagination? She began to move about with clumsy slowness, and her brain was no more agile. Dazed and sluggish, it could not cope with the pictures that shifted dangerously in her head.

Even through the muddle of her thoughts, she was aware that the expedition had split into two groups. Karel was cold and aloof, watched anxiously by Jean. Finn and Agustin were always close to each other, their heads together, whispering. And she was in between, not knowing where she belonged or whom to trust.

Chapter 12

. . . trusting to the Pachamamma . . .

Dᴵᴾ. Dip. The water swirled round the blade. Puma? Kallawaya? Mist blurred the river and the paddle was heavy in her hands. Feet in the night. In the dark. Black Kallawaya. Golden puma. Mist *everywhere.*

'You're not pulling straight,' Finn murmured. 'Wake up, or we'll go into the bank.'

'Sorry.' She shook her head, angry at herself. How could Finn do it? Hardly trying. Easy strokes. And the paddle so heavy. She dipped again, barely skimming the water, so that the boat veered off sideways. Dimly she saw Finn paddle backwards to correct it.

All the time the mist was rising. Karel and Jean, in the boat in front, were vague humps, and the banks on either side seemed impossibly far away.

Then she missed the water altogether, almost tipping over backwards. Finn shipped his paddle and turned to look at her properly.

'Paula?'

His face was distorted, as though she saw it through a sheet of frosted glass, and when she heard another voice she looked at him stupidly, wondering why his lips had not moved. It was not until she felt Agustin's hand on her arm that she realized that he was the one who had spoken.

'I will come here,' he said, very slowly and clearly. 'Crawl carefully up the boat, Paula. You can sit in the front and rest.'

But her head was so muzzy that she could not work out how to do it. As though he understood, he began to spell it out, movement by movement.

'Bring up your paddle. Good. Now give it to Finn. Now. Gently, gently. So the boat does not rock. Crawl on your hands and knees.'

She felt his cool hands guiding her until, at last, she reached the space between the bundles at the front of the boat. Slipping into it, she leaned her head against a knobby rucksack and half closed her eyes. Her whole body throbbed to a steady beat that echoed the rhythm of the paddles as Finn and Agustin sent the boat shooting forwards.

Ripples. They twisted past her half open eyes, contorting themselves into eerie, gleaming shapes as the sun rose. The mist cleared gradually, revealing the giant, barbaric backcloth of the forest.

Such colours in the forest. They burned against her eyeballs. Scarlet slicing across the green and vanishing as the boat slid on. Orange whorls, erupting like catherine wheels. And, between, the ripples on the river, gold lines intertwining in the sun.

As she stared, they formed into patterns, stiff little figures, like the golden statues of the Incas, gyrating in front of the complicated richness of the forest.

Forest. Incas. Incas and forest. Jewels and feathers and birds and flowers and gold and order. *Order* — oh yes!

Through her confusion, the idea shot like an arrow. Karel was wrong. Not chaos in the forest, but *order*. Like the order of the Inca empire, that had embraced everyone. Here, it took in everything, from the tallest tree to the tiniest grain of soil.

All in the plan
Like every man

The silly rhyme thudded in her head, over and over again.

Like every man
All in the plan

It beat with the terrifying rhythm of her pulse, like a great, booming drum and, in time to it, the golden figures whirled, glittering against the colours of the forest and the black, black shadows beyond, moving faster and faster as the sun rose higher.

All at once, the boat bumped, jarring her. She raised her head and saw that they had hit the bank.

'What?' She looked at Finn. 'Why did you do that?'

'What did you expect us to do?' Finn sounded surprised. 'We'll never shoot the rapids. We'll have to lift out the boats and the baggage and carry them along the bank until the water's clear again.'

Water. *Water!* She looked round and saw the white froth roaring over the ramp of rocks. Thank God! That terrible thudding was not all in her mind.

For a moment her head cleared as she heaved herself out on to the bank, sinking on to a heap of bundles that was already lying there. Dimly she realized that Karel and Jean must have left them. That they must already be further on, in the forest, carrying their boat.

Finn was looking at her. 'Are you all right, Paula? Can you manage?'

'Of course I can.' The effort of speaking made her irritable. Planting her hands on the bundles, she levered herself to her feet. But immediately her legs crumpled and she slumped back, half aware that Finn and Agustin were watching her. They whispered together, and then Agustin nodded and crashed off through the trees.

130

'It's all right,' Finn said. 'You just sit there. Agustin's gone to fetch Karel and Jean.'

His voice was stiff, and he made no attempt to question her or touch her. Gratefully, she closed her eyes and slipped further down, leaning her hot cheek against the damp, cool earth.

Then there was a rustling noise that grew quickly louder and louder. Opening her eyes, she saw Karel come out of the forest, yards ahead of Jean and Agustin. He leaned over her, his face huge, framed by a haze of golden hair and beard.

'Come on, Tabby,' he said roughly. 'There isn't time for that now. We'll sort you out later on. On your feet.'

Gripping her arms painfully, he hauled her up. As her right leg took her weight, she flinched from the pain, and the movement seemed to enrage Karel. Still gripping her arms, he began to shake her.

'You're holding us up! Don't you understand? We have to get past the rapids and on down the river. Before they find us. Pull yourself together!'

Her head lolled backwards and forwards and her teeth jarred together. Somewhere, a long way away, she could hear Jean saying, 'Karel!' but it did not seem to make any difference. The shaking and the shouting went on and on.

But *why*? She felt as though the fibres of her brain had snapped. She was weak and in pain. And it was Karel who was holding her. Why was he so angry?

'It hurts,' she whispered. 'My leg hurts.'

'Do you think you're the only one?' yelled Karel. 'My head hurts. It's been agony for three days now, without stopping. But I haven't whined and moaned and held us up. You're the only one making a fuss. If you couldn't cope, you shouldn't have come, you shouldn't have come, you shouldn't have come . . . .'

The words dinned in her ears, mixing with the thumping in her head and the roar of the rapids until she was barely conscious. The only thing in the world seemed to be Karel's gigantic face, shockingly red and contorted, thrust close up to hers. And his eyes. They glared through her, like torches, shooting flames. A hard, fierce heat. Why didn't he look *at* her? If only she could get to him, behind the burning glare, he would understand that he couldn't possibly be shaking and shouting and shouting.

'It's me!' she wailed. 'It's me, Karel, it's me, it's me!'

Then, miraculously, she felt strong hands pulling her out of Karel's grasp, lowering her gently to the ground. She sank down, sobbing, and saw Agustin step in front of her, setting himself squarely between her body and Karel's rage.

'It is no use, Señor,' he said, quite quietly. 'She is ill. She cannot go on. Feel how hot she is.'

For a moment it looked as though Karel would attack him. Then he slumped. His arms dropped and he shrugged and turned away.

'Malaria, I expect,' he said. 'No reason to get excited. Give her some quinine, Jean, and then we can get on.'

'What about her leg?' Jean spoke very carefully, as though she were afraid of another explosion. 'She said her leg was hurting. Are you sure it's malaria?'

'Of course it is,' Karel said. But Agustin knelt down beside Paula.

'We should look at her leg.' His voice was still quiet, but so obstinate that no one contradicted him. 'Let me see. Paula.'

He caught hold of her, with his large, gentle hands, and moved her body so that he could pull her leg from underneath her. Then he rolled her trouser leg up, almost to her knee. The skin of his fingers felt cool and smooth, although any touch was agonizing, and the memory of Octavio swam suddenly into Paula's head. Then Agustin took hold of her sock. Tears jumped into her eyes, and she gripped his fingers so that he could not move them.

'Please — it hurts so much.'

He smiled. 'Do not worry. I shall not make it worse.'

She went on gripping tightly for a moment more and then, gazing into his steady brown eyes, she suddenly believed him and let go. With soft, careful movements, he began to roll the sock down, pulling the scratchy wool away from the pain.

Chapter 13

. . . and ignoring all doubts . . .

THE whole leg was swollen, from knee to ankle, the skin stretched tight and streaked with red. Just above the ankle was a hard lump, bigger than a golf ball. Agustin rested his hand on it lightly.

'Hot,' he said.

Jean knelt down. 'Paula, you silly girl, why didn't you say something?'

She sounded shocked and Paula was afraid, but she made herself smile. 'You were all so busy. You wanted to get on.'

'It's my fault,' muttered Jean. 'I should have remembered. But even then — What *is* it?'

She turned to Karel, as though he might tell her, but it was Agustin who answered.

'I think I have seen a thing like this before. When my uncle Paz came back from working in the east, in the jungle. He had a swelling like this one on his foot. And fever.'

'What happened?'

'The *brujo* — the doctor of our village — said that it was a grub. From an insect that lays its eggs in men's flesh. There is pain. If the grub dies, there is great pain, and danger. That was what happened to my uncle. And I think it has also happened to Paula.'

'And this *brujo*,' Jean said quickly, 'did he cure your uncle?'

'Oh yes. He made magic —' Agustin pulled a rather sheepish face, '— and then he cut out the grub and gave medicines.'

Finn shuddered, with an expression of distaste, and took a step backwards. Paula touched her leg. *A grub*, she thought. *A dead grub in my leg.*

Jean stood up. 'I don't think we need the magic, but cutting it out sounds a good idea. Who's going to do it, Karel? You or me?'

Karel had stayed at a slight distance, his head bent and his arms hanging slack, but he answered at once. 'I'll do it. I know how. I once had to cut a thorn out of Alfred's arm when it went septic.'

Jean looked him up and down. 'Are you sure you can manage it?'

'I can manage it.' He was almost unnaturally calm now. His wild rage of only a few minutes before seemed unbelievable. 'But she'll need some kind of anaesthetic. It's going to hurt.'

'I've got some morphine in the medicine chest,' said Jean. She caught Finn's quick, surprised glance. 'What did you think it was? A toy nurse's kit? I always knew I'd have to be prepared for things like this.'

Paula was still lying on the ground, only half aware of what was happening. She heard Jean giving orders and then felt herself lifted on to one of the hammocks which was spread flat on the earth. The movement was so agonizing that when the hypodermic needle jabbed into her it was simply another stab of pain. She murmured weakly and lifted her head.

'I'm going to disinfect your leg,' said Jean. 'Then I'll hold both legs down, so you don't flinch while Karel's working. Finn —' she looked at him and changed her mind. 'No. Agustin, please will you hold Paula's shoulders?'

The antiseptic on the cotton wool was cold, and it stung as it passed over the swelling. Paula gulped and bit her lip. But already the morphine was beginning to take effect. Her eyelids drooped as she watched Karel take out his knife and sharpen it, testing the blade against his finger. Jean, meanwhile was making a fire and boiling a pan of water to sterilize the knife. The muscles in their faces were clenched with concentration and they moved without talking, understanding each other. But when Karel was ready to start he looked down at Paula and smiled.

'Be a brave girl, Tabby. It won't be fun, but when I've done it you can start to get better.'

She nodded, too sleepy to feel afraid, and made herself grin back feebly. She could feel Jean gripping her legs and somewhere, far away, there was a pain. But it did not seem to matter much.

'Here goes,' Karel said softly. And moved the knife downwards.

If it had not been for Jean and Agustin, Paula would have wrenched away. As it was, she cried out loudly and closed her eyes. But she forced them open again. If she could not look at what was happening, how could she expect anyone else to bear it?

There was a burst of muddy, yellow pus that oozed out of the incision in a foul trail, trickling down her leg. Karel wiped it carefully away and began to probe the wound, flicking away a small, dirty green clot.

Then the blood came. Feeble and watery at first, streaking the yellow of the pus with bright red. Gradually the red grew more and more and the yellow dwindled, until there was a steady stream of scarlet, unmarked by poison.

'Antiseptic,' Karel said in a low voice. Jean moved to fetch it and, as she opened the bottle, the sharp, icy-clean smell mixed with the heavy dampness of the forest air.

136

Then, for what seemed an interminable time, Karel swabbed at the cut, removing all traces of the infection. At last he held out his hand for bandages and began to dress it, drawing the edges of the cut tightly together with sticking plaster. Behind her head, Paula could hear Agustin breathing. Slow, hard breaths. She was aware of nothing else except the pain of her leg and the black waves of unconsciousness that lapped at the fringes of her mind.

'Not yet,' Jean said. 'Don't go to sleep yet, Paula. I want you to swallow these pills first. Then we'll leave you alone.'

'But I mustn't —' Paula struggled to lift her head. 'We've got to go on. The river — the Kallawaya —'

'Don't worry about the Kallawaya.' Jean pressed the capsules against her lips, forcing her to open them. 'We'll take care of everything. You just sleep. Sleep and get better.'

Paula gulped once, swallowing automatically. Then she slipped away from them all, into the blackness.

She did not know how long she lay half conscious. The hammock swayed. Cold and heat followed each other as night turned into day and back to night again. And once or twice it rained, and people moved round her, tenting her hammock with waterproof sheets on which the heavy drops pattered and trickled.

But all that was vague and shifting. It was the Incas who were bright in her mind, golden and sharp, as they had been on the river. Only now they moved against a background of lurking shadows. Black and threatening, the Kallawaya stalked through her dreams, mysteriously powerful.

The only person who broke through the images was Jean. From time to time she loomed close, holding out pills or giving sips of flat, boiled water. Paula swallowed obediently and fell back into the fire of colours.

At last there came a morning when she woke completely, blinking at the brightness of the sun. All the noises of the forest were sharp and clear. Monkeys gabbled far overhead, a mosquito was buzzing on the other side of the netting and twenty yards away Jean was clattering pots.

Cautiously, Paula put a hand down under the covers and felt her leg. There was still a dressing over the actual wound, but all around it the skin was cool and flat. She smiled and fell back asleep again.

The next time she woke, it was because a shadow had fallen on her face. Karel was standing beside her, quite still. She grinned and lifted herself on one elbow.

'Hallo.'

'Hallo, Tabby. How are you?'

'Floppy. But the pain's gone and —' she realized it suddenly '— and I'm starving.'

Karel gave an absent-minded nod. 'Well, you've timed it right. Jean's just finished cooking. Agustin killed some birds with his sling and she's made a stew. I'll get you some.'

He fetched a bowlful and stood by the hammock, still staring at her, as she began to eat. A little way away, the others were laughing and talking, but he did not pay them any attention. He just went on gazing, frowning slightly as though something troubled him.

Paula thought she knew what it was. Resting the bowl on her legs, she said, 'I'm all right to go on now. Really I am. I'm sorry I've wasted so much time, but I didn't mean to be a nuisance. Please say you're not sorry you brought me.'

'Oh, Tabby.' Karel smiled ruefully at her. 'It's not like that. I'm the one who ought to be apologizing. Because I should have taken better care of you. I should have noticed your leg was getting so bad.'

Paula pulled the netting back and touched his hand. 'You couldn't know unless I told you. It wasn't your fault.'

138

He hardly seemed to hear her. 'I let you struggle on by yourself. All alone.'

'But I wasn't alone. I was with Finn and Agustin.'

'Don't.' Karel winced and leaned closer. 'Don't you *see*? That's what I should have been protecting you from. Because I knew.'

'Knew what?' Paula was bewildered.

Karel leaned closer, talking in a whisper now. 'I knew Finn was an enemy. I've known it for a long time. He's out to wreck the expedition. From the very beginning, he's contradicted everything I've said. Criticized everything I've done. Tried to undermine me. But I thought I could manage him. I didn't realize how much they'd got at him.'

Somewhere in the dark of Paula's mind, fear twitched like a snake, its eyes horribly bright. She glanced at the others. They were just the same as usual, eating and laughing at some stupid joke of Finn's. But Karel's words spread an uneasy shadow over everything. His voice hissed and his eyes stared. Paula tried to be sensible.

'I don't understand. *Who's* got at Finn?'

Karel looked sideways at her. 'Don't you think he's changed since we started?'

'Well — yes.' Paula glanced across again, remembering how exuberant and nonsensical Finn had been in the beginning. As they came down into the forest, he had quietened. She remembered his odd behaviour when Octavio died and his flinching away from her leg. 'Yes. He's not quite the same.'

'That's right!' Karel leaped on her agreement, as though he were relieved. 'You can see it too. And *they're* doing it to him. I knew he was weak, right from the start, but I didn't think they could get such a hold over his mind.'

'*Who*?' Paula wished he would stop. His face had an awful intentness that frightened her.

'Who? The Kallawaya, of course. They've used him to work out their plans.'

'The Kallawaya?' She was so surprised that she spoke more loudly, and Karel held up a warning hand. Lowering her voice she said, 'But he's never spoken to a Kallawaya. We've only seen them from a long way away. Down in that valley and in the boat on the river.'

'What about in La Paz?' said Karel. 'When I went off to see Philip Bellamy? Finn *said* he was going to buy a knitted hat, but he went alone, didn't he? And there are plenty of Kallawaya in La Paz. They wouldn't let a chance like that slip. It's so much easier than fighting us, isn't it? To slide into the mind of someone on the expedition. Use him to make trouble from inside. That's how they defend their city. And I've been a fool to let it go. You could have died from his plotting.'

'But that was an *insect*.' Desperately, Paula looked around, wishing that someone else would come. She did not know what was more frightening. To believe Karel or not. 'I'm sure you're wrong. No one could have had such an effect on Finn. Not from a single meeting in La Paz.'

Karel laughed softly. 'That was what I thought, too. That was my mistake. It was a long time before I guessed about Agustin.'

'Agustin?'

'He's in it too. Of course.'

No, thought Paula. *No, that's silly.* She could — just — have believed it of Finn. All through the journey, she had been aware of something uneasy crouching under the surface of his jokes, black as the Kallawaya. But Agustin? She remembered his calm eyes, his steady hands. 'No,' she said. 'I'm sure that's not right.'

Karel shrugged. 'You'll see. Just be on your guard, that's all.' Glancing over his shoulder, he saw Jean coming and, putting a finger to his lips, he slid away into the edge of the forest.

'Feeling better?' Jean said as she came up. 'Come on, now, eat up your stew. It's delicious and you're letting it get cold.'

Paula hesitated. She never told Jean anything. But she was so worried that she forced herself to speak.

'Karel —'

'Yes?' Jean looked forbidding.

'He's been saying awful things. *Peculiar* things. About Finn and Agustin. He —'

'Oh, you don't want to take any notice of him,' Jean interrupted quickly, her head turned away. 'He's been fretting to get on with the journey and it's made him restless. That's all. He's very excitable.'

He never was before, thought Paula. She made one more attempt. 'Please —'

But she was not even sure what she was going to ask, and Jean gave her no chance to work it out.

'Don't you worry about Karel. I'll take care of him. You concentrate on getting better, so we can get on with the journey. That's what's important. Remember? There's a city in the forest waiting to be found. Now eat up your stew.'

'All right.' Dispirited, Paula picked up her spoon and prodded at the food. 'Do you think — ?'

She was going to ask a straightforward question about how soon they could start again. But Jean had already turned away and moved out of earshot, so that she would not be able to hear any more.

Chapter 14

. . . until, for the third time, a great river flows in on the right hand side. On the bank opposite the place where these rivers join, is the stone tower built by the people of before, which marks the hidden road across the further mountains.

THE banks on either side of them were ten or fifteen feet high, shadowing the edges of the river. Paula leaned her cheek against the bundles beside her and stared up at the narrow strip of sky, letting her mind relax. No thoughts. Just a gentle drifting that matched the gliding of the boat.

'Paula.' Finn's voice, from the back, was pitched just loud enough to carry over the slapping of water against the paddles. Karel and Jean, twenty yards ahead, could have heard nothing. Paula lay quite still and decided that she had not heard either. She was not sure she wanted to talk to Finn.

'Asleep.' He sounded relieved.

'No.' That was Agustin. 'She is not asleep. You must speak to her now.'

'Paula,' Finn said again, 'you must listen to me.'

'Mmm?' She raised her head reluctantly. 'Sorry. I was thinking.'

'About Karel?' Finn said quickly.

She did not answer, and he dipped his paddle again before he went on.

'We should all be thinking about Karel. You can't put it off for ever. I know he's been talking to you. About me.'

She sat up carefully. 'You know what he said? Has he told you as well?'

'He's told everyone.'

Paula looked at him. 'And what do you want to say about it?'

'Oh, come *on.*' Finn was impatient. 'It's nonsense. You know it's nonsense. All that stuff about the Kallawaya creeping into my mind. People can't do things like that.'

Paula shifted awkwardly. 'The Kallawaya aren't ordinary. Everyone knows they have special cures. Herbs that are secret from everyone else. Why shouldn't they have mental powers as well? Karel —'

In the dark of her mind, the snake of fear stirred again. She hesitated and then plunged on. 'Karel's always said that some of these primitive tribes are very strange. That they have ways of influencing people —' Her voice died away ineffectually.

'You see?' said Finn. 'You don't really believe it. No one sane could believe it.'

Sane. The snake reared up and struck at her with sharp fangs. Then, quite suddenly, it began to rain, large fat drops trickling over Finn's bare shoulders. He and Agustin ignored them, being already stripped to the waist, but Paula pulled a waterproof sheet closely round her, using that as an excuse not to answer.

'Go on.' Finn sounded rough. 'Don't just take it from me. Ask Agustin.'

Until then, they had been speaking in English, but Agustin's face was alert, watching their expressions. When Paula began her question, he did not show any sign of surprise.

'Is it possible, Agustin? For the Kallawaya to —' she stopped, hunting words ' — for the Kallawaya to touch people's minds? So that they act differently?'

He smiled, half amused and half scornful. 'The Kallawaya are not a wild tribe. They travel in all the great cities. If they thought you had come to steal gold, they would not need to use magic. They would report you to the agents of the government. And besides —' he glanced at Finn, as though they were sharing a familiar joke '— Finn is not a person to work magic on. He does not believe.'

They were both staring at her now, their faces gleaming with the rain. Agustin looked sympathetic, but Finn was sharp.

'You see?' he said.

Blackness licked at the rim of Paula's mind. 'The forest can do strange things to people,' she said desperately.

'But not to us.' Finn's stare was unrelenting. 'It's Karel who has been strange. All the way. He has been wild for speed.'

'Of course!' Paula snapped. 'Because this journey is the most important thing in the world to him. And to me. But how could you understand that? You're not a dreamer. And Agustin —' She stopped, appalled at what she had been going to say. But Agustin seemed to pluck the thought out of her head.

'And Agustin is an Indian,' he said, 'who is too stupid to understand a white man.'

'I didn't mean that.' Paula looked away, avoiding his eyes.

'I am not ashamed that I am an Indian,' he said quietly. 'It is you who are thinking the thoughts of an ignorant person, if you believe what the Señor Karel says about the Kallawaya.'

'I don't know *who* to believe.' Frantically, she looked up at him. 'Agustin, how can I make up my mind? Don't you see what you are asking me to say?'

'It has been the same for all the journey,' Agustin went on remorselessly. 'Always the *patron* has been wrong. My father died and, if I had not argued, you might be dead also.'

'He can't think of anything except the city,' said Finn. 'He's obsessed.'

Agustin smiled sadly. 'Why do you always hide things in words, Finn? The old man in the village was not afraid to speak plainly.'

'All right!' Finn said hoarsely. 'So will I.' The words seemed to hurt him. 'He's mad, Paula.'

'But he's my *father!*' She felt herself slipping into a dark pit and, in her wretchedness, she shrieked the words.

In the boat in front, Karel and Jean turned round, startled. Without thinking, Paula raised her hand and waved cheerfully to them, so that they would not guess what was being discussed. Then she realized what she had done. She had joined the conspiracy. Her face was white as she turned back.

'Sometimes the truth is like a tiger,' Agustin said gently. 'If you run from it, it will devour you.'

'And you knew anyway,' said Finn. 'Didn't you?'

The rain sluiced over them, flattening their hair, as unrelenting as their faces.

'I knew,' Paula said. 'But I couldn't bear it.'

She gazed down the river at her parents. Karel seemed strangely small. Not the great golden lion that she had always imagined. He was wearing only a pair of shorts, and his shoulder blades stood out sharply in his naked back, as though the flesh had shrivelled round them.

'Help me,' she whispered. 'I can't bear it.'

But before either of them could answer, Karel gave a yell and waved his paddle in the air.

'Look! That makes three!' So that there should be no mistake, he raised three fingers, flourishing his hand triumphantly.

Ahead, the river was rough, churned by irregular waves breaking from the right, stirring up the mud and stones on the bottom. Beyond the overhanging trees, a huge volume of water was pouring in.

Dipping his paddle again, Karel nodded to Jean and the two of them bent forwards, sending their boat faster down the river.

Finn let out his breath. 'No time to talk now,' he said quickly, looking away from the other two. 'We've got to get going.'

It was an escape. A way out of the pit. And Paula took it gratefully. Turning to the front, she deadened her thoughts and strained her eyes to look ahead.

She was not watching the river that flowed in on the right, but staring at the other bank. Searching for a glimpse of *the stone tower built by the people of before.*

She had imagined it rising above the tree-tops. Tall and grey and solitary, like Rapunzel's tower, ridiculously decorated with little turrets and swirls of ivy. That was nonsense, of course. The trees were several hundred feet tall. But she might be able to see a dark pillar amongst the shadows, or a stretch of smooth wall breaking the pattern of leaves.

There was nothing. The green tangle spread along the bank without a gap.

Karel and Jean drove their boat up against the left hand bank, exactly opposite the rough water where the tributary poured in. With a challenging, exuberant grin, Karel waved at the muddy bank. It rose ten feet above his head.

'Great,' Finn said as they drew level. 'I suppose we fly. Or do we get out the stilts?'

Karel chuckled. 'We scramble up. Like moles.' He measured the distance upwards with his eye. 'Don't you fancy it? Too hard for you?'

'I'll race you up it any day,' said Finn. 'Old man.'

'Right. You're on.'

As they wound ropes round their waists, they taunted each other like schoolboys.

'Scared of the water, laddie?' Karel thumbed his nose.

'I'll pull you out when you start drowning, grandpa.' Reaching over the side of the boat, Finn trailed his fingers in the water. 'At least it's not freezing. And we can't get any wetter.'

146

He slithered out of the boat and splashed in up to his hips. Then his feet slipped on the bottom and, by the time he had regained his balance, Karel was already digging away at the bank with his hands, pulling out stones and lumps of earth to make a foothold. With a roar of defiance, Finn copied him, tossing a fistful of mud at his chest.

They're trying to cover up the darkness, thought Paula. *Pretending it's not there. Walking on thin ice.* She was relieved, but amazed that they could do it.

The thought of finding the next part of the path gripped them both and they worked fast, laughing and shouting to each other as they clawed at the bank. By the time they were half-way up, their wet skin was streaked with sticky, red mud, clotted more thickly where they had flung it at each other. They reached the top together and threw themselves face down on the bank, panting.

Then Karel reached out and shook Finn's hand. 'We've done it!'

'Mount Everest, here we come!' yelled Finn.

Jean shook her head at them, leaning backwards to gaze up the bank. 'You look as though you've been swimming in a sewage farm,' she called. 'And you smell like it, too.'

She was right. There was a foul stink of rotting vegetation where the mud had been disturbed. But Karel and Finn both pulled rude faces at her as they began to untie the ropes from round their waists.

'Explorers always smell,' said Karel. 'If you wanted a scented husband, you should have married a hairdresser.'

'I *knew* you reminded me of something,' Finn murmured. Karel seized a handful of mud and rubbed it into Finn's dark curls.

'O.K., O.K., I give in!' Backing away, Finn lowered his rope over the edge of the bank. 'Tie on some of the bundles, Jean. *I* might as well do some work, even if Karel can't be bothered.'

It took them over half an hour to raise the boats and the luggage. Jean insisted that Paula should climb up early on and sit and rest, without doing any work. So Paula sat on the bank, watching as the others splashed about, shrieking with laughter every time the edge of the mud collapsed and slid into the water. If she did not laugh as much as they did, it was because she had time to glance over her shoulder at the forest. And she still could not see any sign of a tower.

But Karel did not seem worried. As soon as everything was safely raised, he began to rummage among the bundles, looking for the machetes.

'Come on, Finn. Let's make a start. It could take us hours to hack our way through this lot.'

But it was not like the cloud forest on the mountainside. Here, behind the tangled façade, the forest floor was almost bare of low plants. Only the trunks of the trees stretched up towards the canopy, impossibly high overhead.

Up there were all the flowers and birds, the riot of life that had been so close before. But down on the ground, in the darkness and the silence, it was like being on the bottom of the world. Paula shuddered.

'It's real jungle,' Jean said, looking around.

Even the rain seemed distant, as though they were in a huge tent. Slowly they began to walk forward, between the trunks of the trees.

'I thought so.' Karel gave a satisfied nod. 'It would have been hell looking for this tower in the cloud forest. But we can see a bit more here.'

He glanced about. They had reached a sort of rough clearing, about thirty feet across. The trees met overhead, but only one or two pushed their way up through the mossy earth, which rose in a gentle mound, highest at the centre of the clearing.

'This wouldn't make a bad base,' he said. 'You can stay here, Tabby. You're not really well enough to go crashing round the forest, and we could do with someone to keep

148

still and call out to us, so we don't lose our bearings. Go on. Sit down and then the rest of us can start.'

'That's right,' said Finn. 'Don't give us a moment off. What happened to your whip and your jackboots?'

'You can rest if you like,' Karel said. 'Wait until tomorrow to look for the tower.'

But it was a challenge and Finn knew it. He grinned back as he picked up his machete again. 'Why not next week? Or next year? Come on. Let's go.'

Paula tucked one of the waterproof sheets under her arm and limped over to the centre of the clearing, climbing awkwardly up the shallow mound. Her leg was still sore, but she could walk on it, and she was disappointed at being left behind. *Don't fuss*, she told herself. *Not when they're all in such a good mood. Don't spoil it.* She sat down with the cover round her shoulders and waved to the others as they moved into the forest, fanning out in different directions.

Almost immediately, Agustin gave a shout. 'Here is a stone come and look, Señor.'

It was so close that Paula could see it herself, between the trees, a stubby pillar set upright in the earth. But when Karel reached it he shook his head crossly.

'No. *Look.* It has not been worked, and the shape is awkward. It was never part of a tower.'

He sounded impatient, as though he were tired after the race up the bank, but he plunged straight back into the trees. After a few moments, Paula could not see anyone. She began to call 'Yoo-hoo!' at regular intervals so that they could keep in touch with her. And so that she did not feel totally deserted. It was eerie, sitting alone in the half-light. As the answering calls grew fainter and fainter, dwindling into the trees, her excitement dwindled as well. Now that she had time to think, her thoughts were as gloomy as the forest.

Because they might not even be in the right place. Somewhere back along the path, they could easily have

149

made a mistake. Or perhaps the whole thing was a bitter practical joke, played hundreds of years ago by a tortured man. A joke that had lain dormant for centuries, until someone was found, foolish enough to be taken in. If that were true, they might go on and on into the jungle, until they were hopelessly lost. Because it would not be easy, after all they had been through, to admit that the journey was a wild-goose chase. Even if they had all been sane and happy, it would be almost unbearable to turn back.

And as things were . . . . She dreaded the idea of what Karel might do if they could not find the tower. He might fly into a terrible rage. He might even attack Finn. She called again, as much to stop her thoughts as anything else.

'Yoo-hoo!'

'Yoo-hoo!' The answers, from four different directions, did not comfort her. They sounded weary and dispirited.

Suddenly, she felt a sharp, stinging pain in her right leg. Automatically protecting her wound, she clapped her hand over it and immediately felt the same pain in the palm. Looking down, she saw a large red ant, squashed against the skin and, as she brushed it off, she realized that there were more of them. They were running over her boots and up her leg. Pulling a face, she stood up and began to knock them off, stamping her feet and kicking at the ground so hard that she scattered lumps of moss.

Then it occurred to her that she might, idiotically, have been sitting on a huge anthill. Bending down, she peered at the surface of the mound to see if she were right.

Instead, she saw something that stopped her, utterly still. Sticking out of the hummock, where she had knocked the moss away, was a sharp right angle of stone, perfectly straight and regular and about a foot long.

Forgetting all about ants, she knelt down and began to pull at the moss and the earth, tugging them away in handfuls. There were more of the stones, tumbled together and overgrown, silted with earth. As she continued, she started to laugh, almost hysterically, and then to shout.

150

'Hey! Hey, everyone! Come back!'

And all the time she was pulling at the moss, grazing her fingers on the sharp angles of the stones.

Finn reached her first, sliding between the trees as he ran. 'What's the matter? Are you all right?'

She could not say anything except, 'Look! Look!'

He had seen, even before he crossed the clearing. Letting out a great whoop, he bent down and ran his hand along one of the stone edges. 'She's done it! She's found it!'

As Jean and Agustin came through the trees, he turned to grin at them. 'Paula's a genius! She didn't move a step, and she's found it. It's fallen down completely.'

Jean let out a huge breath, half closing her eyes. 'Thank God. I thought we were never going to find it.'

'The last puzzle,' Finn said triumphantly. 'The final link. Now we really *are* on the road to the hidden city.'

'The road,' Paula said slowly. She had been so excited by her discovery that she had nearly forgotten why it was so important to find the tower. Now she looked round the clearing and frowned. 'But there is no road. And if there were — why did none of you find any sign of it in the forest?'

'It must be here somewhere,' Jean said impatiently. She kept glancing over her shoulder, waiting for Karel to appear through the trees. But Finn and Agustin both looked serious.

'I've been worried all the time,' said Finn. 'Because I don't see how there *can* be a road. There's no stone in the forest. It must have been hard enough to bring this here.' He tapped his hand against the rocks of the tumbled tower, beside him. 'But to bring enough to make a *road*?'

Agustin nodded. 'And they would sink. Look at these. There must be many more under the earth.'

'But a track, worn by feet, would disappear even faster. The forest grows so quickly.' Finn frowned. 'What do you think, Jean?'

'Oh, I don't know.' She flapped a hand, still gazing away through the trees. 'I wouldn't try to make a path at all if I were doing it. I would just mark the line somehow. Make cuts in the bark, or something.'

'That's no use,' Finn said.

But Agustin had grown very quiet. Without saying anything, he walked forward into the forest, in the direction he had taken before. They saw him almost vanish between the trees, but before he was quite out of sight he paused and looked around. Then he came hurrying back.

'Look.' He pointed to where he had been. 'Paula, Finn — what do you see?'

Paula peered. 'I can see the stone you found before. But Karel said that was not important.'

'No use for a *tower*.' For almost the first time since they had known him, Agustin was looking excited. 'But from there I can see another stone like that. I found it before, but I took no notice, because of what the Señor Karel said. And from *that* stone —'

'*Another* stone?' said Finn. 'Can you really?'

'Perhaps. I have not tried.' Still blazing with excitement, Agustin turned to Jean. 'I am sure this is right. We must follow the stones. Will you come and look?'

'But we can't go anywhere,' Jean said. She was still watching the trees. Then, with an effort, she looked at Finn. 'Do you think we should go and search? I can't understand why he hasn't come. He must have heard you shout.'

'He'll come back sooner or later.' Finn did not sound sympathetic. 'When he's ready. Listen. I think I can hear him moving about.'

As he said it, Paula could hear it too. There were faint rustlings in the forest beyond, as though someone were approaching. But very slowly. She tilted her head sideways to catch the sounds and wondered why the movements were so erratic.

'Karel!' Jean shouted. 'Is that you? We're here. We've found the path.'

Still at the same, jerky pace, the noises grew closer and closer. At last, Karel appeared between the trees. He was moving with great difficulty, shuffling one foot after another and pausing from time to time to lean against a tree trunk. As he got nearer, they could see that his face, in the shadows, was very white, tense with effort.

'Finn!' snapped Jean. 'The medicine chest!'

She ran forward and caught hold of Karel's arm, leading him gently towards the clearing. As soon as she touched him, he lurched heavily against her, so that she staggered, her body bending sideways to take the weight. When they reached the clearing, she lowered him to the ground and stretched out a hand for the medicine box that Finn had put down beside her. Her eyes glared at the others.

'Go away,' she hissed. 'All of you. At once.'

She was so forceful that, without understanding, they began to edge backwards through the trees, towards the river bank. Finn lingered for a moment in the shadows and Paula heard Jean snap at him, her voice rising above the short, painful gasps of Karel's breath.

The next moment he came through the green passage they had hacked and out on to the bank where Paula and Agustin were sitting. His face and his hair were still streaked with the mud that Karel had flung at him earlier on, but there was nothing comic about his expression. Squatting down beside the other two, he whispered, 'It's worse. Much worse than we thought. She's giving him morphine.'

Chapter 15

*When he has crossed the mountains, the steadfast traveller
will see at last . . .*

I⊤ was a long time before Paula fully understood what
happened the next morning. When she opened her eyes
she lay for a moment, watching the leaves shimmer high
in the air, hundreds of feet above her hammock. Then she
took a deep breath and sat up, feeling the day clamp on her
like a heavy weight. What were they going to do, now
that everything was altered? She could see the others
beginning to move around, and Jean was already getting
the breakfast. When would the discussion begin?

There was no discussion. Jean was cold and silent, as
though she held a shield between Karel and the rest of the
world. He was drowsy and befuddled, giving vague
orders. Jean repeated them loudly, making the details
clearer. Once or twice, Finn approached her, trying to say
something, but she froze him out, staring hard at him and
asking why he had stopped work. They sorted everything
they could leave behind with the boats and hid it a little
way from the river and still nothing had been said.

Paula edged up to Finn. 'Aren't you going to do anything? You've got to say something to her.'

'Have I?' Finn raised an eyebrow. 'You know I'm the
world's worst coward.'

'But we can't just —'

154

He shrugged. 'So? Do it yourself, if you want it done.'

She understood, then, what he meant, when she imagined herself going to stand in front of Jean. Planting her feet squarely. Forcing Jean to look at her. And saying . . . And saying . . . No, it was impossible.

'You could say you *can't* go on,' murmured Finn. 'Because of your leg.'

'What's the point? We can't just stay here. And I *can* walk — if Karel can.'

Karel was visibly winding himself up for the journey, so absorbed in the effort that he was unaware of the others. Staggering, he heaved his rucksack on to his shoulders and began to plod towards the first stone marker, without waiting for anyone else.

'Come on,' Jean said, with false brightness. 'We're wasting the day.' She hurried after him, struggling to put on her pack as she went.

Finn and Agustin had been whispering together. Now they each picked up a machete and set off at a steady lope, to overtake Karel. There was not much clearing to be done, except where the branches thinned overhead and plants clustered densely in the patch of light. But by being in front they could find the stone markers and shout to the others, leaving them to follow at a comfortable, unbroken pace.

Paula walked last of all, still weak from her fever. Ahead of her, Karel tramped mechanically, his shoulders hunched forwards. Like a robot. Paula knew that Jean must have given him some more morphine, but it was hard to avoid the nightmare feeling that the figure in front of her was only a husk and that Karel, her father, had gone for ever.

After a couple of hours, they were forced to stop, because there was no marker in sight. A huge tree had fallen, tearing a hole in the darkness of the forest. Over its corpse, bushes and creepers and young saplings had rioted, the green of their tangle as loud as a shout of triumph at the sight of the sun. Finn and Agustin plunged into it,

155

cutting their way and casting about for a sight of the next marker, and the other three sat on the ground, grateful for the rest.

Paula was close beside Karel and she glanced at him as he sat slumped forwards, his eyes closed. Suddenly, he opened them, looked straight at her and smiled fleetingly. Very low, so that she could barely hear, he said, 'I'm near the edge, Tabby.'

'Do you —' she was whispering herself, afraid to disturb him. 'Do you want to stay here for a while?'

'No. Got to get on. Don't you realize?' The smile flicked beautifully across his face again. 'We could do it today. Get up on the mountains. *We could see the city today.*'

His voice was full of unendurable longing. He did not say anything else, but closed his eyes and began to breathe deeply, as though he were gathering up his remaining strength.

Then Finn and Agustin shouted together. 'Here!'

Paula got up quickly and limped towards them. She did not think she could bear to go any further if she had to watch Karel. It was too painful. And she wanted to ask Finn about something new that had begun to worry her.

As soon as they were through the tangle and into the dark forest again, she caught up with him.

'Have you thought?' she murmured. 'About the mountains. We've still got mountains to cross.'

Finn nodded. 'I know what you mean. If there's cloud forest on the slopes, like there was back beyond the river, it'll be murder.'

'Not just murder,' Paula said. 'Karel won't — He can't — Oh, *Finn!*'

She turned towards him, wanting him to say something comforting, to make things easier. But he looked away and walked a little faster, so that she had to hurry to keep up with him.

'Could be O.K.' he said briskly. 'We've been climbing for a bit, actually. Very gently. And the forest hasn't got any thicker. Don't forget these slopes will face west. The cloud forest was facing east. That could make a difference. Agustin —' They had drawn level with him, '— do you think there will be thick forest ahead?'

Agustin grinned. 'Forest? What do I know about forests? I am from the mountains. All forests are strange to me. We must be brave and trust to the Pachamamma, that she has left our way clear.'

He turned aside to hack at a creeper that hung diagonally across his path and Paula fell into step behind him, settling to a regular limp, an alternation of long and short steps. Her leg was aching now, but she was beginning to understand how Karel kept going. Don't think. Don't look around. Don't talk. *Screw up your mind, like clenching a fist.* The words seemed familiar — something to do with fear — but she did not chase them round her memory. She concentrated all her attention on the small patch of ground in front of her, between the tree trunks. Nothing mattered except the place to put her right foot. And then her left foot. And then her right foot again.

Towards midday, the markers began to lead them up a steeper slope. The flies and the mud and the darkness of the forest were harder to bear when they had to struggle with climbing as well. But gradually the forest began to thin out. At first that made the way more difficult. Each time a patch of blue sky showed overhead, they had to stop and wait while Finn and Agustin chopped at thickets of bushes. But as the ground firmed under their feet, becoming stony instead of soggy, the lush growth dwindled away. They could see the hills rising in front of them, their upper slopes bare. And they could feel the sun on their faces.

Suddenly, Agustin turned and waved an arm. 'There is a path. Now we shall go more easily.'

Paula could not move any faster. The rhythm of her footsteps seemed to be fixed by something outside her. But when she caught up with Agustin, she saw a narrow, cobbled track stretching up the scrubby slope ahead. On either side, the hills billowed, dark green in the clefts where the forest ran up the sheltered valleys, pale green and rocky on the bare tops. Glancing back, she could see how the forest fell away behind, sloping down towards the hidden river.

'You can walk?' Agustin looked anxiously at her. 'It is not too hard?'

'I can walk.' She smiled briefly, surprised and pleased that he should worry about her. Then she went on plodding, because it was better not to think about her legs. And much better not to think about how everyone else was managing.

The path led towards a slight break in the ridge ahead and, as they laboured on in the full heat of the sun, Paula knew that they were all thinking the same thing. *Perhaps over this ridge . . .* But over the ridge there was another. And then another. The track wound its way over them, between patches of scrub and scattered thickets, climbing with merciless steepness.

They were moving painfully slowly, keeping a pace that Karel could match, but although she knew he was struggling, Paula could not bear to help. She could not even bear to look over her shoulder and see him as he leaned on Jean's arm, his face haggard and his eyes fixed on the path in front of him.

It was the gathering darkness that made them stop. The colours dimmed on the hills ahead and the track running up the slopes could not be distinguished from a distance. Agustin stood still and folded his arms.

'If we go on, we shall lose the path.'

Finn nodded. Once or twice already they had strayed from the line of cobbles and if it grew any darker it would be hard to find it again. He called backwards. 'Jean! Do you think we should stop?'

In a loud voice, so that they could all hear, Jean said, 'Karel, do you think we should stop now?'

158

Keeping up the pretence he's still in control of the expedition, thought Paula. It made her throat dry with misery. And yet, almost incredibly, Karel reacted. Raising his head, he said, with an effort, 'To the top of the next rise. Then we'll stop.'

There was a desperation in his voice that made them all obey him without argument. Automatically they moved on up the path, testing the ground before each step to make sure that there were still cobbles underfoot. It took another half an hour to reach the highest point and by that time it was dark. In front and behind, the downward slopes disappeared into blackness, so that it seemed they stood on a solitary knife-edge beneath the stars.

'We'll have a fire,' said Jean. She sounded tense, as though any relaxation would set her screaming. 'There's nowhere for the hammocks. We'll just have to wrap ourselves up and lie on the ground round the fire.'

No one even suggested keeping a watch. They were far too exhausted. Stumbling round in the light of a torch, they made the fire and began to eat their hastily-prepared meal.

All except Karel. He sat hunched forwards, his bowl on the ground, staring dully at his feet. Jean touched his shoulder.

'You must eat.'

He did not respond at all. After a moment, she picked up the bowl, lifted a spoonful of food and held it to his lips. He swallowed, messily, a trickle running down into his beard. Jean wiped it away with her sleeve and took up another spoonful.

It was agonizing to watch. Finn winced and turned away and Agustin stared soberly into the fire as he ate. But Jean simply went on feeding Karel as though he were a small child, patting his hand from time to time to encourage him.

When he had finished, she put the bowl down and he

159

slipped sideways, almost asleep. Lowering him to the ground, she tucked a blanket round him.

Into the silence, Finn said, 'Jean —'

'Not now. Please.' She sounded defeated. 'We'll talk about it in the morning, I promise, but *not now*. I can't bear it. Let's all go to sleep.'

By Paula's ear Agustin said, as though to himself, 'I have heard talk, all my life, of spirits who steal men's minds from them. But I thought it was the foolishness of old women.' Turning away, he pulled his poncho round and wrapped himself in his blanket, settling to sleep. Paula copied him, because there was nothing else to do. Black despair hung over all of them.

When she woke, it was dawn. The sky ahead was a bright, rosy pink and, outlined against it, she saw a huddled shape, sitting on a rock. Stepping round the sleeping bodies, she walked up behind him.

He spoke at the sound of her footsteps, without turning his head or moving a centimetre. 'It was all true, Tabby. Every word of it. Look.'

Down the forested slope in front of him ran the deep groove of a valley, its stream tumbling to the level jungle at the bottom. And beyond that, there was nothing but more jungle, stretching away into the misty distance.

'You see?' murmured Karel. 'On the right-hand bank of the stream? The city is just at the bottom of this slope.'

He has gone completely mad, thought Paula, cold with misery. She could not see any buildings at all. No walls, no towers. Nothing broke through the forest canopy.

'Well?' Karel said impatiently. 'Can't you see?'

And suddenly, with grateful delight she *did* see. There, among the leaves, was a regular, scarlet line of blossoming trees, marking out a precise, sharp-angled square. A pattern that could not have grown naturally. It blazed in triumph against the green and she felt her pulse stop and then begin to thud fiercely.

160

'They must have been such a small part of it,' said Karel softly. 'Just a decoration. But they've grown with the forest and they still proclaim the city, even though the other trees have swallowed it up.' A faint frown crossed his face. 'I'm not imagining it, am I?'

'Oh no. It's really there.' Paula twisted her fingers together. *Atahualpa's city. My city.* It was like seeing the past rise up solid in front of her eyes. 'We'll be there by tonight,' she whispered. 'We'll be standing in the middle of it.'

'No.' Karel sounded quite calm. 'I shall never stand there.'

Paula slipped down and knelt beside him, looking at him. It seemed to her suddenly that there was something peculiar about his unwavering stillness. Only his eyes moved, flicking from side to side as he gazed at the panorama in front of him. Every muscle in his face was tense.

'It's unbearable, Tabby.' He said it without complaint. 'If I moved my head, even an inch, the pain would make me scream out loud.'

Paula stretched out her hand and then drew it back quickly, before she touched him. 'There must be something. What about the morphine?'

'I had that when I woke up.' His voice stumbled, slurring as though he were falling asleep. 'Hours ago. It doesn't make much difference.'

'But you've *got* to get there. Somehow. We can't just turn back after all this way.'

Cautiously, Karel smiled, a small, bitter smile. 'You still haven't noticed everything, have you? Look the other way. By the left hand bank.'

Paula looked. Set back a little way from the river there was a small, rough clearing, dotted with tiny huts so like the tops of the trees that she had hardly noticed them crouched there.

'It's only an Indian village,' she said. 'What difference does that make?'

161

'Not there.' Karel was sounding very muzzy now. He screwed up his eyes and blinked once or twice as though to clear his mind. 'By the bank. Close in, under the trees.'

She had taken it for a patch of yellow flowers overhanging the water, hidden in the shadows. But as soon as she looked directly at it, there was no mistaking it. The small, yellow motorboat of the Kallawaya.

'Must have gone. Straight down the river. To the Beni,' murmured Karel, barely audible now. 'Then up this one. Funny really. We could have come that way. If we'd known.' He chuckled faintly, a chuckle as thin as the wisps of mist over the stream. 'They knew. Where we were going. All the time. Cat and mouse.'

She thought she had forgotten all Karel's black, obsessive fears of the Kallawaya, but now they flooded over her again. And there was the little yellow boat, lurking like a sentinel under the trees.

She sat gazing at it for a long time while the thoughts whirled in her mind. When she turned back to Karel, his eyes were shut and his head had dropped forwards on to his chest.

'Karel?'

He did not answer.

'Karel!' She said it louder, afraid. Then she touched his hand. It was quite warm, but utterly limp and he did not move. For a moment, appalled, she thought that he was dead, but as she leaned closer she felt his breath on her cheek. Desperately, she shook at his shoulder.

'Karel! Wake up!'

Briefly, his eyelids stirred, without opening. Then he slid sideways, his whole weight against her so that she had to let him down on to the ground.

Behind her, there was a quick, agitated rustling. Finn and Agustin were sitting up beside the dead fire and Jean was already running towards her.

'What is it?' Finn said loudly, across the space.

162

Falling to her knees beside Karel, Jean lifted his eyelids and then picked up his wrist to feel for his pulse. 'It's all right,' she said. 'He's not dead.' Then, more slowly, 'He's in a coma, I think.'

Finn stood up, shaking his blanket away impatiently. 'So what now? I suppose we have to think of some way of getting him back to La Paz. Getting him to a doctor. Before it's too late.'

Jean laughed, a tight, sour laugh, and sat back on her heels. 'You don't understand.' There was no expression at all in her voice. 'There's nothing a doctor can do. It's much too late already. It was too late even when we started out.'

Rain Forest

Deep deep

On the wet, still floor of the forest,
Cathedral-dim,
The tree trunks rise majestic
Through the gloom

Where weak green light drops slow
And not a stir
Of wind breaks the enchantment
Of the air

Up up

To the riotous sunburst of leaves, where flowers
        in fountains
Embroider the canopy spread as a home to harbour
The scamper of monkeys, the raucous, squawking flash
Of azure, magenta-winged, green-bodied birds that pass.

The rainbow blossoms gape for the vibrant probe
Of whirring humming-birds, vie for the cobweb touch
Of butterflies, black-velvet-edged, electric-bright,
For the crucial brush of pollen on stigma before

Down down

Through the ever-darkening layers,
Branches moult
Seeds and leaves and flowers
In a slow silt

To the wet, still floor of the forest,
Cathedral-dim,
Where life decays to new life
In the gloom

Deep deep

Chapter 16

*. . . that which you will never see, because you will die soon
. . .*

The breeze ruffled the hair on the back of Paula's neck, but the sensation was infinitely remote. Her whole body seemed like a stone, in the centre of which her mind crouched, numb and paralysed. Finn was just as still, staring at Jean. Only Agustin moved. He had not understood her words and he came stepping lightly round the fire to look down at Karel.

'He is not dead?'

'It's time to explain, Jean.' That was Finn, the words jerking roughly out of his throat. 'Everything. You can't hold out on us any longer.'

'No, of course I can't.' She nodded dully. 'Let me cover him up first.'

She began to tuck a blanket round Karel. No one made any move to help her. Finn had come to stand beside Agustin and the two of them were staring down the slope, scanning the valley ahead without a word. When they finally gathered in a circle round the dead fire, Jean did not speak for a long time. She sat with her face buried in her hands, drawing long, slow breaths. Then, at last, she raised her head.

'I've been dreading this moment. I suppose I knew it would come in the end, but I didn't believe — I never thought it would be so *soon*. And it's hard to explain.'

'Not like that,' Paula said. 'You've got to talk in Spanish. So that Agustin can understand.'

'All right,' Jean said. 'It will be harder. I have the least Spanish of us all.'

'We'll help you,' Finn said shortly. 'Just *tell* us. Is Karel mad?'

'It is not quite like that.' Jean rubbed a hand over her face and sat up straighter. 'He has —' She hunted for a word, failed to find it, and began again, more simply. 'When he came back from Samoa last year, he had a swelling on his leg. High on the — on the upper part. I could not make him go to a doctor. He said it was not serious. But I should have known. I should have forced him to go.'

'Was he afraid?' Finn said.

'I think so. But he is not a man who will speak of his fears. Even to himself.'

If I screwed up my mind, like clenching a fist, I could freeze the bit of me that was afraid, thought Paula. *Oh God.*

Jean was staring at the charred twigs. 'When I tried to speak to him about it, he grew angry. He said that the swelling would go.' Her mouth twisted painfully. 'I could have helped him better if — if I had not wanted so much to believe him.'

She wrapped her arms round her body and sat quite still, small as a child.

'Go on,' Finn said cruelly. He caught Paula's eye and added, 'She *must*. We should have made her do it before.'

'Can't you see —?' For the first time in her life, Paula wanted to protect her mother. But Jean lifted her head.

'Finn is right.' She gulped for breath and then went on steadily. 'When we got the message from Peter Laban, telling us to come to Rome, it seemed like a signal. Because — of course — we went to stay with Matteo Pascoli.' Paula nodded, but Jean went on, explaining to the others. 'He was once, long ago, a doctor on one of the expeditions. And he is now a famous man in Italy. So Karel trusts him. And he agreed to let Matteo make . . . to let Matteo make tests and . . . .'

Her voice cracked, and Paula saw her bite her tongue fiercely, to keep herself from crying out. 'It's no good,' she said in English. 'You'll have to translate this bit to Agustin. It's too difficult to —' She paused, and then spoke in a rush, as though that were the only way she could get the words out. 'Matteo told me that the cancer had spread into the whole of his body. And that there was no hope of a cure. Not so late. Only that Karel's life could be spun out — a little — if he had massive, disfiguring surgery. And drugs. Powerful drugs, all the time, to keep him out of pain.'

Finn translated, deadpan, and Agustin looked puzzled.

'I do not understand,' he said slowly. 'Is it the fear of this death that has made the Señor Karel act so strangely?'

'No.' Jean bit her tongue again and struggled with the Spanish words. 'He does not know. At least — Oh, he has guessed, of course, but Matteo and I did not tell him. So he does not know exactly. His strangeness comes from something worse. Matteo said that it could be —that it was likely — that the disease would grow also in his brain. He told me to expect —' She choked. 'Ever since we started, I have been waiting for this, and watching it happen.'

Paula felt herself choking with pity. To have known what was happening. And stayed calm and capable. It was Jean's apparent ordinariness that had kept them together all through the journey. But *that* was what had been underneath. Fear and a terrible knowledge. And she had borne it all alone. Paula wanted to reach out and take her in her arms.

But Finn reacted quite differently. He was white with fury. 'So you *knew*? All the time? And you let him set out just the same?'

'I had three days,' Jean said, with a kind of dull stubbornness. 'All by myself in Rome while Karel was going over the Martinez papers with Peter. He was alight. He came back every evening unable to talk about anything else except the Incas and the city. And I went and sat in St Peter's. I sat through a whole mass, without hearing a word, thinking. At the end, I promised myself that Karel should have his city.' She lifted her head defiantly. 'Do you blame me?'

'Of course I blame you,' Finn said coldly. 'You must have been mad. You let him bring us all into the forest. Even children. Even your own *daughter*. When you knew he was in no fit state to cope. No wonder Alfred Moon wouldn't come!'

'Alfred didn't know Karel was ill,' Jean said. 'He just thought that we were being hasty. That we should wait and make investigations first. And I would have agreed with him, only — only I *knew* there was not enough time for that. But I thought that, if we went quickly, Karel might make it.' She looked straight at Finn. 'And I was nearly right. He's been extraordinary. *None* of you knows how much pain and weakness he's been suffering. But he's made himself go on. I didn't know anyone had such strength. Even Karel. If Paula had not been ill, we would have got there. And even after that, I thought he might just — couldn't believe —'

'You didn't *care!*' Finn had jumped to his feet and was standing over her. 'You didn't care what happened to any of us, as long as Karel had what he wanted.'

'That's right!' All at once, Jean was angry too, with a splendid, triumphant rage. 'I didn't care! Should I have made him stay at home and spend the rest of his life — the tiny rest of his life — in a hospital bed, drugged into silliness and eaten up with despair because of what he had missed? He would have withered away. I would have had to watch him vanish in front of my eyes, until he was not Karel at all. At least I've saved him from that. If he dies here, he'll be dying among the forests and the mountains, where he wanted to be. And I've given him that. I've kept him, to the very end of his life.'

For a moment, Paula caught the passion and the defiance, seeing, as though Jean had described it, the vision of Karel striding golden across the mountain tops. Then it shrivelled. That was Jean's dream, just as the city was Karel's. But not hers. Not any more. She was not the sort of person to fling everything into the flames and rejoice at the blaze. She had to look straight at reality, and her reality was Karel, dying. Karel. Dying. She had to make sense of that unhappiness in her own clumsy, stumbling way. Thinking, not crying.

'What do we do now?' she said.

'That's right.' Finn was almost sneering. 'Do we just wait here for Karel to die? Sit and do some knitting?'

Very softly, as though to himself, Agustin murmured, 'The Kallawaya is in the valley.'

'Oh, that's all right.' Jean gave a bitter laugh. 'We need not worry about *that*, at least. That was part of the illness. When Karel said he had seen them, when the puma came round the camp, that was the moment when I knew for certain.' She looked at Finn. 'You were right. He couldn't have seen that. It was a hallucination.'

'Of course,' Agustin said gently. 'I knew that the Kallawaya would not behave so. They come down into the forest for their own reasons. To gather herbs for their medicines. But you have not understood me. You say that even if we take the Señor Karel back to La Paz, there is no doctor who can help him?'

Jean smiled sadly. 'There is not, in the whole of Bolivia, a doctor as good as Matteo Pascoli. And he has despaired.'

Agustin spread his hands. 'Among my people, when a life is despaired of, the sick one is taken to the Kallawaya. So it was with me, when I was small. So it is even with the White Faces in La Paz sometimes. Because the ways of the Kallawaya are different from the ways of white doctors.'

'For God's sake!' Finn ran his fingers through his hair, sending the curls wild. 'Is that what we've come to? Talking about witch-doctors?'

'You are afraid, Finn,' said Agustin. 'Afraid of what you do not understand, like a painted savage.' He leaned forward. 'I am not a savage. I have been to school and, one day, I shall be a man who fixes engines in La Paz. But I *know* that the Kallawaya can heal. I have a strong, straight arm that tells me so. And even if I did not know, I should still tell you the same thing. Now that there is no hope for the Señor, what harm is there in asking for help from the Kallawaya?'

Finn pulled a revolted face and turned away. And Paula felt her mind shrink back. The shadow of that black figure in the boat had loomed in all her fears. Like a demon, it had stalked the expedition, stirring up arguments and discord. To go down there on purpose and seek out the Kallawaya would be to confront that terror.

But she knew it was a foolish, irrational terror. She made herself face it, looking straight at it in the full light. Made herself think. And, in its usual plodding way, her brain brought her an answer.

'Agustin is right. I'm not sure I believe that the Kallawaya can really work wonderful cures, but we would be mad not to *try*. There's nothing to lose.'

'What about civilization?' Finn said sarcastically. 'Science? Reason? Little oddments like that. Once you start running off after primitive superstitions, you're hacking at the whole thing.'

'Civilization isn't going to collapse just because we go down that valley,' Paula said, irritated. He was playing some stupid game of his own, she thought. But Agustin was gazing at him, pityingly.

'It is hard to step over the edge of what you know,' he murmured. Then he turned to Jean. 'You have not spoken yet. What do you want us to do?'

172

She had sat still while they were arguing, slumped back into her earlier dullness. Now she looked up. 'When you have carried something for as long as I have carried this knowledge of Karel's death, hope hurts almost more than despair. How can I decide? Of course I want to believe that the Kallawaya can cure him. But if I let myself believe and it isn't true — how shall I bear it?'

Suddenly, Paula became aware of strength inside herself. Not tension, like the strength that had kept Jean going, but a firm, solid certainty. She knew what ought to be done. She had thought it out and, in the very centre of her mind, she knew that her decision was sensible.

'Don't worry.' She put an arm round her mother. 'We'll do it. We'll take Karel down into the forest. Perhaps he'll live and perhaps he'll die, but at least we'll know that we've tried everything.'

Feeling Jean relax slightly against her arm, she looked up at the others. Finn pinched his lips impatiently and turned away, but Agustin's eyes met hers over the dead embers. Steady brown eyes. No wild enthusiasm like Karel's. No fierce defiance like Jean's. Nor fearful logic like Finn's. Just the calmness of a person who had worked out a decision that seemed sensible to him. And in the middle of Paula's misery, there was room for a small, warm thought. *He's like me. He's the same sort of person.*

Chapter 17

'We could have chosen something easier to do,' Jean said grimly, staring down the valley. Now that they had eaten, she was calmer and she pulled a sudden comic face as she looked down the pathless slopes where the forest gathered thickly on each side. 'How are we going to manage it? Make a hang-glider?'

Paula had been thinking about it all through breakfast. Because it was safer to think than to feel. Now she said, 'We'll have to go down the stream. It's the only way. And then we'll be able to see where we're going.'

Jean frowned. 'But what about Karel?' He's not going to wake up, you know.' She sounded quite detached.

'We can make a stretcher.' Paula squatted down, tracing in the dusty earth with one finger to illustrate her idea. 'Look. If we take one of the hammocks and cut slits along the edges — like this — we can slide poles through the slits. If you look down there, just below where the forest starts, there's a stand of saplings. They'd make good poles. And we've got enough cord to lash them to the hammock.'

She spoke confidently, certain that she had worked it out right. But when she looked up she saw that Jean was smiling.

174

'What's the matter? Don't you think it's a good idea?'

'Oh yes, it's a very good idea.' Jean touched her lightly on the head. 'It's just strange to hear you sounding so practical. I've always thought of you as Karel's child. With nothing of me.'

Guiltily, Paula remembered thinking the same sort of thing herself. Pride that she could share Karel's dreams. When she sat by the fire, listening to him talk, there might have been only the two of them, absorbed in a single idea. But now, as the memory of those evenings came back, she seemed to see the figure on the other side of the fire for the first time. Bent over her sewing or her knitting, shut out of the conversation but somehow adding to the atmosphere by her calmness. *I love you*, Paula thought, with sudden fierceness. But she knew that she could not say it.

'Don't worry,' Jean muttered. 'We've got the rest of our lives to work it out. Let's get going on that stretcher of yours.'

Finn refused to help at all. The others left him while they climbed down towards the copse and came back dragging two young trees, roughly trimmed. By then, Finn had clambered a little way up the hill that rose to the right of the path. He was sitting on a small ledge, nursing his camera on his knees and gazing backwards over the ridges they had crossed the day before. From time to time he moved his position to take a photograph, but he gave no sign that he had seen them come back.

Agustin set down the ends of the tree trunks. 'Finn has shut himself away.'

'Selfish.' Paula picked up a machete and began to chop off the remaining stubs of the branches. 'He knows we could do with his help.'

'Let him alone. He doesn't need us to attack him. He's got problems of his own.' Jean selected one of the hammocks and cut a short, neat slot along the edge. 'Is that about the right size?'

'Very good,' said Agustin. 'You are a good workman.'

Jean grinned at him and nodded her head in thanks. It all seemed unreal to Paula. An awful, nightmare thing had happened. But there they were, sitting together on the ground, working away and talking quite normally, as though Karel were not lying unconscious only a few yards away. Somehow the work was a relief. After the struggle over the hills and the terrible story Jean had told, it was comforting to be able to deal with a small, manageable problem.

Agustin finished trimming his pole and slid it carefully through the slots on one side of the hammock. Then he picked up the coil of thin cord and began to lash the pole and the cloth tightly together. Jean stood up.

'Finn,' she called, 'we're nearly ready. Are you going to come and help lift Karel on to the stretcher? And we ought to sort out our rucksacks. We'll have to leave the other hammocks and most of the food behind, or we'll never make it. Come down and say what you want to bring.'

As though to be deliberately annoying, Finn did not answer at once. He waited until he had finished taking the picture he was preparing. Then he shouted over his shoulder, 'Take what you like. I don't care. I've got my camera, and that's all that matters.'

'He is like a child now,' Agustin said mildly. 'It is no use to argue with a child. We must tell him what to do.'

But when the time came to tell Finn, it was not so easy. He scrambled down the slope and stood for a moment staring down at Karel who was lying on the stretcher, tied into placé by ropes round his body. Then he lifted his head and his sharp face was sombre. 'I won't do it. You can take him down there if you like, but I won't be a party to it.'

'But we need four people to carry the stretcher,' Jean said. 'You'll have to help us.'

'Help you behave like idiots? Why should I?' He turned away and began to climb the hill again, ignoring their shouts.

'All right.' Jean bent down to pick up the ends of the poles, her face set. 'If he won't come, we'll do it without him. Agustin, you and Paula take the two ends by his head. That will be the heaviest part. I will carry the other two myself.'

They bent down and lifted, straining at the weight, and Agustin glanced at Paula. 'Your leg?'

'I can manage.' She smiled reassuringly. In fact, it was already aching, but she refused to think about it. Instead, she looked down at Karel. He lay in the hammock, slung between the two poles, his unconscious face very thin. Jean grinned ironically.

'Perhaps it's a good thing he has lost so much weight. We could never have carried him otherwise.'

With a jerk of her head, she motioned to them to start and they began to move forwards, taking short steps, the hammock swaying. In spite of what Jean had said, Paula almost panicked as she looked down the steep valley. *We'll never do it. Not down that slope.*

But she had learned from her journey up the hill. Never think about where you are going. Just take each step as it comes. Step by step by step. Like that, they left the end of the path and walked into the bed of the stream, searching for safe footholds among the rocks.

They had gone no more than twenty yards when there was a loud splashing behind them. Finn came rushing up and caught at Agustin's pole. 'Give it to me,' he said hoarsely. 'Go and help Jean with the other end.'

Taking the weight as Agustin let the pole go, he started to shuffle down the stream beside Paula. He did not say anything and his face was stern.

Gradually, as they made their slow, painful way down the valley, mist thickened over the water and the forest began to rise on either side. It encroached on the stream, sending long tendrils across their path and threatening to tangle their feet. Occasionally, it grew all the way from one side to the other, so that the stream was dark under a low bridge of branches and Agustin had to leave his pole to Jean and hack at the trees with the machete that he had hung round his neck.

As the forest became closer and darker, Finn began to pant, his breath coming in short gasps.

'What's the matter?' Paula said at last. 'Are you getting tired?'

'Of course not!' He turned his head away and she let it go. It was better not to interfere with him. But a little later he spoke again. 'I bet you're thinking bad things about me.'

'I was.' She could not bring herself to be dishonest. 'But not now. You're here.'

'I didn't —' He shook his head angrily, as though the words would not come. 'I wasn't playing games back there. I didn't think I could force myself down into the forest like this.'

'But it's not the first time.' Paula was surprised to see that his forehead was covered in sweat. 'The forest never bothered you before.'

'No.' He smiled wryly. 'Before, it was as I had imagined it. Like Karel's expeditions have always seemed to me. We were in charge. Cutting our way into the darkness so that we could bring light. So that we could *understand*.'

'But now it's different?'

'Of course it's different! We're giving ourselves up to the darkness.' He was so fierce and intent that he didn't watch where he was going. His foot slipped on a loose rock and he staggered and almost fell, jarring the stretcher so that Karel's head lolled sideways. Finn winced. 'Can you understand what I mean?'

'I'm not sure I can.' Paula considered. 'I've never been afraid of the dark.'

'Not of the dark *outside*. But —'

'But the dark *inside*?' Paula looked down at the stretcher. Karel was still again now, the bones of his face showing sharp where the flesh fell away into deep grooves. He seemed infinitely fragile and helpless. 'That's where he is, isn't it? In the dark. Perhaps we have to go into it too. To get him back.'

'That's just talk,' Finn muttered angrily. 'You don't *know*. We none of us know what we're doing. Or what we're going to find.'

He seemed to withdraw, his face darkening. Paula decided to leave him alone and concentrate on picking her way so that she did not strain her sore leg.

The further down stream they went the less steep it became, so that in some ways it was easier to walk. But all the time the stream was growing deeper, rocks rising more and more rarely above the surface. The water began to swirl around their ankles and then towards their knees. Jean glanced up.

'We shall have to go up on to the bank, or the water will reach the stretcher.'

Paula looked down towards the little yellow boat moored under the bank. It was no more than a few hundred yards away now, beyond the last outcrop of rock. But the smooth water where it floated looked very deep.

Agustin had been watching the bank. Now he gestured sideways with his head. 'There is a clearing. If we go up to it, we can lay the *patron* down and then, maybe, cut a path through the forest.'

Jean nodded. 'Finn, you and Paula go first. I think we can get straight through to the clearing. But watch Karel's face on the branches.'

Lifting the end of the stretcher so that it rested on the bank, Finn and Paula scrambled up. They heaved on the poles, sliding the stretcher over the ground so that Karel was lying among overhanging bushes. Then the four of them lifted again and pushed their way through to the clearing. As soon as they set the stretcher down in the open space, Jean knelt down and picked up Karel's wrist to feel his pulse.

'Stupid!' She smiled apologetically. 'But all the way down I was thinking, *Suppose he's dead already?* And I couldn't touch him to find out. I —'

Agustin prodded her shoulder and put a finger to his lips. She looked up.

'What? What is it?'

'I am not certain.' He glanced around at the trees. 'I thought I heard a noise. Close in the forest.'

Immediately they were all tense, listening hard. But the only sound they could hear was the rushing of the water and the rustle of the wind among the trees. All around them, the forest spread dark shadows and the gathering mist blocked their view. Then Paula turned her head slightly and gave an involuntary gasp.

On the far side of the clearing, which had been empty a second before, were three Indians. They must have stepped out of the trees in that time, but they were so still that they might have grown where they stood, the red lines daubed over their bodies and faces as fiercely bright as the flowers on the trees. Long bows were slung on their backs, but they made no move to reach for them. They stood motionless, staring at the travellers without any expression.

'Are they from the village?' Paula whispered.

Agustin nodded. 'I think so.'

'Can you talk to them?'

Agustin shrugged. 'Perhaps. But they are Indians of the forest. They may have a few words of Quechua, but no more.'

He stepped forward and began to speak, sounding stiff and guttural. The three Indians did not react at all. They went on staring. Then the tallest of them walked further into the clearing. Ignoring the stretcher, he signalled to Jean and Agustin to take off their rucksacks, pulling impatiently at the straps when they did not obey him fast enough. The other two Indians moved closer and squatted down, tugging at the flaps until they broke the buckles.

180

Roughly, they emptied out the contents of the packs and shuffled through them with their hands.

'What are they doing?' Paula whispered.

Agustin frowned. 'I do not think they want to steal. Perhaps they mean to frighten us. So that we go away.'

The tallest Indian approached Finn and began to prod at the pockets of his waistcoat. Crossing his arms protectively round his body, Finn backed away.

'No!' he said loudly, in English.

'Finn,' murmured Jean, 'let them look. It could be dangerous if you don't.'

The Indians were glancing at each other. One of them reached over his shoulder and unslung his bow, tightening the string. Finn's face tensed obstinately.

'I saved for five years to buy this camera. Do you think I'm going to let some — some *savage* — snatch it away and drop it on the ground?'

The Indians had begun to mutter now, but their faces were still impassive. It was impossible to guess what they were saying. Paula moved closer to Agustin.

'Please try to talk to them again. You must be able to make them understand *something*.'

'I will try.' Agustin stepped deliberately in between Finn and the Indians and stared straight at the tallest Indian. This time he spoke very slowly. So slowly that Paula could make out the word 'Kallawaya' repeated again and again. For a moment it did not seem to have any effect. Then one of the Indians nodded.

'Ka — lla —wa —ya,' he said in a loud voice, with an odd intonation. Turning round, he pointed to Karel. 'Ka — lla — wa — ya.'

It was impossible to tell if he were asking a question, but Paula, Agustin and Jean all nodded vigorously and said, 'Kallawaya' again. Only Finn did not move. He was standing with his back close to a tree and his waistcoat clutched round him, waiting for another attack on his camera.

But the Indians took no notice of him. The leader gestured to the other two who stooped down and picked up the stretcher. Without any sign they plunged straight into the forest at a trot.

'Come on,' said Jean. 'We'll lose them.'

Paula glanced quickly at the mess of baggage lying spread on the ground. No time to rescue it. Then the medicine box caught her eye and she scooped it up as she moved towards the trees.

There was no clear path through the forest. The trees grew tall and straight on every side, towering up towards the distant canopy which shut out the sun. But the Indians did not hesitate for an instant. They wove their way between the trunks at such a speed that Paula found herself limping painfully in her efforts to keep up with them. She was just beginning to flag when they suddenly stopped.

In front of them was the clearing that had been visible from their camp that morning. Blackened tree stumps showed how the forest had been burnt away to make the space and, between the tree stumps, the earth was reddish and bare, trodden bald by the passing of feet among the small, rough huts.

Beyond the empty space in the middle was a bigger building, square and strongly made. Next to it, a roof of branches spread over a curious raftered frame. The four corners of the roof were supported on poles, but the sides had been left open and lines of creeper stretched between the poles. From each line hung dull bundles of dried leaves, silver-grey and brown.

The clearing was completely empty, but in one of the huts a child was crying. Paula guessed that the villagers had hidden at the sound of strangers approaching. It was a comforting thought. If they were afraid, they could not be utterly ferocious.

The tall Indian raised his arm, pointing across the clearing at the square hut.

182

'Kallawaya,' he said, very slowly so that they should all understand. Then he nodded and the other two began to carry the stretcher forward between the nearest huts.

Jean followed first, paying no attention to what was around her, her eyes on Karel. Then came Paula and Agustin. Agustin was glancing inquisitively from side to side and when he looked at Paula he smiled encouragingly. Finn walked last, still holding his waistcoat round him, his face pale. And in front of them was the black doorway of the Kallawaya's hut.

Chapter 18

. . . which only the loyal shall reach . . .

After all their fears and arguments, he seemed very small. A wrinkled old man in black sitting cross-legged on a blanket. The garish colours of the blanket were muted by the dimness, but the shadows seemed to emphasize the contours of his face instead of muffling them, the bones standing out strong and heavy.

He did not move as they came into the hut, nor did his expression alter as the Indians set down the stretcher and spoke to him. He simply gazed at the travellers. On his shoulder the little monkey crouched, mimicking his stillness. Its dark brown fur merged into the blackness of the old man's shirt and its white face, with the ears set high and far back, seemed oddly human. Only its eyes were alert, shrewd and glittering.

As the Indians backed out of the doorway, the Kallawaya looked down at Karel's unconscious body. Then his eyes flicked from one face to another, as though he were deciding who led the group. But when he spoke, it was to all of them, in clear, fluent Spanish.

'Why have you come here?' He sounded hostile and suspicious, without any trace of kindness, but Jean answered at once.

'We have come to ask for help for my husband.'

The old man's eyes flicked backwards and forwards again, sharp in the gloom. At last he said, 'This is a strange place to come to if you are looking for help from the Kallawaya. Everyone knows that the Kallawaya are people of the mountains. Why did you not go to the *ayllus* round Charazani?'

'Our journey had already brought us here,' Jean said. 'And we saw your boat from the top of the hill.'

'So. There was another purpose for your journey.' The Kallawaya looked coldly at them. 'This is not a place where strangers are welcome.'

'That's obvious,' said Finn. 'Those Indians turned out our luggage. Threw it all over the place.'

Jean clutched at his arm, hushing him, but the old man gave a satisfied smile. 'They were obeying their orders. But this — this bringing you here — that was not according to their orders.'

'They understood,' Jean said quickly. 'When they saw my husband. They knew that we wanted to see you.'

The Kallawaya was not softened. 'They should not have brought you.' He tapped the tips of his fingers together. 'I am not certain that I should speak to you. I am bound by an oath to protect the secrets of this place.'

Paula tensed in the shadows. It was like a confirmation of Karel's imaginings. The knowledge of the city across the river burnt in her brain. What would he do if he knew that they were looking for it?

But Jean plunged on, desperately. 'We don't *care* about your secrets. Only about my husband. *Please* will you help him?'

The old man pursed his mouth, sucking at his bottom lip. The monkey on his shoulder thrust its fingers into his hair and chattered crossly. At last the Kallawaya said, still in the same frosty voice. 'First you must tell me why you came here.'

'Of course I'll tell you.' Jean could hardly say the words fast enough. 'We came to find the city that was prepared for the Inca Atahualpa. We have travelled a long way, across the mountains and through the forests. But if you will only help my husband, we will go away and not tell anyone that the city is here.'

Paula held her breath and crossed her fingers. Then, as she watched, a smile spread over the old man's face. He leaned forwards and caught hold of Jean's chin between his thumb and forefinger. 'You are telling me the truth? You came to look for the city? You think that that is the secret of this place?'

'Yes,' Jean said, sounding bewildered. 'That is what we thought.'

The Kallawaya looked thoughtful, as though he were not sure whether to believe her, and Agustin spoke suddenly into the silence. 'I understand you, Señor. I had heard that there are secret places in the forest where the Kallawaya come to gather their herbs. And I have seen the plants drying in the sun. But you do not need to be afraid for your secrets. These people are from a far country where the wisdom of the Kallawaya is not properly understood. It was not for this that they came.'

Finn gave an impatient snort and Paula glanced anxiously at him. But, somehow, that snort seemed to reassure the Kallawaya more than Agustin's explanation. He relaxed visibly and smiled again.

'Well. Perhaps I shall believe you.' Sitting up straighter, he suddenly became brisk and businesslike, nodding to Agustin. 'Tell me about the man who lies here. What is his sickness?'

'You should not ask *me* —' Agustin began. But the old man stirred restlessly and so he went on. 'The Señor has been very strange, all through the journey. First there was the death of my father . . . .' Slowly and awkwardly, he went through the whole story, pausing every now and then to gather his thoughts. As he spoke, Jean's face grew stony and when he started to describe the scene on top of

186

the hill that morning she closed her eyes. But the Kalla-waya paid no attention to her, concentrating on Agustin's words.

'. . . and now he is as you see,' Agustin finished. 'We cannot wake him and the Señora says that the doctors of her country can do nothing for him.'

'I understand.' The Kallawaya looked down at Karel. 'I have seen this sickness before. Once, or perhaps twice.' Leaning forwards, he picked up Karel's wrist in one hand and, with the other, pulled open the slack eyelids. Then he gave a low, fluting whistle.

Immediately, the monkey leaped to the ground and scampered into a corner of the hut. Chattering softly to itself, it raked through a pile of objects and came back carrying a small, red, plastic torch. Absently, as he took the torch, the Kallawaya scratched the monkey's head and it jumped back on to his shoulder, curling its tail round his neck.

The narrow beam of light from the torch seemed to make the hut darker, as though there were nothing in the world except Karel's face. The spot of light travelled along his nose and came to rest directly over one eye. Pulling back the lid even further, the old man leaned close and peered down.

The eyeball gleamed eerily white and Paula found that she had clenched her fists and stopped breathing. Looking quickly at the others, she saw that they too were intent, watching the light. Even Finn was staring, as though the old man's stubby finger held him fascinated.

The torchlight moved to the other eye, catching the lashes so that they glittered pale gold. Then the switch clicked and for a moment Paula could see nothing in the darkness.

'Now,' said the Kallawaya, 'I shall read the coca.'

He gave a different whistle, through his teeth, and the monkey leaped again, its long tail waving. This time it brought back two things — a small crimson bag, woven with orange figures, and a brown cloth which it carried draped over its head and round its shoulders, so that it looked like a little old woman going to market. Taking the cloth, the Kallawaya spread it on the ground in front of him, between his feet and Karel's body. Then he opened the bag and began to select coca leaves from a small bundle, turning them over and over, rejecting some and choosing others that looked identical to Paula. Every now and again he held one up to the light from the doorway, as though to assess its colour.

Jean was twisting the edge of her jumper in nervous fingers and Finn had turned his face away in disgust. Only Agustin was relaxed, with the air of someone watching something familiar.

The Kallawaya spread his selected leaves on the brown cloth in a neat pattern. Then he rolled the cloth into a bundle, lifting it and twisting it round in his hands while he muttered something under his breath. Laying it down again, he unrolled it.

The leaves lay jumbled, most of them clustered together, but one or two clinging at the edge of the cloth. For a long time the Kallawaya stared at this pattern, tracing it out with one finger and chewing thoughtfully at his bottom lip. On his shoulder, the monkey moved its finger in the same way, in solemn imitation.

Finally, the old man gathered the leaves together. Dropping one or two on the ground, he rolled the others into a ball which he put into his mouth. He chewed slowly, his eyes half closed.

'Now,' he said at last, 'I shall tell you what is wrong with this man.'

'We *know* what is wrong with him,' Jean burst out, as though she could not stop herself. 'What we want to know is —'

The Kallawaya held up a hand and opened his eyes staring icily at her. 'First you must believe. It is not the habit of your people to believe my people. Listen, therefore.'

188

She nodded and folded her hands, but Paula could see how tightly the fingers gripped each other.

'Your husband has been robbed of his soul by evil spirits in his brain,' said the old man. 'First they made him wild and then they grew more powerful and possessed him completely, so that he is as you see now. If they are not checked, his life will be squeezed from him and he will die.'

'For Heaven's sake!' Finn said, in English. 'How much longer are you going to go on listening to this rubbish?'

Jean turned on him fiercely. 'What do you know about it? Why don't you *listen*? You think he's wrong because he's using different words. But he's not wrong. What he says is exactly what's happening to Karel.' She looked back at the Kallawaya. 'It is as you say. But what can be done to save him?'

The old man spread his hands. 'It will not be long. Two days or maybe three. Then there will be no more room for his soul inside his skull and he will die.'

'Unless you help him.' Jean's voice was very low, hardly more than a whisper. 'You are the only hope I have. What can you do?'

The old man glanced away from her, looking at Finn's averted face. Then he closed his eyes.

'I can do nothing.'

Jean arched forward soundlessly, both fists pressed hard against her mouth. Paula did not move, but she felt her mind convulsed with the same despair. It was all over. It was no use. Karel was going to die.

But she felt Agustin's arm brush her lightly as he stood up. His shadow fell across Karel's body and darkened the Kallawaya's face.

'Most honoured healer,' he said gravely, 'I have always been told that the Kallawaya could treat all parts of the body. That they could work even on the head. Even on the brain.'

189

The old man leaned back slightly, to look at him, and gave a slow, hoarse chuckle. 'You are a child of the new times. Can it be that you believe these tales of your grandmother?'

Agustin stood steady. 'If I do not believe them, they will be lost. And your people and mine will be swallowed up in the ways of the white men. Soon no one will remember that there was also a way of the Indian.' He dropped suddenly to his knees, facing the Kallawaya across Karel's body. 'If you want to preserve the old ways, show me, and I shall believe.'

The old man stretched out one finger and drew it down Agustin's cheek. 'Why do you want to help the man who killed your father?'

The reply came so softly in the darkness that Paula had to strain her ears to catch it. 'When I set out on this journey, I was ashamed of being an Indian. I wanted only to learn the ways of the white men and be like them. But, as I have come down the mountain, it has seemed to me, more and more, that my people still have the wisdom that I thought was lost.'

The Kallawaya was silent for a moment, watching him. Then he spoke, not to Agustin, but to the others. 'The boy is right. I can heal this sickness, as I heal other sickness. But before the cure can even begin, it is necessary to wake the sleeping soul. To weaken the pressure of the evil spirits. In the past, the Kallawaya had a way of doing this. By making a hole in the skull.'

Paula winced, a dim memory stirring, and the Kallawaya smiled. 'Yes, it is a hard way. And the government has forbidden it for many years. When I was a young man, I agreed, with the rest of my people, not to risk the anger of the government by going against this rule.'

'But you *have* done it? In the past?' Jean lifted her head eagerly.

As though her words added a last, unbearable shadow to the darkness that licked round them, Finn jumped up, stooping his head under the poles of the roof.

'You're *mad*! You've all gone mad! Don't you understand what he's saying? He wants to carve away at Karel's skull. It's demented! *You can't believe it.*' Pushing past Paula, he burst out of the doorway and they heard his feet running across the clearing.

'You understand?' murmured the Kallawaya. 'It is because of that one that I cannot do it.' Jean gasped and he made a gentle movement towards her. 'Señora, I am a healer. I see, as clearly as you, that your husband has no other hope but my help. And it could perhaps have been done. Here in the jungle, who is to know what happens? And your own country is far away. When you returned there, we should all be safe.'

He paused and stared down at Karel's face. 'I do not want to let this man die. For the sake of the boy, if for nothing else, I want to heal him. But I cannot do that without first using the forbidden way to rouse him, and I must think of my people. Your companion who has left is angry in his heart. How can I trust him to be secret?'

'He would. I'm sure he would,' Jean pleaded. But the old man looked at her with stern sadness.

'Always there are men who try to take away the lands of the Kallawaya. They hunt for reasons. If it became known that I had done this thing, they would have their reasons.'

'Oh no,' Jean whispered. 'Oh *please.*'

Paula felt herself near to screaming. With an effort, she forced her mind to be calm. She *had* to think of something. Agustin and Jean had done their best and Karel was unconscious. She was the only one left.

'Suppose,' she broke in diffidently, 'that I speak to Finn — to the man outside. Is there anything he can do to make you change your mind?'

'Only this.' The Kallawaya sounded reluctant, regretting his earlier sympathy. 'If I am to change my mind, I need two things. First, this man — this Finn — must come to me himself and ask me to make the cure. So that I know his heart is altered. And also you must pay me. I am a man of business, and it will cost you five hundred American dollars.'

Jean and Paula had not even thought of that. They looked at each other, horrified, and the Kallawaya laughed at their faces, an edge of bitterness in the sound.

'What? Did you think I was a painted Indian from the forest, to risk my life and the land of my people for a handful of beads or a few blankets? I know the ways of the modern world as well as you do. I have worked in great cities and in these hands — ' he spread them above Karel's head '— is the skill of many years. If you need it, you must pay for it. And if you cannot pay —' He shrugged.

Paula stood up. 'Wait,' she said. 'Please. Just wait for a little while.'

As she pushed her way out of the hut, she did not know what she was going to do. She only knew that she had to speak to Finn.

He was standing on the far side of the clearing with his hands in his pockets, staring into the darkness between the trees. As Paula approached, he looked round with a small, shamefaced smile.

'Come to tell me how badly I've behaved? Don't think I don't know. But I would have exploded if I'd stayed there any longer. All the shadows and the superstitious hocus-pocus. It was like — like being squashed into a black box.'

'But it needn't be just hocus-pocus,' Paula said. 'I've read —'

'I know, I know.' Finn flapped his hand wearily. 'Trepanning. I've done my homework as well. I know the Andes are littered with thousand year old skulls drilled full of holes. Whoopee. Wonders of Inca brain surgery. But haven't you ever asked yourself how many of the poor devils *lived* after the operation?'

'Karel will die anyway.'

The words made a small pool of silence. Finn stood looking at her, his face very grave, and swallowed hard.

192

Then he smiled again, with his familiar charming, half apologetic smile.

'Well, it doesn't make any difference what I think. Is he going to do it?'

'No. Not unless you ask him.'

'Me?' Finn raised an eyebrow.

'He wants to know that you'll keep the secret. And he wants us to pay him five hundred dollars.'

'That's it then, isn't it?' Finn laughed lightly and Paula saw his whole body relax with relief. 'He's not going to take a cheque, is he? And I don't suppose Jean could scrape up that much anyway.'

'No,' said Paula, 'I don't suppose she could. Certainly not in the middle of the jungle.'

He looked at her as though he expected her to say something else, but she did not speak. She just let her eyes travel down from his face towards the two big pockets in his waistcoat that bulged with his equipment. He understood her at once. Backing away, he clapped his hands over the pockets.

'*Oh* no. My camera's all I've got in the world. It's the only thing that makes sense in this crazy jungle. Not on your life.'

'Not on *my* life,' said Paula.

Finn flinched and dropped his arms. She stared at him, wishing she could tell what he was thinking. It was like gazing at the surface of a dark, scummy pond. She was afraid to take a stick and stir up the depths underneath. But, when he did not speak, she added, very softly, 'Do you hate Karel so much? Is that why you won't save him?'

'Hate Karel?' Finn looked oddly at her. 'Me?'

'Oh, I know you *admire* him. But that's a cold word, isn't it. You don't really *feel* anything for him. And now you're going to let him die.'

For a moment Finn's mouth worked and then he began to speak harshly, not looking at her. 'Feelings are hellish. As long as you can think and plan and organize, you're in

193

control. But once you start to *feel* things for people — then you're really down in the dark. And the more you care, the more it hurts.'

'And — Karel?' Paula hardly dared to speak.

'Of course I don't hate him, you silly little girl.' He glared at her with fierce eyes. '*Nobody* is more important than Karel. Nobody and nothing. Watching what's happened to him on this journey has been the worst thing in my life.' His voice cracked. 'Do you really think I'd grudge my camera — do you think I'd grudge my arm or my leg — if it would make him well again? But how can I bear to let that old — that old *witch-doctor* — hack away at his head?' He shuddered. Paula felt weak with pity. But also with relief. Because she knew that she could do it now.

'I love him too,' she said quietly. 'But I could bear it. Because anything's better than knowing he'll be dead in two days.'

Finn winced.

'But I can't help him, Finn. No one can. Except you. And if you're too afraid of the darkness —'

She let the sentence die away. There was nothing more to be said now. All she could do was wait.

Slowly Finn raised his head. He did not speak to her. He did not even look at her. He began to walk across the bare earth with steady, even strides. Paula followed at a distance. It was his moment, not hers.

But she was near enough to see him enter the hut. Near enough to hear his words as he squatted down in front of the old Kallawaya.

'I have not got five hundred dollars. But my camera and my equipment are worth four times as much. I will give you a paper to say that they are yours and I will tell you where to sell them in La Paz. Please will you save Karel's life?'

Slipping his arms out of the waistcoat, he leaned over Karel's body and laid the whole thing at the Kallawaya's feet.

194

Chapter 19

. . . after great hardship . . .

Somehow, in spite of the urgency of it all, Paula had not expected anything to happen straight away. But the Kallawaya reacted instantly. Scooping the waistcoat towards him, he nodded.

'Very well. I shall do the first part — to wake him — while it is still light.' He pursed his lips. 'This is not a good place for healing. Up in the mountains, the air is clear and the mountains themselves watch over what we do. Here the air is full of spirits to corrupt the flesh. But I shall give orders to protect against them.'

'I have — medicines.' Jean hesitated and then pushed the box forward. 'From our country. You can use them if you wish.'

The old man drew in his breath. Paula saw Agustin's fingers tense and realized that what Jean had said was an insult.

'You have asked for my help,' the Kallawaya said coldly. 'If you have more faith in the wisdom of your own doctors, you can take your husband back to them.'

'No, no,' Jean said, all in a rush. 'Forgive me. Everything shall be as you say.'

The Kallawaya nodded, still disapproving, and began to heave himself slowly to his feet, reaching for a stick. He leaned heavily on it as he shuffled towards the doorway, calling out orders.

The effect of his words was dramatic. From every hut, all round the clearing, Indians hurried out. They began to run in all directions, making the preparations that he commanded.

It took them less than an hour. In the centre of the clearing, a wooden framework was set up, with long poles lashed across tree trunks to form a rough bed about two feet high. On this Karel was laid, his arms hanging slack, ropes of creeper running round his body to tie him to the bed. On either side of him, three tall stakes were hammered into the ground and to the top of each one was tied a crude torch, made of a thick stick with a bundle of cloth wrapped tightly round one end. The cloths had been saturated with a sticky green liquid so that when they were lit they burned with a sour, choking smoke that drifted over the clearing. It pricked at Paula's eyes and stung the roof of her mouth. She blinked hard and rubbed her face.

Agustin grinned as he too wiped his eyes. 'I think this is to keep off the flies and the evil spirits in the air. And also to give light if the darkness comes too soon.'

'Floodlights,' muttered Finn. His face was very pale. 'Do we have to watch?'

'I think we should,' Paula whispered. 'Unless he sends us away. Whatever happens, it won't be as bad as what we'll imagine if we can't see.'

She and Finn and Agustin ranged themselves in a line beyond the torches, facing the wooden bed. Jean had moved closer. She was kneeling on the other side, her face unreadable as she bent over Karel.

The spirals of smoke rose into the air, twisting lazily, as the Kallawaya emerged from his hut. The monkey was still crouched on his shoulder, gripping with all four feet and swaying slightly as the old man walked. He came steadily into the middle of the clearing, still issuing orders to the Indians. Passing between the torches, he settled

196

himself cross-legged on the ground behind the top of the bed, so that his face was almost level with the fair hair on the crown of Karel's head. Then he began his preparations.

Taking a few coca leaves from the bag he wore, he rolled them into a ball which he chewed slowly, muttering in an undertone. Then he removed the ball, squashed it in his fingers and dropped it on the ground.

'He is asking the *Pachamamma* of the earth to bless the work of his hands,' murmured Agustin. Finn shuddered.

For a moment there was no sound except the damp hissing from the torches. The Kallawaya was staring at the top of Karel's head, studying it closely. At last he spoke a few words and one of the Indians moved forwards, holding out a small earthenware pot. Its sides, which bulged grotesquely, were pierced with holes through which the glow of burning embers was visible. The Indian set the pot down beside the Kallawaya. On top of it, he placed a shallow tin lid.

The old man nodded. Taking a little bottle from his bag, he poured a slow stream of liquid into the tin. It hissed and spat as it hit the hot metal. Then he began to select more leaves from the bag, choosing them carefully. This time they were not coca leaves. They were narrow and lance-shaped, about three inches long, with a strange purple tinge.

He put a handful of them into his mouth, his face twisting as though they tasted unpleasant. When he had chewed them to a soggy lump, he dropped them into the tin lid, poking them about with a cautious fingertip until they began to break into shreds.

As he worked, his eyes had taken on a distant, intent expression, his attention focused on the little brazier. Without looking round, he clicked his fingers and one of the Indians brought up a torch like those tied to the stakes. The smoky flame danced close to the Kallawaya's face. Too close for the monkey on his shoulder. With a chatter of outrage, it leaped on to Karel's chest and jumped to the ground, its tail arched. Paula saw it scurry away to the far side of the clearing where it crouched motionless, watching.

Still staring at the brazier, the Kallawaya slid a hand into his bag and pulled out a short knife. Without looking at it, he turned it over and over in his hands, as though to re-acquaint himself with all its angles. It was a curious shape, the blade narrow and curving backwards like a crescent moon. As it caught the light from the torch, it glinted gold.

The old man stretched out and held it steady in the flame for a moment while the blade changed colour subtly. Then he placed a hand on Karel's head.

'No,' Finn said softly. 'No, I can't.'

'You've got to.' Paula caught hold of his hand and gripped it hard. She saw Agustin, on the other side of him, do the same, so that the three of them were linked in a chain.

Very delicately, using the outward curve of the golden blade, the Kallawaya began to shave away the hair from the front of Karel's skull, letting the fair strands drop to the earth below. As the scalp began to emerge, Paula realized for the first time quite how thin Karel had grown. Freed from the softening aureole of hair, his face was all angles, the flesh hanging from the bones, the eyes deeply sunken.

Brushing a hand across the bare half-circle of scalp, the Kallawaya looked at it for a moment. Then he drew a line with the point of his knife, slightly to one side of the centre. Where the knife passed, blood oozed in a thin, scarlet line and Paula felt Finn clutching at her hand.

Every inch of her body was aching to look away. But she knew that if her self-control wavered, even for a second, Finn would crack. He might shout. He might even leap forwards. And anything except total, silent stillness would be a danger to Karel. So she forced herself to

198

keep staring straight ahead, as though her neck were a pillar of stone, her hand steady in Finn's painful grip.

The old man began to work away at the flap of skin, peeling it backwards. Trickles of blood ran down into the remaining hair at the back of Karel's head, leaving long, sticky trails.

Then, appallingly clear in the silence, came the sound of metal sawing at bone. Paula swallowed hard and bit her tongue. It seemed impossible that Karel could remain unconscious, that his whole head was not shot through with fiery pain. Something she had read somewhere swam into her mind and repeated itself desperately. *The brain is incapable of feeling pain.* But she could not believe it. In her own skull, imagined nerves throbbed agonizingly. But Karel did not stir as the knife ground on and on.

As the old man worked, the forest had grown darker around them, shadows edging between the trees. Although she did not turn her head, Paula was aware of everyone and everything in the clearing, as if she could see through her skin.

Jean was plain in the circle of light, her face no more than a foot from the knife blade. Not a muscle moved. Only her eyes glinted backwards and forwards, following the motions of the Kallawaya's hand. Next to Paula, Finn and Agustin were just as still. Paula could feel, through her fingers, Finn's almost unbearable tautness, but Agustin looked relaxed, his breathing soft and regular.

Out and beyond, in the shadows, were the village Indians, forming a circle round the clearing. Their broad, dark faces were impassive, even the children standing in quiet awe. And beyond again, enclosing everything, was the dim, rustling forest that took no heed of what was going on. She could almost feel its upward thrust, rising from the roots buried in earth, through the heaped layers of growth that were home to millions of alien creatures, to the great outburst of colour and life high above in the canopy. And, in matched and contrary motion, the dead

199

leaves and flowers dropped slowly downwards to rot on the forest floor, so that the whole unending cycle could begin again.

Four times the Kallawaya's knife sawed into the bone, cutting two crossing pairs of parallel lines. As he finished the fourth cut, he inserted the point of the knife into it and levered gently. The small square of bone in the centre came loose and he removed it, dropping it into the tin over the brazier. He stirred the mixture round with the knife and then lifted out the disintegrating mass of leaves on the tip of the blade. They hung limply, steaming in the smoky air.

As the steam died down, he took them in his fingers, setting the knife down beside Karel's head. Very carefully and slowly, he squeezed the juice out of the leaves on to the wound, moving his hand round and round until the purple liquid covered the whole area and ran down the back, mixing with the clots of blood in Karel's hair.

With his other hand, he smoothed the flap of skin back into place and pressed the leaves on top, spreading them so that they formed a poultice which he held in place with splayed fingers.

In a low voice, too soft to be distinguished beyond the torches, he said something to Jean. She blinked, as though she were coming back from a long way away and he had to repeat the words before she understood them.

It was almost completely dark now. The figures on the far side of the clearing were invisible, merging into the wall of forest behind. Only the three in the circle of torchlight were distinct, as though they were on a stage. Jean moved sideways, opening the medicine box which she had carried out with her. Obeying the Kallawaya's directions, she began to dress the wound, taping a pad of cotton wool over the leaf poultice and then swathing the whole of the top of Karel's head in a great bandage. Against the whiteness of the dressing, his skin suddenly showed as a dirty yellow, pale and unhealthy.

200

His whole body lay slack, the hands drooping over the sides of the bed, the feet splayed out sideways. Only the very faint rise and fall of his chest showed that he was still alive.

The Kallawaya, too, seemed drained. As Jean finished her work, he closed his eyes and let his head slump forwards, deep grooves forming on either side of his mouth. But his body had a kind of solidity, as though the batterings of life, which had made Karel as frail as paper, had turned him to stone.

As Jean taped the last piece of bandage into place, he raised his head and half opened his eyes. Still holding Finn's hand, Paula moved nearer, to catch his words. He spoke in a weary, dragging voice, no longer brisk and businesslike.

'He must rest. What I have done will not cure him, but it will gain time for a cure. Now his spirit is exhausted. If you try to move him, you may put it to flight. Watch him. I shall order the villagers to keep the torches burning.'

'And then?' said Jean, her voice rough from the long silence. 'What happens next?'

'Next,' the Kallawaya said, 'he will waken. Maybe tomorrow, maybe the day after. When he does, I shall begin his cure. Now I go to rest. I am an old man and tired.' He paused, then added sharply, as though he sensed some impatience in Jean, 'I can do nothing to heal him until he is awake. He must know what I am doing, so that he can trust me. That is a part of the cure. He must share in it. Without his trust, I am helpless.'

He uncoiled himself, reaching for his stick, and strained to rise to his feet. As he shuffled across the clearing there was a shrill gabble and the monkey appeared out of the shadows, swarming up the old man's clothing and settling itself on his shoulder. Together, they disappeared into the hut.

Nobody spoke until he was completely out of sight. Then Paula said desperately, 'What are we going to do?'

'I don't know.' Jean buried her face in her hands. 'Oh, I'm *stupid*. It never occurred to me that *Karel* would have to agree to all this. Once we'd persuaded Finn, I thought those problems were over.'

'Perhaps,' Agustin said quietly, 'the *patron* will feel differently about the Kallawaya when he wakes. When he learns what has been done for him already.'

'Perhaps.' Jean did not look convinced. 'But he is a very stubborn man. And he is not cured yet, remember. He could be just as full of strange ideas when he wakes as he was before.'

They crouched round the bed, all staring down at Karel. He looked tranquil and undisturbed.

'We can do nothing,' Agustin said softly. 'Only wait.'

Chapter 20

. . . the secret city of the East . . .

'KEEP still, Karel,' Jean said quietly. 'Keep still. Don't move.'

Paula lifted her head and rubbed the sweat from her eyes. Under the rough canopy they had set up to shield him from the sun, Karel looked exactly the same as before, his limbs motionless and his eyes closed. She had been staring at his unconscious face for hours and she could not see any difference now. But Jean's voice went on, murmuring into the silence.

'Don't move an inch. Keep quite, quite still.'

This time they all saw it. The faint twitch of an eyelid.

'Very still, my dear.'

Both eyelids twitched. Then, slowly, they opened, the eyes vague for a moment until they focused on Jean's face. She leaned over and picked up a cloth, dipping it into the bowl of water she held. Still crooning, 'Still, keep still,' she held the cloth to his lips and let him suck the drops of water that dribbled down into his mouth. As his throat moved, swallowing, his eyes flicked from face to face. When she took the cloth away he spoke, his voice weak and grating.

'What's happened? Where — ? Tell me.'

Be careful, thought Paula. *Oh, be careful.* With nightmare clarity, she could imagine Karel leaping up at the word *Kallawaya*, wrenching free of the ropes and dislodging the clumsy bandage from his head.

But Jean had had hours to plan what she was going to say. For a while she looked at him, assessing how clear his mind was. Then she began to talk in a calm, even voice.

'We're in the forest, Karel. You've been very ill. You nearly died. Remember?'

A frown crumpled his face. 'I remember — pain in my head. Worse pain than I've ever known. On and on and on. And then sliding slowly down. And the city.' He tensed and moved his fingers as though he wanted to lift his arm. Obviously he did not realize that he was tied down, because he frowned again, puzzled. 'Did we reach the city?'

'Not yet. But we're very close to it,' Jean said. Before he could say anything else, she held out the cloth to give him more water. His eyes darted about all the time he was sucking and when she left his mouth free to speak his voice was wary.

'We're in the village? The one we saw from the hills?'

Jean nodded. 'We're in the village and someone here has saved your life. He's taken a great risk for your sake and we're all very grateful to him.'

Every muscle in Paula's body was clenched. She was willing Karel not to ask the next question. Not to guess what had happened until he was stronger. And for a moment it looked as though that would happen. He stared muzzily at Jean's face and then closed his eyes.

But over at the far side of the clearing there was a movement. Turning her head slightly, Paula saw the Kallawaya shuffle out of his hut, the monkey on his shoulder. Slowly he began to move towards them. She nearly held up a hand to him, as a signal to keep away, but before she could stir, Agustin laid a finger on her wrist and shook his head. All she could do was watch the old man shuffling closer and closer until his shadow fell across the bed.

'You are awake,' he said.

Karel's eyes opened again. His face showed no expression, but, low in his cheek, a muscle tightened. He stared up at the Kallawaya, who stared gravely back.

At last the old man said, 'You are afraid of me. Why is that?'

Paula could see Karel bracing himself to the effort of understanding and speaking Spanish. He blinked rapidly for a moment and then said, 'We are enemies. You have followed me all through my journey. Because you knew that I was looking for a secret of your people. How can we not be enemies?'

Faintly, at the corner of the Kallawaya's mouth, a smile stirred. 'You are speaking of the city of the Lord Atahualpa? The refuge that was made for the Sapa Inca?'

'You know that is what I am speaking of.' Karel caught his breath suddenly, the noise sounding loud in the silence. 'And you have won. You have made certain that I shall never see it.'

The old man nodded calmly. 'You are right. You will never see it. You are too ill even for that short journey.'

Karel screwed up his eyes hard, as though he were in pain, and for a second he was totally silent. Then his mouth pinched. 'You have made me as I am. You are a destroyer.'

Agustin glanced apprehensively at the Kallawaya and, behind her, Paula heard Finn mutter, 'Oh, no *more!*' sounding immensely tired. But the old man did not look insulted. He turned aside to Jean.

'It is the spirits in his head who are speaking. They fear being cast out. Do not distress yourself.' Then he looked back at Karel. 'The city is nothing. I do not care if a hundred Americans come with spades to dig it up. But it is not good for you to blame me. I cannot cure you unless you will trust me.'

'Trust you?' Karel laughed bitterly. 'Does a man trust his enemy?'

The Kallawaya stood staring down until he stopped speaking. Then he said crisply, 'Listen to me. The fear in your heart is bad, even though you are strong to hold it back. If you do not trust me, I shall not be able to drive out the evil spirits. If I could win your trust by sending you to the city, I would do it, but I cannot. As you are, you would die on the way. But suppose — suppose I send others there, so that you know I am speaking the truth when I say that the city is of no importance. Will you trust me then?'

Karel did not answer, but his eyes were alert.

'I will send these others, with a guide.' The Kallawaya's hand swept round the little group. 'They can be there tomorrow, within an hour of setting out, and they shall come back and tell you of it.'

For a moment the gaze held, the two men staring into each other's eyes. Then Karel looked away with an expression of despair.

'It is a trick. You are trying to deceive me.'

The Kallawaya shrugged, giving up, but before he could move Jean dropped to her knees and caught at Karel's hand, squeezing it hard.

'Listen to me, Karel Staszic,' she said fiercely, 'you're supposed to be brave. Mountains, oceans, lions, tigers — I've seen you face them all and I know they don't really frighten you any more. But you're afraid to trust this old man, aren't you? Well, he can't do anything else to prove he's your friend. He's risked his safety to stop you dying and he's offered to send people to the city. You're never going to trust him unless you *dare*. Are you too much of a coward to do that?'

For an instant, sheer cold rage showed in Karel's eyes. Then, very slowly, a smile spread over his face. 'Damn you, Jeanie,' he said softly, 'you're a wicked woman.

Other wives take care of their husbands, you know. Pamper them and warm their slippers. You just keep flinging me into one danger after another.'

He laughed weakly and closed his eyes.

'It's all right,' Jean said, without turning round. 'He will trust you now.'

She went on kneeling there, completely still, holding Karel's hand in both of hers.

She refused to go to the city. Folding her arms stubbornly, she insisted that she was staying with Karel.

'But it's what you came for,' said Finn. 'How can you bear to be so close and not see it?'

'I came because of Karel. I'm not leaving him.'

In case he dies, thought Paula. For a second, she panicked, certain that she could not bear to go either. Then she caught Karel's eye. Bending down, she leaned close to him to catch his voice. He was tiring and he could hardly speak above a whisper.

'You'll have to be in charge, Tabby. Make sure it's all done properly. Are you sure you know what to do?'

She nodded, forcing herself to sound cheerful. 'I ought to by now. After all the times we've talked about it.'

'Good girl.' He smiled at her. 'I shan't mind so much, you know. Not if you can come back and tell me all about it. It'll be almost as good —'

But I wanted us to go together. The words wailed themselves in Paula's head, but she would not let them out.

She had to make the journey by herself. To find the city and save Karel's life. Now it was doubly important.

And quite different from what she had imagined. In all the years she had dreamed about the city, she had seen herself going with Karel, adoring and unquestioning, dancing beside him through the forest. Instead, there was only a fixed determination driving her along.

As they crossed the river in the little yellow boat, with

the guide the Kallawaya had given them, she gazed feverishly at the opposite bank, looking for the track that they would follow. But there was no track. The guide borrowed their machete to cut a way through the snarled wall of forest, while the three of them waited impatiently.

'Thunderstorm coming,' said Finn. He was pacing up and down, his hands thrust into his pockets.

Paula could feel the tension in the air. Then the first heavy drops of rain began to fall, making the surface of the river dance in a pattern of interlocking circles. Finn turned and pushed his way into the forest behind the guide, the violence of his movements setting the branches swaying and rustling.

In the tree-tops above his head, there was a flurry of wings. Out of the leaves flew a bird so beautiful that Paula caught her breath. Its back was metallic green, glinting in the rain, and as it flew over her head she saw the crimson flash of its breast. It darted over the river and plunged into the forest on the other side.

She stepped forward into the darkness as the first flash of lightning glanced up the river. For an instant, it lit the gloomy forest like a stage and, for the first time, Paula's eyes opened to the strangeness of it.

She saw. A hundred details leaped at her in a single glance, each one different from the next and all of them eerily alien. By her feet, delicate as lace, a patch of white fungi spread fragile netted veils. High on the trunk of a tree, a brilliant red gall swelled gigantically, its surface convoluted like coral. And further on, in the shadows, an orchid grew, grotesque and fleshy, from a hump of roots.

Understanding flared in her mind like the star-burst of a rocket. She had been right, in her fever. The forest *was* a huge, ordered system. But it was too huge to grasp, embracing more kinds of life than she could begin to imagine.

Suddenly she was afraid. How could the city, which had been the central dream of her whole life, match this infinite splendour? Even now, walking through the forest, she was free to conjure up palaces and treasures, but what gold, what elaborate carvings, could live up to her dream? With every step, it wavered, growing misty and insubstantial.

Finn rounded on her in a rage of impatience.

'What's the matter with you? Don't you *want* to get there? Come on.'

She shook herself and walked faster, but she did not leave her doubts behind.

After about half an hour, their guide stopped abruptly, folding his arms.

'What is it?' said Finn. 'Why have we stopped?'

Agustin looked amused. 'I think we are near the city. He will not come any further, because he is afraid of spirits.'

'Huh!' Finn said. He moved a few steps ahead, frowning slightly as he gazed around the forest. It spread all about him, shadowy and dim, busy with its own life. Far above, the thunder crashed, but the brightness of the lightning could not reach where they stood. On the forest floor, it was as dark as late evening.

Suddenly he shouted, 'There!' and charged forward, dropping to his knee beside a low, mossy clump. He began to scrape with his hands.

'What is it, Finn?' Agustin ran across and Paula followed more slowly, almost reluctant.

What Finn had found was clearly the remains of a wall. But the stones had been shaped only roughly and they were tumbled about by the plants that had grown up between.

'A house.' Agustin was working his way round the clump, pulling away the moss. 'Yes. Look, here was the doorway.'

'Let's get *on*,' said Finn. 'It's nothing important.'

But Paula was fumbling in her pockets, pulling out a compass and a pen and some paper. She had promised Karel that it would be done properly. Illogically, she felt that if she kept that promise he would be all right. *Every-thing* would be all right.

'We can't go yet,' she said. 'We must make a plan of the house.'

Agustin nodded and began to pace round the walls, calling out measurements while Paula drew, but Finn crashed on, shouting wildly as he discovered another ruined house and another.

Gradually, as the hours passed and they pushed on into the forest, a pattern began to emerge. There was a cluster of small houses, about twenty of them, set with their backs towards the river. Some of them were totally ruined, rising only a few inches above the ground, but others were almost complete except for the roofs, their floors neatly paved and their walls head-high.

Paula concentrated on the plan that she was making, not letting herself think, hardly aware of the thunder crashing overhead or the rain that dripped down her neck. When her hair grew so wet that it dribbled on to the paper, she simply pushed it back impatiently, shielding the pad with her hand, and crouched over her drawing.

Then, quite suddenly, the houses stopped. They cast around in all directions, but the forest floor was level and bare. Paula looked down at the dull, neat squares, the tiny figures she had written.

'Do you think that's all?' she said in a flat voice. 'It's not a city, is it? Just a village.'

But Agustin was standing with his head tilted back, staring up into the trees. The storm was over, although Paula could not have said when it had stopped, and the green leaves of the canopy showed bright far above. All at once, he pointed.

'Finn, Paula — can you see? Up there?'

'Oh, come *on*,' said Finn. 'We haven't got time to start admiring the scenery.'

But Paula had seen it too. A small patch of scarlet blossom among the green. She followed it with her eyes and, very faintly, made out another. 'The square?' she said. 'That we saw from the hill?'

'What?' With a single leap, Finn was beside them, peering upwards. When he managed to pick out the red flowers, he gave a great yodel. 'That's it! There must be more on the other side of the square. No one makes a square on the *edge* of a city. But I can't find any more of the wretched flowers. The leaves are too thick.'

Quietly, Agustin had been studying the trunks of the trees, following the line down from one of the patches of scarlet. Now he touched a trunk.

'I think it is these trees.'

Now that he had pointed them out, Paula could see. The trunks were distinctive, their bark smooth and grey, with a silvery gleam, and there was a line of them among the other trees, perfectly straight.

'Let's follow it round,' said Finn. 'Come on. Quickly.'

For the first time, Paula felt a stirring of excitement, but she had not forgotten her promise to Karel. 'We must pace it,' she said. 'Whatever's on the other side won't go away. It will wait for us.'

They began to move from trunk to trunk, measuring the size of the square. The line of trees ran from north to south, across the front of the houses they had already explored, and then turned at right angles and ran eastwards for fifty yards or so. They peered from side to side as they went, but there was no sign of any other building. Then they reached the far corner and the trees began to run back again, parallel to the first line.

'There must be something here,' Finn said. 'There *must*. Facing the other houses.'

He started to cast out into the forest, not waiting for Paula to finish marking the square on the map.

And he found it almost immediately. It was too big to miss. A long, low building, stretching for nearly fifteen yards along the eastern edge of the square. It was quite different from the houses they had already found. The stones were shaped precisely, set in regular courses, and the walls rose for eight feet or more, masked by bushes that had grown up where the trees thinned.

Half-way along the front wall there was a gap, each side edged with tall, stone pillars that leaned slightly inwards. The top of the doorway was missing, but the pillars stood steady. Paula ran her fingers down one of them.

'What do you think it is?' she said.

'I think it is the palace of the Sapa Inca,' said Agustin.

He sounded awed, and Paula was touched by the same feeling, as though a huge, invisible figure had laid hands on her shoulders. *Here,* she thought. *If we find anything special, it will be here.* In her mind, the shape of the Inca steadied and came clear and her lips shaped the word soundlessly, *Atahualpa.*

'What are you waiting for?' Finn said roughly. He pushed past her and led the way into the building.

They stepped into a small room, no more than ten feet square. Its walls rose above their heads, shutting out everything except the green dome of the forest, arching like a distant roof. To right and left, doorways opened in the side walls, giving a clear view of other small, square rooms. And all of them were completely empty.

The floor beneath their feet was paved with large, flat stones, undisturbed except in one corner where a fuchsia bush had rooted in a crack and forced the slabs aside as it grew. It billowed outwards from the angle into which it had squeezed, its crimson flowers vibrating on their slender stalks.

All three of them stood perfectly still. The rustlings of the forest seemed deadened, as though they were infinitely far away. There was nothing close except the dull grey of the stones and the red eruption of flowers.

Then, from the corner by the fuchsia bush, came a low-pitched whirring. A small blue humming-bird had flown down and was hovering in front of one of the flowers, poking its tiny beak into the centre. Its wings blurred in a vigorous whirling, the ceaseless movement keeping the minute body immobile in the air. In the dull light, it was as precise and precious as a jewel.

'Oh!' said Paula.

Instantly the bird had gone, darting up and away, over the wall. The only sign that it had been there was a blue feather, like a flake of brilliant dust, floating gently to the ground. It settled on a patch of tumbled earth, gleaming between two stones. And below it, in the earth, was a duller gleam of black and white.

With an odd feeling, as though what she was doing were the final stage of the journey, Paula walked across the room and knelt down, parting the branches of the fuchsia so that she could work the soil aside with her hands and free the object that was embedded there.

It was no more than three inches long, a cat's head with small rounded ears and teeth bared in a snarl. The red surface of the pottery was indented all over with a pattern of tiny circles, striped black and white, but it ended in a jagged break. The head was severed at the neck and the raw edge of the earthenware was crumbling.

'*El tigre*,' murmured Agustin. 'The jaguar.'

Paula nodded. Brushing the dust from the crevices of the head, she laid it in the palm of her hand and stared down at it, wondering why she did not feel anything.

Then Finn said harshly, 'Is that all?'

'What do you mean?' She looked up at him.

'I mean, is that all that's left?' He swept an arm round, taking in the city and the whole of the forest in a single, angry gesture. 'Think of all we've been through. That terrible journey. Death. Madness. All the hours we've spent today, searching in the forest. And for what? A few ruined walls and a bit of broken pottery.'

It was as though he had screwed her head round and made her look at it. And suddenly, bitterly, she felt cheated. She had done everything right — endured to the end of the journey, kept her promise. And, all the time, she had been expecting the magic flash that would let her see the city, whole and glorious, as she had imagined it. But Finn was right. The magic had not worked. And the plan she had made was only a scribble of lines on a scrap of paper.

Agustin had not understood. 'What did you expect?' he said, puzzled.

'I thought it would happen to *me*.' Finn banged his fists furiously together. 'Like it does to Karel. I thought there would be a moment when the darkness and the shadows cleared and I could *understand*. But no one will ever understand this city like that. It's too far away, too deep in the jungle to be excavated. It will be lost in the dark for ever. And it's obvious the Indians don't care about it. If it was ever golden and splendid, the way Karel described it, all that was stripped away years ago, before any of us were born. Karel was *wrong*.'

Looking around at the bare walls, the broken floor, Paula felt the emptiness inside her. Oh, she knew that Finn was exaggerating. There was plenty here to make a tale to take back to Karel. But now she knew the truth behind the tale. And she would never again be able to imagine the people who had once moved among these ruins. The city was dead, made for a king who had been murdered hundreds of years ago.

'You can see it too, can't you?' Finn said cruelly. 'Your precious father's let you down this time, hasn't he? He was wrong.'

She swallowed the realization and stood up, bleak but controlled. 'So? Karel was wrong. Is that the end of the world?'

Finn stared at her as though she had said something quite extraordinary. 'You've changed. You couldn't have said that at the beginning of the journey.'

Paula remembered, dimly. 'You're right. I couldn't. But this journey has been enough to change anyone.'

'Even me.' Finn gave a short, hoarse laugh. 'I thought I could be the same for ever. Clever Finn Benjamin, with the world tidily sewn up, ready to take his neat pictures of the forest and jump back on to an aeroplane. A hit and run photographer. It never occurred to me that the forest could do anything to *me*.'

'And has it been so bad?' Agustin said softly.

'Like Paula says — not the end of the world.' Finn's smile was bitter. 'But I've lost my camera, and everything I thought was certain and secure has been knocked sideways, dropping me into the darkness. And all for this — this *nothing* in the forest. Funny, isn't it?'

He turned abruptly and walked out through the doorway. They could hear him crashing away through the trees. Slowly Paula wrapped the jaguar's head in her handkerchief and put it in her pocket. The room had grown shadowy and the silence was like deep water. Only she and Agustin, stained and spattered with mud, stood in the place that had been made for the great king, the son of the Sun on earth.

'I have tried to tell you,' Agustin murmured. 'That the Incas were long ago. But it does not matter. I thought it did. That the Indian had died with the Incas. But I was wrong. Empires die, but the people who make them — they go on. And the dreams with them, maybe?'

'I don't see how they can,' said Paula wretchedly. 'I've been dreaming of this place all my life and now the dream is over. It may not be the end of the world, but it *feels* like it.'

As if it were a picture, she saw her life stretching ahead of her, grey and practical. Like Jean. But like Jean without Karel. In that moment, she felt that he had died in her head, leaving nothing but an infinite bleakness.

Very gently, Agustin reached out and took both of her hands, turning her to face him. 'Sometimes,' he said, 'it is good to wake up, Paula.'

215

She could feel the warmth in his eyes and in his hands, but she did not know what he meant and, before she could ask, Finn called from beyond the walls, hectically gay.

'Come on, you two. I want to go home. It's getting late, and I'm *scared* of the dark.'

For the first time, Paula understood his ridiculous play-acting. Tugging at Agustin's hands, she pulled him through the doorway and into the forest, running back along the edge of the square and then away from it between the little houses, chasing Finn.

They saw their guide's head jerk round, startled, as they approached him, and he followed them at a steady trot until they burst out of the forest and found the boat waiting for them, awash with rain water.

'We'll be soaked to the skin!' Finn said dramatically. With a ludicrous gesture, as though they were not drenched already, he took out his handkerchief and dried a seat for Paula, handing her into the boat like a duchess.

'Set sail, Columbus!' He waved his hand at the bewildered guide. 'And let us pray that we do not drop over the edge of the world before we reach the further shore.'

'O brave and intrepid explorer!' Paula played up to him. Because now she knew why he did it. 'Can we truly discover the Americas?'

'They lie at your feet, my lady!' He swept his arm in a wide arc, nearly upsetting the boat as it chugged out into the middle of the stream. 'Gadzooks, I am as hungry as a bear! I hope the great chief in the village has prepared a feast for us.'

As soon as they touched the opposite bank, he leaped from the boat, landing on one knee and clawing at the earth. Agustin shook his head.

'You have gone mad, Finn. What strange animal has bitten you?'

'A tiger!' shouted Finn. 'I've been bitten to the heart by a tiger!'

He began to run down the path towards the village. The rest of them followed, but he was still ten yards ahead when they saw him skid to a halt at the edge of the clearing. Heard him say, in quite a different voice, 'What's happening? They haven't waited for us to get back. What are they doing to Karel?'

Chapter 21

. . . from whence our Lord shall rise again to destroy the invaders and bring again the glory of the people of Tahuantinsuyo.

THE torches were flaming again on the stakes in the middle of the clearing, but now they burned with a steady yellow light. And the space in the centre was bare except for two figures. Karel was kneeling in the middle, sitting back on his heels, with the heavy bandage still on his head. He wore nothing but a pair of shorts and the whole of his skin was a strange mottled green. For a moment Paula thought that the colour was an odd trick of reflection, caused by the torchlight on the surrounding forest. Then she realized that his skin had been daubed all over with some kind of paste, so that he looked like a jade goblin. He was utterly still, his head tilted back as he stared into the Kallawaya's eyes.

The old man was standing in front of him, leaning on his stick. He was chanting in a loud voice and, as he chanted, his body swayed from side to side so that long shadows flickered from it in all directions, dancing rhythmically over Karel's face and outwards, into the forest.

Beyond the torches, the villagers were clustered, with Jean among them. When he saw her, Finn took a step forwards as if to run to her, but Agustin and the guide caught quickly at his arms and held him steady so that he could not move.

218

'It is dangerous to interrupt,' whispered Agustin.

Finn gave him a ferocious glare and then stood still, watching the scene in the clearing with a look of revulsion.

Suddenly the Kallawaya flung his stick away and stretched up taller, raising both arms to the air. His loose black garments billowed, but beneath them his body seemed incredibly small and frail, as though only his will held him upright. And as he reared up, so did his voice, rising higher and higher, until the words merged into a single, formless shriek that tore through the shadows, going on and on without pause.

At the culmination of the cry, he dropped to his knees and pressed his mouth to the green-smeared skin on the front of Karel's thigh. Without moving, Karel stared down at him. The old man sucked vigorously and then, darting his head back like a snake, spat hard. Something small and round flew from his mouth and hit the ground with a thud. He did not look at it, but moved higher, setting his mouth to Karel's chest and sucking again.

Paula's whole mind rebelled. She had been able to believe in the trepanning, with its strange herbs and queer golden knife, because at least it was like a form of medicine. But this — this sucking out of a disease — was pure witchcraft. For a moment she shared, utterly, the disgust and rejection that she saw on Finn's face.

And still the eerie process went on, the Kallawaya's mouth moving upwards over Karel's armpits and neck. Finally, he reached up and caught Karel's head with both hands, tilting it downwards so that he could reach the forehead. Paula could almost feel the pain of that touch, the hands gripping tightly, the mouth pressed hard to the skin so near the covered wound. But Karel showed no sign of it. His whole attention was on the Kallawaya and, even from the other side of the clearing, Paula could feel the thread of concentration stretched between them.

Spitting hard for the last time, the old man crumpled suddenly, lurching sideways to lie in a small heap on the ground. He looked exhausted. After a moment, the sound of his voice came faintly, murmuring something. Karel reached out for the discarded stick and gave it to him. Very slowly and with great difficulty, the Kallawaya levered himself up, leaning forward with his weight on the stick. He bent his head to Karel, in a silent salutation, and then began to shuffle away to his hut, resting on the stick after each step, to pant for breath.

Jean had already come out of the crowd and was running between the torches. As Paula started forward, she saw her mother reach Karel, fall to her knees and stare at him with a strange, shy look of enquiry. In answer, Karel stretched out a forefinger and ran it lightly down her cheek.

Finn and Agustin were close behind Paula and as they came into the smoky brightness of the centre of the clearing Finn said sharply, 'What was going on? What's happened?'

'Ssh!' said Jean. 'Don't make a noise.'

Karel was turning his head about and clenching and unclenching his fists, as though his fingers were numb. Then he looked at Finn, a smile beginning at the corner of his mouth. 'You know what's happened.' He sounded very tired. 'I didn't dare wait. In case I faltered. So I asked the Kallawaya to heal me today.'

'But you're not telling me —' Finn looked angrily from Karel to Jean and back again. 'That's ridiculous! You can't believe that rubbish. You can't believe it's *worked!*'

'Can't I?' Karel raised an eyebrow at him. 'You mean *you* can't believe it's worked. I believe it. I'm cured.'

'But you can't *know*,' Finn said stubbornly. 'Not without examinations and tests and —'

'Oh, I'll have those.' Karel nodded, his eyes glazing over with weariness. 'Later on. When we get back to England. I'm not stupid. But I know what the results will be. I can feel it —' he grinned suddenly ' — I can feel it in my bones.'

220

Slowly he stood up. His body sagged, leaning heavily against Jean's shoulder, but his face was peaceful.

It might be true. The words hummed themselves in Paula's brain. *It's not impossible.* Very cautiously, she let herself try out the idea and Karel seemed to read her thoughts. With his free hand, he reached out and tickled her ear. 'Well, Tabby?'

'You're not in pain?' she said.

'I'm not in pain. I can walk. I can talk.' He took a deep luxurious breath and grinned at her. 'Tomorrow there will be another day and I shall be alive to see it. And then you can tell me about the city.'

Jean put her arm round his waist. 'That's enough for today. You ought to go to sleep. The Kallawaya's lent us a hut.'

Her body braced to take his weight, she began to lead him away from them, across the clearing, letting him rest from time to time as they walked. When their figures started to merge into the shadows, Paula said again, aloud this time, 'It might be true.'

She turned to look at Agustin. Solid, steady Agustin. And he nodded. 'It might be true. And we shall all wish for it.'

'Even me,' said Finn. Suddenly he looked as exhausted as Karel and the Kallawaya. 'Even I have my good moments. I'm not a complete monster. I'll wish for it to be true, even though that would mean I have to start everything again in the dark.'

'Time to say goodbye,' Karel said. 'I'm sorry. I should be coming back over the mountains with you.'

'It would not be wise,' the Kallawaya murmured quietly.

They were all standing on the bank of the river, half their luggage loaded into the little boat and the other half packed in rucksacks for Finn and Agustin. Nothing, it seemed, was left except the farewells. But those were more difficult than they expected. The sky was brightening, ready for the sunrise, but still they lingered, making excuses to go on talking to each other.

At last Finn shook himself and picked up one of the rucksacks. 'Well, we can't stay here all day,' he said, defiantly cheerful. 'It's all right for you three. You've only got to sit in a boat. But Agustin and I have mountains to cross.' He turned. 'Come on, Agustin. No delaying. Put on your pack.'

'Ah, you are the *patron* now,' Agustin said teasingly, hoisting the rucksack on to his shoulders. 'I can see that you will be worse than the Señor Karel.'

'Of course.' Finn twisted his face into a stern scowl. 'That was a journey for pleasure. This is work. We have boats to collect, mules to take back to their owners. Everything has to be put back as it was before we started.'

No one bothered to contradict him. They all knew that that would never be true. Solemnly they began to say goodbye.

Agustin shook Karel and Jean by the hand and then came across to Paula. 'I do not think that we shall ever meet again,' he said.

'No.' She shook her head miserably. Because there was no way of telling him everything she felt. All she could do was grip his hand hard, to try and make him understand. 'I hope — that you have a good life, Agustin. And that your dreams about La Paz come true.'

'And you —' Whatever he had been going to say, he changed his mind. 'May the *Pachamamma* of the earth keep you always in her care.'

Then he and Finn had gone, beginning to work their way up the bank to the shallower water where they could wade in the stream.

'Goodbye!' called Jean. 'Goodbye, Agustin, and good luck. Goodbye Finn. See you in England.'

222

Finn turned, waving both arms in an extravagant, dramatic gesture of farewell. Then he and Agustin settled to a steady tramp, beginning their journey back along the secret road.

'So,' said the Kallawaya. 'It is over. You are disappointed?'

'Me?' Karel shook his head. 'You know I am not. What I have found here — what you have given me — is more than I can ever repay.'

'And what you have given me,' Jean said. She squeezed Karel's hand.

'It is well.' The old man smiled at them. 'Señor, you have the spirit of the condor who flies over the high mountains. And you, Señora, have the heart of the jaguar who hunts in the forest. May it go well with you both.'

'And with you,' said Karel. Carefully, his legs still weak, he began to climb into the boat, letting Jean help him. But Paula lingered on the bank. As though he sensed that she still had something to say, the Kallawaya turned towards her. He did not speak, but his eyes were shrewd.

She reached into her pocket and pulled out the bundle of her handkerchief. Unwrapping it, she let the jaguar's head lie in the palm of her hand.

'I found this,' she said. 'In the city of the Inca.'

'Ah.' The old man looked down at it. 'And it troubles you?'

'Perhaps I should leave it?' She had meant to explain that it belonged in the city. But that was not really why it troubled her and, as the Kallawaya's eyes scanned her face, she let her voice die away. He went on studying her for a moment.

At last he said, 'I think it is a long journey you have made.'

Paula glanced up the stream. Ahead were the forested hills and beyond, high above and far away, the dim, snow-covered peaks. For a second, the whole of their travelling flashed through her mind, from the bare, high plateau, down through the tangle of the cloud forest to the silent darkness on the floor of the jungle, the bottom of the world. All part of the same mountains.

But, as she met the Kallawaya's eyes, she knew that he had meant more than that.

'Yes,' she said slowly, 'and it was not only a journey down the mountains.'

The Kallawaya nodded. 'If you have come to the bottom of yourself, then you have truly travelled.' He reached out his hand and closed her fingers round the jaguar's head. 'You should keep this. To remind you.'

'But it doesn't remind me of that!' Paula had not meant to say it, but now it burst out. 'All it means to me is that the Inca is dead. Dead for ever.'

'So that is what troubles you.' The old man smiled. 'You are wrong. The Incas helped to shape this land. Like my people, and all the other peoples in all the years. Nothing is lost.'

'My dream is lost,' Paula said stubbornly. '*The secret city of the East, from whence our Lord shall rise again.*' She looked down at the broken jaguar in her hand and then across at Karel, his face gaunt under the growing stubble on his head. 'I don't believe the Inca will ever come back. And you don't either. Do you?'

Almost tenderly, the old man took her shoulders and turned her to face across the river, towards the eastern bank where the city lay hidden.

There, above the dark spread of the forest, encircled with a halo of brilliant rays, was the disc of the rising sun. In the jungle canopy, the flowers opened at the touch of its warmth, flaring in trumpets of blue and scarlet and orange. The tangled layers below stirred more slowly with the waking of the millions of creatures which lived in the half light. And far down, on the forest floor, where the sun itself never penetrated, the effects of that rising drew up new life from the buried roots and set the dead plants

224

rotting to nourish those roots and play their part in the ceaseless cycle.

'My child,' said the Kallawaya, 'there is truth in every old tale, and He comes again each morning from the East.'

★

'You broke your promise,' said Fettis. 'You said you'd tell me what happened.'

He was standing outside the street door, his hair damp with the November drizzle, his hand resting lightly on the box of oranges at the edge of the greengrocer's display.

Paula blinked at him. She had been alone in the flat, absorbed in a complicated piece of trigonometry. His sudden, unexpected appearance had confused her, as though he had startled her out of a deep sleep.

'I couldn't come back to school,' she said.

Fettis glanced past her, up the narrow, uncarpeted stairs that led to the flat.

'Money?'

'Something like that.'

He nodded, and Paula stepped backwards to let him in.

'You're getting soaked. Come upstairs and I'll make you a cup of tea.'

'Thanks.' He lumbered up the stairs after her and, as she pushed open the door of the flat, she could feel him taking in the shabby furniture and the scuffed walls. But he did not say anything until he had sat down. Then he murmured, 'I told you I wanted to know what happened to you. So here I am.'

'It was clever of you to find me. With the move and everything.' Suddenly Paula realized that she was pleased to see him. Pleased, and a bit flattered. She moved towards the kitchen. 'I think I'll make the tea first. It's a long story.'

When she came back, he was standing up again, walking round the room. Jean had pinned up the photographs that Finn had sent — magnificent shots of distant mountains

225

and close-ups of strange, intricate plants. They opened tantalizing windows in the cramped stuffiness of the flat. But Fettis had stopped in front of the one clumsy picture. The one that showed Paula herself, slightly askew, standing in the middle of a dusty plain. He jerked his head at it.

'That's a bit different from the others, isn't it?'

'Yes. That's not one of Finn's.' She put the tray down carefully. 'It was taken by — by someone who's training to be a mechanic in La Paz.' All at once, as clearly as though he stood there, she could see Agustin's delighted face as he looked up from the camera. Could hear him say, 'I have done it? I have made a picture?' For the first time in all the months since they had come back to England, she felt that she really wanted to tell the story. Sitting down, she started to pour the tea. 'Come and have a cup. Then I'll begin.'

He listened to her all the way through, without interrupting once or shifting his eyes from her face. When she finished, he picked up his cup of cold tea and drained it at one gulp. Then he put it down on the saucer.

'It's a shame there aren't any pictures of the city,' he said. 'I'd like to have seen those. How will your father manage without them in his book?'

'I'm not sure he'll ever write it. Not now. It doesn't seem important to him any more.'

Fettis nodded thoughtfully. 'But he's O.K.? He's cured?'

'It seems like it. You can't ever be really sure, of course, but there's no sign of a relapse.'

'Funny, that.' Fettis ran a finger round the rim of his teacup. 'Do you think it was all in the mind? You know, like faith healing? Or was it that green stuff the old man covered him with?'

'I think —' Paula hesitated. 'I think perhaps it was both together. Mind and body. I'm not sure you can separate them.' *All part of the same mountain.*

'It doesn't matter really, does it?' Fettis dropped his chin forward on to his chest, brooding. 'Be nice to know how

226

it was done, though.' Then he looked up. 'What about Finn? Is *he* going to write a book?'

'That's the last thing he'd do.' Paula smiled wryly. 'He wouldn't even keep copies of the photographs. As soon as Karel had paid him back for his equipment, he went off to New York. I'm not sure we'll ever see him again.'

'So it's all still there,' murmured Fettis. 'A secret city and a secret cure, both hidden in the jungle.' Suddenly he grinned, the smile filling his heavy face with light. 'I knew I was right to come. It's a fantastic story. Thank you for telling me all about it.'

I haven't told you any of it, thought Paula. *Not so you could understand. No one could understand without making the journey.*

Eerily, he answered her thought, staring down at her as he stood up. 'You know — someone ought to go back there, one of these days. Find out a bit more.'

'Perhaps someone will,' said Paula. 'One of these days.'

He was silent for a moment, still staring down at her. His heavy, dark head was outlined against the street lamp outside. It looked very solid and real.

Then he muttered, 'I could come and see you again after Christmas. If you like.'

Paula stood up to face him. 'Yes,' she said slowly. 'Yes, I would like that.'

He smiled again. 'See you after Christmas, then.'

She went to the top of the stairs with him and then wandered back into the sitting-room and over to the window. It looked cold and damp outside. She wriggled her shoulders, glad of the shabby warmth of the flat.

Then the door clicked downstairs and footsteps sounded on the pavement. Leaning forwards, she watched Fettis shambling away up the street. Both his hands were thrust deep into his pockets and he walked with his head bent, ignoring the rain. Thinking of the journey that he would make himself, one day.

★

227

In the heart of most of us there is always a desire for
something beyond experience. Hardly any of us
but have thought, some day I will go on
a long voyage, but the years go by
and still we have not sailed.

Richard Jefferies

Author's Note

When I first thought about writing this book, I knew that the Kallawaya were travelling healers at the beginning of this century, but I had no proof that they still exist and practise their mysterious cures today. I spent several years trying hard to find out about the modern Kallawaya and I was beginning to despair when I happened to visit Nottingham one day. Quite by accident, I walked into the library there and found Ross Salmon's book, *My Quest for El Dorado*. It describes his visit to a Kallawaya village in 1977 and tells how he watched a Kallawaya doctor healing a small boy, apparently by 'sucking out' his disease.

When I opened the book and realized what I was holding, I was almost speechless with excitement. I shall always be grateful to the understanding librarian who listened to my gibbering and made it possible for me to borrow the book so that I could study it in detail.

I should also like to thank all the other people who have helped me with my research and answered my often peculiar questions. Two people, in particular, have given me invaluable assistance. Dr Peter White, who diagnosed Karel's disease as a lymphoma, also read the book in manuscript and corrected my medical errors. John Wainwright, of the Library of the Taylor Institution in Oxford, translated the directions for finding the lost city into correct sixteenth century Spanish. I am very grateful to both of them.

Gillian Cross